"God knows I ne ___ ___ to hurt you, Addie," Deke said.

But you did, she thought. *And I'm so afraid you'll do it again.*

She simply couldn't let it happen! Angrily she swiped away a traitorous tear. "I promised myself I wouldn't do this!"

"Do what?"

"That I wouldn't cry over you ever again! Because I cried rivers over you, till I thought I'd die. Damn it, it took years to stop my heart from pounding at every ring of the phone or trip to the mailbox. You can't do this to me again, Deke. You can't come barging back into Bridgewater and m-make me—" She broke off, her heart thundering in her chest.

"Make you what?" he persisted.

She scraped at her wet cheeks. "Damn it! Make me love you again!"

Dear Reader,

Have you ever been so excited after reading a book that you're bursting to talk about it with others? That's exactly how I feel after reading many of the superb stories that the talented authors from Silhouette Special Edition deliver time and again. And I'm delighted to tell you about Readers' Ring, our exciting new book club. These books are designed to help you get others together to discuss the brilliant and involving romance novels you come back for month after month.

Bestselling author Sherryl Woods launches the promotion with *Ryan's Place* (#1489), in which the oldest son of THE DEVANEYS learns that he was abandoned by his parents and separated from his brothers—a shocking discovery that only a truly strong woman could help him get through! Be sure to check out the discussion questions at the end of the novel to help jump-start reading group discussions.

Also, don't miss the other five keepers we're offering this month: *Willow in Bloom* by Victoria Pade (#1490); *Big Sky Cowboy* by Jennifer Mikels (#1491); *Mac's Bedside Manner* by Marie Ferrarella (#1492); *Hers To Protect* by Penny Richards (#1493); and *The Come-Back Cowboy* by Jodi O'Donnell (#1494).

Please send me your comments about the Readers' Ring and what you like or dislike about what you're seeing in the line.

Happy reading!

Karen Taylor Richman,
Senior Editor

Please address questions and book requests to:
Silhouette Reader Service
U.S.: 3010 Walden Ave., P.O. Box 1325, Buffalo, NY 14269
Canadian: P.O. Box 609, Fort Erie, Ont. L2A 5X3

The Come-Back Cowboy

JODI O'DONNELL

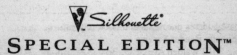

SPECIAL EDITION™

Published by Silhouette Books

America's Publisher of Contemporary Romance

To my fellow St. Ambrose C&M-ers—
thanks for being a big part of why I love my job.

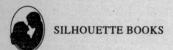 SILHOUETTE BOOKS

ISBN 0-373-24494-0

THE COME-BACK COWBOY

Copyright © 2002 by Jodi O'Donnell

This edition published by arrangement with Harlequin Books S.A.

® and TM are trademarks of Harlequin Books S.A., used under license. Trademarks indicated with ® are registered in the United States Patent and Trademark Office, the Canadian Trade Marks Office and in other countries.

Visit Silhouette at www.eHarlequin.com

Printed in U.S.A.

JODI O'DONNELL

grew up one of fourteen children in small-town Iowa. As a result, she loves to explore in her writing how family relationships influence who and why we love as we do.

A *USA TODAY* bestselling author, Jodi has also been a finalist for the Romance Writers of America's RITA® Award, and is a past winner of RWA's Golden Heart Award. She lives in Iowa with her two dogs, Rio and Leia.

The Journal of Addie Gentry

June 15

Our son was born today. Deke's and mine. Which means it's been about nine months since he left— left without a word of explanation or even a goodbye. Left before his promise to me had died on his lips: that he'd love me forever, would never leave me....

Still, he's beautiful, this tiny baby the two of us created. And when I look into those eyes that are so like his father's, I know that even with all the tears I've cried over Deke's leaving, the prayers I've sent up to heaven begging for his return, the words of hopelessness I've written on these pages...even with all these, I could never regret this child we made.

And so as much as I'll curse myself for doing it, I'll keep on praying in my heart of hearts: come back, cowboy. Oh, cowboy, won't you come back...?

Chapter One

"*Jace!* Jace, come back here this instant!"

The sound of a truck door slamming in the distance tempered the sheer panic in Addie Gentry's voice as she burst through the same door that seconds before her son had shot out of like a pellet from a BB gun. She'd be blasted, though, if she'd duck her head in embarrassment. She wasn't about to give her son the notion he could get away with such behavior just because one of the ranch hands happened to be within earshot. Nossir.

Thank goodness that at her order, Jace stopped short of the weathered gazebo halfway across the yard. She could see he still radiated pent-up emotion, fists nailed to his sides in barely leashed frustration, telling her he was spring-loaded to take off again. And making him look like another who'd up and left.

It raised the fine hairs on the back of her neck.

"You are *not* running away from here, Jace," Addie said, sparing not a glance toward whoever it was who'd slammed the truck door and marching toward her son. Her progress was hindered by the heels of her one and only pair of nice pumps suck-plugging in the turf with every step, which escalated her own frustration this morning yet another count. The expensive shoes would be ruined in this mud, which only added insult to injury: they'd already punished the tender tissues of her feet, widened by miles in cowboy boots.

The hair she'd spent forty minutes coaxing into order in the damp mid-April weather frizzed up around her face like she'd stepped on a live wire. Now, there was a thought. As good a solution as any. Unfortunately, she had barely enough time as it was to get the situation with Jace taken care of, much less find a moment to fix her hair—with Connor due any minute.

"I will not stand for this sort of behavior," Addie informed Jace when she reached him. "You got a problem with what's goin' on, you stay and work it out. Runnin' tear for bear out the door is *not* an option!"

He at least had the grace to look ashamed, as he scuffed a boot toe against the gazebo's worn wooden step, making him seem more like the boy she'd raised and not the rebel who'd taken over her son's six-year-old body ever since her announcement last month. *This* boy she had some hope of reasoning with.

"Jace," she said, gently taking him by the shoulders to turn him toward her, still ignoring the figure at the corner of her vision who had the decency not to intrude on their private business, even if they were conducting it practically in public. "Hon, why won't you at least give him a chance?"

"'Cause…he's a phony, Mama!" He looked up at

her, amber-green eyes again turning contrary in his boyish face. "He says he's a rancher, but he can't hardly rope a cow or nothin'. All the boys laugh about how he's the only rancher they've seen who gets slicked up *before* he goes to work every day."

It sounded as if she needed to have a talk with the hands, Addie thought severely, perhaps starting with the one who'd set out toward them from across the ranch yard. She narrowed her eyes, trying to make out his identity, but the drab light and misty air obscured even the edges of the red barn behind him.

She bent back to Jace. "Just because a man's got some things to learn, that doesn't mean he's a phony, hon."

His small shoulders twitched impatiently under her palms. "But he's always callin' me his pal—and we're not!"

"He's only trying to be friendly! I know for a fact that Connor is one-hundred-percent earnest about being your dad—"

"But I don't want him for my dad!" Jace broke in, getting upset all over again. "I don't wanna go live somewhere else 'sides here!"

His struggle against her hold on him nearly broke her heart. It just wasn't like Jace to be so desperate—which made Addie realize how deeply the feelings in her son went regarding this particular issue, feelings she'd believed long ago resolved.

Well, she sure had been wrong.

What was she to do, though? It was time. Time for her to lay the past to rest once and for all and get on with her life—and take definite steps toward putting a father into Jace's.

"Jace, please," Addie said huskily, her fingers tightening on his shoulders. "I know this is a lot of change to take in right now. But I really do think you'll feel differently if you just give Connor a chance." She hesitated, then went on in soft appeal. "Give us all a chance to be a real family."

This sent him into an absolute frenzy. "No, we won't! He can't be my dad!"

"But why not, Jace?" she asked, completely stumped.

"'Cause!" His eyes filled with rare tears, disturbing Addie even more. "I don't want a dad, ever!"

With that, Jace broke free, whirling around and taking off like a locomotive at full speed away from her, head down, jeans-clad legs pumping. Addie could only look achingly after him. She'd never felt more helpless in her life, for she didn't believe for a moment that Jace didn't want a father. That wasn't the problem, but she was confounded as to what really was.

And just as at a loss about how she might find out.

Then the boy was suddenly swept from his feet with a deep "Whoa there, Slick," and swung around in a movement as smooth as a dance step, dislodging Jace's cowboy hat from his head. The move surprised him enough that he struggled not at all, but only stared up at the stranger who held him under the arms like an eight-week-old puppy.

For this man, Addie now saw, wasn't one of the Bar G's ranch hands...although there was something uncommonly familiar about him. She couldn't make out his expression under the shading brim of his black Stetson, but his stance was like stone as he, too, stared down at Jace in surprise.

Leaning a hand against the railing, Addie straightened as she took in the whole of him—lithe and lean and tense as a jungle cat, vigilant. Dangerous.

A steel rod of shock shot through her spine, making every muscle in her body go rigid. *It couldn't be!*

The sun broke through the clouds, cranking the humidity up another couple of notches and distracting her from the danger swirling around her. It was getting late. She needed to get Jace taken care of, needed to batten down this thicket of hair and scrape the mud off her heels. Needed to remind Opal, the wife of one of the ranch hands who tended the house, to pick up Daddy's prescription at the pharmacy when she was in town for groceries. Needed to do the thousand and one things that signified life going on as usual.

The problem was it couldn't—not when the danger wasn't around her but within her. For in that instant her traitorous heart rose up in her with the force of a hundred-year flood, drowning out every other sound in the world with its jubilant cry: *At last! At last, he's come back.*

Oh, I knew he'd keep his promise!

He had a son.

The realization rocked him, tipped his world and set each ever-so-carefully placed piece on it careening perilously toward the rim.

Deke Larrabie scrutinized the dark-haired boy that he held; his hawk eyes that could spot a case of scours in a calf before it started looking peaked were hindered not one whit by the overcasting clouds. The air hung heavy around him, though, making it hard to breathe, hard to think.

For it changed the whole picture—his whole life— if he'd left Addie Gentry pregnant.

Could he be wrong? A skirmish over the question broke out in him. Even as Deke did a review of the events of the past couple of months that had brought him to this moment, he clung to the possibility as he would a rope over a yawning canyon.

But why else would Addie's father have labeled his call providential, even if Deke had been phoning in direct enquiry to Jud Gentry's ad for a ranching consultant at the Bar G? Except that when Jud hadn't mentioned Addie, Deke had assumed life had taken her away from the ranch and that she no longer lived there.

Of course, he hadn't had the guts to assign the label "happily married" to the situation, even in his own mind. But when he'd first spotted her a moment ago with the boy who was obviously her son, he'd felt nothing but relieved gratefulness that after he left she *had* gone on and found happiness.

That hadn't exactly been evident in the tone of their words, unclear to him except for the last—that heart-wrenching cry of *I don't want a dad, ever!*

Desperately, he peered at the boy as he slowly lowered him to the ground, the small hands continuing to clutch Deke's shirtsleeves. The smattering of freckles across his nose, like splatters of tan paint, was all Addie, he thought. So was the wide lower lip that gave the youngster the appearance, at least at this moment, of being able to bend without breaking, being able to yield precious ground while not giving it all up.

But the Will Rogers cowlick in front and those cat-colored eyes looking up at him with an even more impossible mixture of hope and doubt—those were pure Larrabie, come by in a straight shot from Deke's father D.K., to Deke, to this boy.

He had a son. *They* had a son. He and Addie.

And the past seven years he'd been living a lie.

Another depth charge of emotion buffeted Deke, as nitro-potent as he'd experienced in ages. What a fool he was, thinking he had a chance to make anything up to Jud or in any way change the fate that had been written for him the day he was born.

Because it was not this boy, but Addie who changed everything. Everything.

At the realization, his heart set up a pounding cadence, its pace growing stronger and faster, like a clock wound too tight after years of never being wound at all. Holding his breath, he focused on slowing down the sound until it beat out a nerve-steadying rhythm, metronome-like. *One-two…thud-thump.*

Deke knew the mantra; it had become a part of him. *You and you alone are in charge of your destiny.* He was not at the mercy of his inclinations. At the mercy of his emotions.

Slowly, he raised his head and found her gaze.

''Hello, Addie,'' Deke said, speaking for the first time in seven years the name of the woman he'd loved—and left.

He knows, Addie thought wildly. *He knows about Jace.* But perhaps that was all he knew at this point.

She had to get both herself and Jace safely away, though, from the force that was Deke Larrabie.

''Jace. Come on back here, hon,'' she said as calmly as she could, holding her hand out to her son. Thankfully, he came, although the whole way he craned his head around to stare at the stranger as if he were Duke Wayne in the flesh.

Once he'd reached her, she couldn't prevent herself from pressing him close to her side, obstructing his sight of the stranger. Or was she blocking Jace from Deke's view?

His eyes were only for her, though, as he started toward her. Amber-green, eerie in their detachment, yet as intense as ever.

In fact, everything about him was more intense. More...Deke-like. He'd always filled out a Western shirt and pair of Wranglers in a way that was uniquely, devastatingly *him.* Had always worn a Stetson at that exact angle, pulled low over his eyes, in a way that had her believing the cowboy hat had been invented just for him.

Now, though, he wore everything with even more command, so that the fit of the shirt stretching across those wide shoulders, the cut of the jeans hugging those long legs, even the shade over his eyes created by his hat's wide brim—all of them seemed branded by Deke Larrabie...as *she* once had been, and as her son now was.

It took every bit of her willpower to silence her heart, which continued to beat against the walls of her chest like a captive hostage, because she knew that the real moment of reckoning had yet to come—the one in which she'd discover why Deke Larrabie had really come back.

Whatever the reaction showing on her face, at least it stopped him ten feet from her and her son. Addie seized the advantage and pressed it home while she could.

''All right, hon.'' She brushed back Jace's thick, burnished-bronze hair. ''You don't have to go with us to Houston if you don't want, but then you need to go help Granddad in the office.''

"Why?" Jace stalled, pulling away from her, his questioning gaze trained on her face.

Her own eyes remained on Deke. She almost expected from him a lightning move or sleight of hand that would snatch away some precious belonging, leaving her feeling dispossessed and bewildered by what had happened and how.

But that had already occurred, hadn't it?

And, by God, it wouldn't happen again.

"Do as I say, please, Jace," Addie said more sternly, giving the boy a helping push in the right direction.

"I'm not leavin'." He planted his booted feet in front of her.

Exasperated, she glanced down. Her son had sure picked a fine time to go from running away from conflict to hanging tough. She wondered whether to kill him or kiss him, but she knew that her first order of business must be to protect him.

"Please, hon," Addie said, trying for a reassuring smile. "I'll be all right."

"But you know him, don'tcha, Mama?"

"Yes," she said, praying he'd take the rest of her answer on trust. Yet how could you convey such a feeling if you'd given it up a long, long time ago?

"Then, who is he, Mama?" Jace asked. "Who's that man?"

The boy's question was like a wake-up call, breaking the spell he'd been under.

Deke found his feet moving from the spot where Addie's warning look had riveted him. He started toward her again, still not knowing what he would say, how he would say it, if he should say anything at all.

Regardless, any explanation Addie chose to make shouldn't have to be made alone.

He stopped in front of her, trying hard not to put a label on the nature of the emotion radiating from her. Trying not to anticipate his own reaction.

Yet the sight and sound and smell of her filled his senses to the brink. Her eyes were even bluer than he remembered, the shade of blue that could bolt a man to the wall or drown him in desire. That flaming red hair spilled over her shoulders in a thick flow, like lava over a mountainside, as it swirled and waved with a life of its own. She wore a form-fitting skirt and short jacket in yellow, making her look as out of place as a daffodil sprung from the winterscape—and yet fitting as much as she ever did the definition of Texas ranch royalty.

Of course. *He'd* been the one who hadn't fit in here. Sons of alcoholic cowboys who were surviving only by the grace of such royalty weren't included in that class. Especially after his father had repaid the Gentrys' kindness by letting a hundred-thousand-dollar ranch building burn to the ground around him, too drunk to save it or even himself—although, in truth, he'd already been dead inside for years....

At the thought, Deke felt his heart speed up, like a time bomb inside him just waiting to explode.

No! He must remember: Sure, he was D. K. Larrabie's son. And yes, they bore the same name. But he was not *his* father. *This* D. K. Larrabie had set his every fiber to taking charge of his future, just as he'd set his mind to becoming the best damn ranch manager in Montana.

"Might be best to do as your mother says," Deke said, trying to help Addie out.

"Yeah?" The youngster stared up at him with a mixture of youthful hope and distrust that again spoke to Deke of his own boyhood. "Who are you to tell me what to do?"

"Jace!" Addie clutched him to her almost frantically.

Deke heard the outright panic in her voice and realized she hadn't answered the boy's question because she didn't want their son to know who he was. She looked not the least inclined to respond to either question put to her—this one, and *Who's that man?*

So what had she told their son about his father? For the first time, it struck Deke that for six years he'd had a son. And although he had taken off for parts unknown, why hadn't Addie or Jud tracked him down and let him know?

For that matter, why hadn't Jud seen fit to tell him when Deke had called? And from the looks of it, it seemed Addie was as surprised to see him as he was her.

What the hell was going on here, anyway?

Deke didn't want to jump to conclusions without having all the facts, but still he couldn't resist asking, "Why not answer the boy, Addie? Or have you forgotten exactly who I am?"

She leveled a look at him with eyes of glacial blue.

"Go on along now, Jace," Addie said, her gaze still on Deke. "If Granddad doesn't need you, I'm sure the boys can use your help dosing calves out in the west pasture."

"But what's going on?" the boy protested. He'd turned back to his mother. "Mama?"

She soothed her palm over his hair in a loving gesture that made Deke's own hands tingle with the remembered warmth of touching his son. "I'll explain things to you later, when there's time. I promise."

Seeing she'd have no more words on the matter, he turned back to Deke, who knew this time that keeping his mouth shut was going to be the winning ticket. For now.

When he realized that neither adult would give up anything while he remained, the boy muttered a resigned "Yes, ma'am." He marched over to his hat, dusted if off with a *whap* against his thigh, then screwed it down on his head in a gesture of pure disgruntlement before heading in the direction of ranch HQ.

The ensuing silence fell like a deadweight between them.

Addie shifted on her feet, one long bare leg thrust forward, hand planted upon her hip, looking cool as cubed ice and just as frosty.

It took him aback for a moment, after the way he'd seen her with her son. *That* had been the Addie he remembered: passionately unreserved and loyal to a fault with those she cared for deeply.

And therein lay the danger.

"Didn't mean to intrude on your conversation with... Did you call him Jace?" And Deke spoke his son's name for the first time, even in his mind.

"Yes, it's Jace," Addie replied, lifting her chin. "Short for J.C.—Judson Charles Gentry."

Deke absorbed the fact. So Jace had been named after his grandfather and not his father. But Jace also went by a shortened version of his initials, just as Deke was short for D.K.

It was a meager concession, but he'd take it.

"Well, he seems like a real fine kid," he commented.

"Normally, he is," she replied, fist still on her hip. "But you'd have to be blind not to see just now that he's a confused boy who's struggling to make sense of some of the changes in his life and comin' up short all around. Which is why I'll thank you to let me handle it myself—just as I've handled everything for six years now."

Abruptly, she turned and climbed the steps to the old gazebo that had been her mother's pride and joy. Not that Deke had known Addie's mother, who'd died, as had his own, when Addie was just a girl. But the structure had become a kind of memorial to the woman— one, he knew, to which Addie had often come to connect with her mother.

Of its own volition, his gaze went to the gentle rise at the far edge of the ranch yard, where grew an ancient cottonwood tree, its contour lopsided as if a giant mouth had taken a bite from its branches. Standing to one side was a crumbling chimney.

At the sight, Deke's heart gave another of those warning thumps. Fine, he'd let her have her space, but he wasn't going to be put off so easily. He waited until she sat on the wood bench seat to say purposefully, "It sure didn't have to be that way, Addie—you takin' care of Jace's needs by yourself."

"Didn't it?" she asked, her rich alto voice gone bone dry with sarcasm.

He'd let that one go. "So what did you tell him about me?"

"The truth. That his dad and I split up before he was born."

In what struck him as another avoidance tactic, she

leaned forward to slide her feet out of her high-heel shoes. Except, it worked this time. The movement caused her neckline to gap and exposed the upper swell of her full breasts.

And abruptly plunged Deke headfirst into another memory—of holding her in his arms, his lips pressed to that very spot. Then, however, Addie had been skinny as a fence rail. At considerable peril to himself, he'd called her Boney Gentry—when he wasn't teasing her with his other nickname for her. Wasn't whispering it while he made love to her that first and last time, before reality thundered down on top of him in a suffocating avalanche, just as it was doing now.

Because somehow he'd been able to convince himself over the past half-dozen years that the passion he'd known with her hadn't been as powerful as he remembered. He saw now, however, how he'd methodically bleached all the intensity out of those feelings, allowing him control over them.

You are *in control,* he told himself. But he needed to keep his distance if he was to hang on to that control.

His jaw clamped reflexively, and Deke scrutinized one of the gazebo's peeling posts, blue faded to gray. ''And that's all you told Jace?''

From the corner of his eye, he saw Addie examine her muddy shoes as she held them before her, elbows on her knees.

''No, it wasn't—''

Her voice had turned businesslike, he noticed, as if she, too, needed distance.

''I told him his father had chosen not to be a part of his life.''

''You what?'' he asked, deadly low.

''I had to, Deke. I couldn't have him pining his heart

out over a man I had no appreciation would ever return, much less be able to give us—Jace, I mean—what he needed.''

''So he's grown up believin' his daddy never cared enough about him to stick around.'' He noticed his own voice sounded calm. ''But that was obviously not true, because I didn't know, Addie. About Jace.''

Idly, he slid the pad of his thumb across the husked surface of the railing. ''You could have found me and told me about him. I'd've come back and lived up to my responsibility to him.''

Now, *that* got a reaction, for Addie sprung from her seat and in an instant was across the plank floor and hovering over him.

''You don't think we tried?'' she asked, shoes clenched in either hand, her blue eyes blazing down at him. ''Daddy had just about every rancher in the Southwest keepin' their eye out for you for nine solid months! If we couldn't find you, Deke, it was because you didn't want to be found!''

No, it hadn't taken long for her indifference to dissolve. For some reason, he was relieved that at least that aspect about her hadn't changed. Yet something else had changed about Addie, something he wasn't able to pin down yet.

So deal with it, Larrabie. Deal with just that one comment.

He drew in a deep breath and blew it out through loosely pursed lips. ''All right. I deserved that.''

''You deserve a hell of a lot more, and you know it,'' she said with a chilliness that rivaled a blue norther.

That's when he was able to put a label to the real change in her. It was there in her features—not an icy coolness so much as just the opposite. A hardness, to be sure, but more like that of something left too long in the sun.

In his years on the range, he'd seen many people who had, by design or necessity, let the relentless sun cook their skin to a leathery brown. It *was* leather, tanned and oiled as any cowhide stitched together to make a pair of chaps.

Not that Addie's skin had weathered the same way. Indeed, it was still as white and smooth as ever, with only that sprinkling of freckles to mar its creamy surface. Rather, it was the particular look of being overexposed to the harsh glare of life's disappointments that had baked anything tender or flexible or trustful right out of her expression.

That, it occurred to Deke in another bolt of realization, was the real legacy he'd left to her. And the one he had most desired to spare her of.

The enormity of his failure sliced into him, razoredged as the blade of a newly whetted knife. Somehow, though, wasn't a sharp, clean cut better than being on the jagged side of such pain? Sure, a rough cut wasn't as deep, but it caused a lot more damage, a more painful wound and an uglier scar as each shark's tooth made its notch in tender flesh.

But God, how to explain that to Addie?

Grasping the post, Deke swung himself up on a level with her so he could look her square in the eye. "That's what I'd been thinking about you when I left. That you deserved a hell of a lot more, a hell of a lot better, than what I'd be able to give you."

She took a step back even as she retorted, "Oh, what a crock of bull! You obviously wanted to leave!"

"It's the truth," he persisted. "It wouldn't have

been good for either of us for me to stay, not after what happened…''

Say it, damn it! *I didn't want to leave at all! I had to, though, because I knew if I didn't I'd end up like my father, maybe not in the same way, but just as completely, totally lost.*

He tried again. ''There're things you don't know about what happened that night. That's why I'm here. You've got to believe me. This wasn't the situation I meant to leave you in—''

''Oh? And what would have been a suitable situation to leave me in?'' She gazed at him, the pain he knew now that she'd only been hiding from him stark in her eyes. ''You gave me your promise, and when you did, I gave you my trust in return. My innocence. And you took it and left without a word. So now you're wonderin' why I kept to myself the one thing you did leave me?''

Eyelashes batting, she made a half turn away from him, a bid, he could see, for control. Even so, her voice shook as she went on. ''Well, you can just go to hell, Deke Larrabie. You gave up any say about anything having to do with my life when you left me and the Bar G seven years ago without a backward glance. I had to protect my son, and I've got no regrets for doing so.''

''He's my son, too.'' Deke fixed her with a resolute look. ''Neither of us has said it straight out like that, have we? But yes, Addie—he's my son, too. Now that I know about him, you've gotta see there's no way I'll shirk my responsibility to him.''

''And there's no way I'll let you just blow into his life, announce you're his father, then leave again!''

She graced him with as cynical a look as he'd ever

seen in his own mirror. "I don't know why you've come, anyway. Surely no one's got a gun to your head, makin' you stay. Besides, why do anything different? That's the Larrabie way, isn't it? Always lookin' for the exit sign."

Oh, but that cut him! Like the jagged rasp of a hacksaw. The hell of it was, her barbed words almost had him turning on his heel and hitting the highway.

And that's exactly what she wants, he realized. Addie didn't want him to know his son, didn't want Jace to know who he was. And he couldn't help concluding that it was for the same reason she had told Jace his father was never coming back. Because she saw Deke as being made in the image of his own father—an irresponsible cowboy rambler and rover.

Or, in Deke's case, a card-carrying cowboy leaver.

Which caused that timer inside him to speed up again in that dangerous tick-tick-tick, of the second hand edging ever closer to…to what?

To nothing! Deke told himself. He was Jace's father, damn it! No matter what had happened between the two of them, he deserved to know his son, deserved a chance to be a father to him!

Maybe that had been Jud's plan: to bring Deke on to do some troubleshooting and give him the opportunity to know Jace while he was here. But if so, there was still a puzzle piece missing, because Addie had just said she didn't know why he'd come to the Bar G, and it had obviously been a surprise when he showed up.

"Jud didn't tell you, did he," Deke said abruptly.

She went as wary as a cat. "Tell me what?"

And God help him, he couldn't help taking some satisfaction in informing her. "He hired me as a ranching consultant to put the Bar G back on solid ground. Which means I'm here to stay, Addie."

Chapter Two

Addie felt as if she would be sick right there in the ranch yard, her thoughts were whirling around her head so fast, while hurt and betrayal flip-flopped in her stomach.

"Daddy hired you?" she asked through numbed lips. "That's why you came back, to be a ranch consultant?"

"That's right—me, Deke Larrabie." His gaze had gone back to that stoniness that was frightening, so different was he from the emotionally charged twenty-two-year-old she'd last known. Just a split second before, though, she'd seen the spark, hot and fiery, leap to his eyes.

Yet make no mistake: The endearing rough edges of the half-boy, half-man she'd fallen in love with had been whittled away and sanded down, so that little showed that wasn't meant to be seen.

Yes, that boy was gone. But she'd come to terms with that fact seven years ago. Hadn't she?

"I don't know what Daddy was thinkin', telling you there was a job for you to do here," Addie said desperately, trying to come up with some valid arguments while not knowing the terms Deke and her father had discussed. It was difficult to concentrate for just that reason. What had her father been thinking? Why would he take such a step behind her back? Sure, they'd discussed whether a ranching consultant would be able to do anything for the Bar G that she couldn't do herself, given the time and the money. Which of course they'd have once she'd married…

Connor.

Sheer panic hit her like a tornado. She had to get Deke out of here before—

But it was too late. In the distance, a fire-engine red dual-wheeled pickup sped along the blacktop toward the Bar G.

Addie stepped closer to Deke, hoping to keep him from turning to see what had caught her eye.

"First of all," she said quickly, "the Bar G's already got someone capable of revamping its operations—me. I've been practically runnin' the ranch since I was eighteen."

"Then, why would Jud think it necessary to bring me in?" Deke asked with all reasonableness.

"I don't know!" Oh, but she intended to find out the next time she saw her father! "Second, we're just breaking even right now, which means there's no room in the budget to put anyone else on the payroll."

It near to killed her to admit such a thing, but she *was* desperate. The dually was turning under the lintel sign at the end of the lane.

Deke had an argument for that one, too. "Jud and I agreed I'd be workin' without pay for the time being," he said, adding quietly, "I thought it the least I could do to make up for the damage my daddy caused seven years ago."

For the moment, Addie forgot all about the red pickup. "We don't need your charity, Deke Larrabie!"

"Then, you'll understand real well why I couldn't hang around here those years ago and take yours without raisin' a word of protest," he replied with that maddening calm.

No way would she let him turn the fault back on her!

Yet Addie closed her eyes against the tide of emotion that rose in her at his words, for even now the memory of that night could make her weep with unconditional sympathy. She'd never forget Deke's face, streaked with sweat and soot, as he stared at the smoldering wreckage containing his father's remains, in his hand the empty bottle of Jim Beam that moments before Mick Brody had shoved at him in disgust. Still filled with the power of the bond she and Deke had just forged between them, Addie had felt the last particle of her heart that hadn't already been his go out to him.

Yet, then came the other memory, just as heart-wrenching, of when she'd laid her hand upon Deke's arm in silent comfort, and he'd bent upon her that sightless gaze—in which she'd seen the kind of devastation she could only imagine—before turning away from her, shutting her out like the door of a vault slamming shut.

Addie pressed the back of one hand against her lips. Suddenly, it all seemed too much to handle. She didn't care that the damp had crept through her clothing to her skin, had invaded her very bones. Didn't care that in her fervor she'd gotten a swipe of mud on her skirt from her shoes, still clutched in her hands. Didn't care that she looked like anything but a woman on her way to pick out her wedding ring with the man who would place it on her finger and give her the security, if not the all-encompassing emotional connection, that she so craved.

It was a choice she made gladly, because she'd had the other—and while it had been as wild and exhilarating as a Texas thunderstorm sweeping through her heart, it had left just as quickly, with nothing for her to do but pick up the pieces alone.

Yes, she must remember: such emotion wasn't worth the heartache.

Addie opened her eyes and gazed at the man who'd caused that heartache. "Maybe you did think you were doing what was best for me by leaving, Deke. And maybe you're hoping that by coming back you can make up for…oh, for a lot of things. Like helpin' out the Bar G to make up for your daddy's accident. The problem is, there're some things you can't make up for. Because the thing I can't forgive you for is that you never let *me* decide what was best for me. You took that choice with you when you went away. And when you did, you took away Jace's choice, too."

Addie spread her arms in front of her in a simple gesture. "This time I have a choice, and I mean to use it by doing what's best not only for me, but for my son."

Gripping her shoes in her hands, she pointed them both straight at her heart. "Yes, *my* son, Deke. I will not let you turn Jace's world on end."

She almost believed he hadn't heard her, he seemed so caught up in his thoughts, those amber-green eyes boring into her, yet looking at a place only he could see. When their focus clouded, then came back to her, the expression in them was haunted.

"I've got no intention of upsetting Jace," he finally said. "But I'm not leavin', either."

She saw he was dead serious. Deke Larrabie, the man who'd left her then so easily, now wouldn't budge an inch. She'd find the irony amusing if it didn't make her want to cry.

Because she saw, too, how very, very difficult it was for him to stay.

"Look, Deke," she said, trying one more time. "If you're truly serious about wanting to make up for some of the pain you've caused us, then leave."

The shiny red dually pulled up a few yards behind Deke. "Now. Please." She couldn't keep the urgency from her voice.

"No, Addie." Shaded by the brim of his hat, his face looked carved in stone. Yet set within the stone, those eyes glittered like gems. "This time, I've got a choice, too—and I'm choosing to stay."

"Then, I can't let you reveal who you are to Jace, Deke," Addie said fiercely. "I can't let you do him that way! Promise me right here, right now, that you won't, not without my say-so. You owe me that much."

He looked about to argue, and her heart stopped. Then he gave a nod, making the promise. "I won't tell him."

Deke seemed to realize at the exact moment she did, what had just transpired: Once again, he'd given her his word. And once again, she would have to give him her trust.

And where was the choice in that? she almost asked him but didn't. There was no time, for just then the door of the truck opened and out stepped Connor Brody—the man who would be her husband.

And Jace's dad.

Deke turned at the sound of a vehicle door slamming to see a man in a Western-cut sport coat, stand-up stiff blue jeans and spit-shined ostrich-skinned boots. When he doffed his white Stetson, the sunlight glanced off the shine on his dark hair and clean-shaven face, while at the same time carving out the Clint Black-deep dimple in his cheek.

There was something familiar-looking about the guy, but Deke couldn't put a finger on it.

"Mornin', darlin'," he said, sparing not a glance toward Deke, the smile on his face all for Addie.

Deke's antennae sprung to full alert. He shifted an assessing eye toward Addie, who was pushing her hair back from her suddenly flushed face. What was going on here?

"Mornin'," she answered. Obviously not wanting to make introductions, she went on briskly. "I'm all set to go."

The man glanced toward the house. "What about Jace? Isn't he—"

"No! No, he's not fit company this morning."

She wouldn't look at Deke, which made him even more suspicious. Who was this city slicker to Jace, anyway?

He sure looked disappointed, some aspect in his

downcast face making Deke wonder again where he'd seen him before.

"Well, shoot. He ought to be with us, y'know, when we make our decision, if we're going to start out like a real fam—"

"No!" Addie interrupted again. "Believe me, we're better off lettin' him get out whatever burr's under his saddle on his own. So! We'd better get on the road. Don't want to be late for our appointment."

It was pretty apparent to Deke that Addie wanted to be shed of him as quickly as possible. Hopping from one foot to the other, she shoved her toes into her high heels while trying to get past him without so much as a by-your-leave.

The man gave a huff, which distracted Deke again with that sense of familiarity he'd be damned if he could place.

"Well, sure, but how about a hello kiss from my fiancée first?"

That sure enough came through loud and clear. *His fiancée?*

As luck would have it, Addie's heel caught in a crack in the plank floor, and she stumbled beside Deke.

He bent down to pull the heel out, just as Addie stooped to do the same, his gaze seeking hers, hoping he was wrong.

Her face was even more flushed than before. She refused to meet his eyes.

Damn her! he thought as the reason for her guilt became abruptly clear to him: she intended to slot this guy into place as a father for Jace—and just seconds ago she'd extracted his promise that he wouldn't tell Jace *he* was the boy's father!

"I guess I'm not used to wearin' these shoes," she mumbled by way of an excuse.

He wasn't going to let her get away with it. Even knowing he shared some blame for her situation, that he hadn't the least right to be anything approaching angry, Deke still was. Deathly so.

"But somehow you seem to think you can fill mine for Jace pretty well, don'tcha?" he said.

That brought those blue eyes flashing up at him in defiance. Straightening, she lifted her chin before descending the steps to reach her boyfriend's side.

"Of course you get a hello kiss—darlin'," she said sweetly, offering him her lips.

Obviously about as mashed for a woman as a man could get, the fellow wrapped his arms around Addie and enthusiastically pressed his mouth to hers.

Sure, Deke could have made as big a show of not watching. He wanted nothing less than to give her the satisfaction of knowing she'd gotten to him in this instance.

But the truth was, he couldn't have looked away if his life depended upon it, and so he stood there in a hell of his own making, as this man with his shiny boots and country-singing-star looks kissed the stuffing out of Addie Gentry.

Finally, she broke the kiss and turned toward him, the other man's arm lingering at her waist. It did Deke some good to see in her eyes the defiance, and not the look of a woman who'd been thoroughly and satisfyingly kissed.

He held her gaze without a flicker of emotion.

Her intended finally seemed to notice the silent byplay between them, for he spoke up. "I don't believe we've met. Connor Brody's the name."

If he'd been stunned before, now Deke felt his blood stop dead in his veins. "Brody? Any relation to—"

"Mick Brody? He's my dad."

Of course. *Of course.* If Addie had wanted to put a fine point on just how unsuited the two of them had been for each other, she couldn't have done a better job than to pick a Brody. He'd never met this particular Brody before, but he'd once had more acquaintance-ship than he wanted with Connor's father, Mick. And from the looks of it, Connor had all the qualities his father had been swift to point out as lacking in Deke's father and Deke, foremost among them responsibility.

No! He had been responsible—if not in those hours leading up to D. K. Larrabie's fatal mistake, then every single day after that. And if Addie would just give him the chance, she'd find that out!

Except, from what she had just said, he had no chance of gaining her regard or her forgiveness. The very thought that he couldn't, nearly sent him back down the road again, in spite of everything.

But he couldn't go. Whatever his failings before, that didn't excuse him from doing his best by Jace from here on out.

And that meant he'd be damned if he'd stand by while she handed any man the right to be a father to his son.

"And you would be...?" Brody asked after the lengthy pause.

Deke couldn't have invited a better opening if he'd laid it out himself.

"Well, seein' as how you asked," he drawled, "I'd be—"

"Don't, Deke," Addie said in a warning that had just enough pleading in it to stir his conscience.

The problem was, she should have stopped there. But in her urgency to keep him from spilling the beans, she stepped forward as she said it. She stumbled again, this time as she caught the toe of her shoe on the gazebo step, which propelled her straight into Deke's arms.

Her breasts came flush up against his chest as she grabbed his shoulders for balance and his fingers grasped her waist. He just barely heard her gasp over his own stifled groan.

Holding Addie the woman as opposed to Addie the girl was as different as night and day—and yet as familiar to Deke as the fit of his leather work gloves. Because every time he'd ever stroked the back of his fingers across her cheek, every time he'd pressed his palm to the small of her back, every time he'd trailed his mouth down her throat and beyond—all came rushing back to him like the wind across the plain. He had no time to set his defenses against the familiar yearning that quickly followed.

Their gazes collided as surely as their bodies had, and Deke saw in Addie's blue eyes what he hadn't minutes before: desire, as strong and stormy—and undeniable—as ever.

He'd have felt some satisfaction if the sight hadn't pushed his own desire even higher.

Deke gritted his teeth.

"Deke, please, don't," Addie whispered, still clinging to him. "Don't stir up any more trouble."

"I stirred up trouble?" How could he have imagined her being hardened? She was anything but, as soft as a down pillow and as pleasurable to sink into. "Damn it, Addie, you're marryin' a *Brody?*"

"Addie?" Brody said from a few feet behind her. "What's goin' on here?"

"Let me explain things to him myself, please," she begged Deke. "Remember, you made me a promise. You wouldn't break it again so soon, would you?"

"That promise was for Jace's sake and you know it!" Deke said, in a low voice.

She had no response for him, only staring up at him in mute appeal, blue eyes shimmering.

"Why only nine months, Addie?" Deke demanded out of the blue, as would a man grasping at straws. But he had to know. "Why'd you give up lookin' for me after just nine months?"

"Why seven years, Deke?" she whispered as insistently. "Why has it taken you seven whole years to come back?"

Damn but it was quick, that wicked sharp blade of guilt slipping between his ribs, cutting through nearly a decade's worth of defenses, so that he'd have done anything to rid himself of the pain.

Then Deke's gaze fell to Addie's lips, still glistening from the kiss of that Roy Rogers wannabe—and a Brody to boot. The sight sure enough bought him a measure of reason.

"What's that sayin', Addie?" Deke murmured. "Somethin' like, Those that can't run with the big dogs shouldn't come off the porch."

He didn't voice the other bromide that had sprung to mind: *All's fair in love and war.*

He set her away from him and gave the now thoroughly stumped Connor Brody one of his friendliest smiles.

"To answer your question, I'm the new ranching consultant at the Bar G," he said.

He let the relief just barely touch Addie's expression before he added, "The name's Deke Larrabie."

Brody frowned. "Larrabie? You mean you're…?"

"That's right—Jace's long-lost daddy, come back to stay."

Connor's expression of stunned hurt tore a patch of anger through Addie a mile wide—yet failed to entirely uproot her own culpability.

Even though Connor and his father were very different, she could see why Deke would take particular issue with the fact that she'd have anything to do with Mick Brody's family, considering Mick's scathing condemnation of Deke and his father the night D. K. Larrabie died.

Of course, everyone also knew Mick had never gotten over it when D.K. ran off with his intended bride years before. Not many county folk had blamed Mick for getting a bit of his own back, even if it couldn't have been done at a crueler time.

But what better reason was there to bury such ancient history for good! Connor wasn't to blame for his father's actions any more than Deke was for D.K.'s.

She noticed Connor concentrating on straightening the silver conchos on his braided leather hatband in the removed manner she'd come to recognize as his way of closing off his doubts about her feelings for him— and Jace's objections to him as his new father.

Blast it! She should have gone with her first impulse and hustled Connor away from the Bar G so she could make her explanations to him in her own way and time. But no, she'd had to provoke Deke, practically waving a red flag in front of him.

It had cost her, too, with that inadvertent contact

between them that had shocked her in its intensity. And rekindled feelings in her she'd thought herself well shed of.

But it'd always been that way between them as they egged each other on, almost dare-like. On the upside, they had spurred each other forward to chart new territory, develop new skills and face down fears. On the downside, they'd urged each other on to greater and greater heights of expressing the kind of passion that was born out of a pair of natures that had never known defeat in their young lives, and so had no reason for caution.

No, Addie was forced to admit, Deke was not to blame for a lot of things, including her own reckless surrender to him.

"You could have told me, Addie," Connor said quietly, bringing her out of her thoughts. "That you'd hired Deke Larrabie to take over the work we were going to do together on the Bar G." He lifted his head and shot Deke a challenging glance. "And to take over the job of Jace's father in place of me."

"Connor." Addie reached for his hand, giving him her most sincere look. "First of all, Deke showin' up this morning was as big a surprise to me as it was to you—and Jace. And second, nothing's changed of our plans." She squeezed his fingers. "Think about it a minute. You know one of the things that's been so important to me is that we get the Bar G's future taken care of while gettin' you settled in running the Tanglewood after we're married. Deke's being hired to do some troubleshooting? Well, that's a temporary thing, as far as I'm concerned."

She couldn't even think of glancing at Deke, she was so put out with him. Connor didn't deserve this. So

theirs was no great love affair. She was very fond of
him. And sure, he might lack in ranching skills, but he
was steady and willing to do what it took to succeed—
and she truly believed that with time Jace would come
around to appreciating that. She and Connor had even
discussed giving her son time to get used to him and
not pushing Connor in the role of father, given the
issues that had come up about Jace's real daddy.

Which brought her back to her own responsibility in
this morning's little drama.

"As for Deke being Jace's father, well, I know
we've never really talked about it, since it's pretty
much common knowledge around here, except to
Jace—" Addie took a deep breath and admitted
frankly, "and Deke. He only just today learned himself
that he was a daddy."

Connor let go of her hand and leaned back on the
front fender of the pickup truck, now clearly confused—and, she could see, completely disillusioned.

She guessed if anyone here had a right to be, he did.

A sparrow landed in a nearby puddle and made a
production out of taking a bath. The rain had finally
let up, and the sun beat down on the three of them as
they stood in a silent triangle.

Addie lifted her hand, rubbing her forehead. She
knew that further explanation was needed, just as she
knew that the damage done to everyone involved was
not going to be easily repaired. It felt, however, as if
the burden of making that effort rested primarily on
her—as had the past six years during which she'd
struggled to raise a child, look after a failing parent,
and keep the family business profitable.

What other choice did she have, though?

With longing, she turned her gaze to her mother's

gazebo. She hadn't taken advantage in a long while of the steadying, perspective-building influence this special place had always provided her. She was simply too busy, with a million things to get done, and a million more to think about doing.

Oh, Mama, how I miss you!

Not for the first time, Addie wished for someone to turn to who might provide her with support. Not necessarily someone to bail her out, nor even someone to lean on. Just someone to…be there—to share the burden.

Addie slowly became aware of Deke studying her with that eagle-sharp gaze of his. Dropping her hand, she didn't bother to hide from him every bit of her world-weariness and discouragement.

And so she was surprised when he took a step forward, his own expression no longer challenging but decisive.

"Look, Brody, I'm as much in the dark as Addie about why Jud never mentioned to her about hiring me back on the Bar G," he said. "Maybe he's thinkin' Addie could use a little help herself—what with her marrying and moving and all—with keeping the Bar G going. Or maybe he just thought that bringin' a fresh pair of eyes to the ranch might be good for it, as it nearly always is in any business. You can be sure I intend to ask Jud what his plans are, first opportunity I get, and I'd recommend you and Addie do the same."

Tipping his hat back a notch, he took an appraising look around the ranch yard and beyond. "I'm willin' to evaluate the operation and give my feedback for how the ranch might be run more efficiently and profitably, whether I'll be involved in that effort or not. That's for y'all to decide."

His gaze came back around to them, and Addie realized she was being treated to yet another side of Deke Larrabie she'd never seen before. "I will say in Jud's defense that whatever his plans, you can rest assured he hired the right man to do the job. In the past five years I've revamped operations on ranches twice the size of the Bar G, so that now they're well into the black."

Connor straightened in surprise. "Well, thanks, Deke. That's sure big of you—you know, considerin'."

"No thanks needed," Deke said tersely. "It's my job."

Then he squared off in front of both Connor and her, but Addie knew Deke's message was for her alone. "As for bein' Jace's daddy, you can be sure I'm as prepared to handle that responsibility, too. I know you've made some plans of your own along those lines, but I'm here to tell you that I expect you to revise them to include me."

His face was a study in fierce determination, and its aspect was so undiluted Deke Larrabie that it caused a frisson of fear to sizzle up her spine, even before he said, "Or believe me, I'll take without askin' what's rightfully mine."

He gave the brim of his hat a tug down in the front, making his eyes stand out even more starkly against his tanned face. "Now if you'll excuse me, until I hear different, I've got a job to do."

Stunned speechless, Addie watched him stride with purpose to the building where the ranch office was located.

Who *was* that man who'd just sized up the situation and taken charge of it? Certainly not the Deke Larrabie she'd known before—except for his single-minded focus that in the past she'd experienced only as directed at her, making her feel as if she were the only other person in his world.

Yet she'd also experienced the loss of that all-exclusive focus, and it had nearly been the end of her.

She shivered suddenly, even in the claustrophobic heat. Deke had certainly sounded as if he meant business about taking responsibility for what was his. For Jace's sake, she'd have to be very careful.

And for her own sake, as well. Because somehow Addie got the feeling that Deke Larrabie's definition of what was his included her.

Chapter Three

Deke stepped into the Bar G Ranch stable. Amazingly, it looked the same as it always had.

Bridles and reins were hung neatly on pegs along one wall. Opposite was a variety of other horse tack and cowboy gear—harnesses, ropes and such. Just beneath, a row of stock saddles, including a hand-tooled one Deke knew to be Jud's pride and joy, sat on their racks. The pungent scent of leather and horse sweat rose up to meet his nose, making him yearn abruptly for that feeling of a well-trained horse galloping beneath him, a rope in his hand and a runaway steer trained in his sights.

At the thought, his gaze searched the rigging for one item in particular. His spirits lifted when he spotted it: a coiled catch rope, its color a dull brown from thousands of encounters with the dusty necks and dirty hooves of as many beeves.

Deke lifted the lariat off its peg, looping the coil over his right hand while taking the twisted nylon between his left thumb and forefinger. Its surface was taffy smooth, its girth still with just the slightest give, even after all these years.

No, neither had it hardened completely in his absence.

He lifted his head, and his gaze went unerringly to the doorway in the opposite wall leading to the small room off the back. Wondering when he'd developed such a masochistic streak, he drifted closer to push open the heavy door and see inside.

Light from a small, high window cast a beam onto the bunk directly under it. The narrow berth traditionally served as a place where the weary cowboy could take a break from roundup or catch a few winks while a mama cow struggled through a difficult birth. For Deke, however, this was where he'd made fumbling, awkward love to Addie Gentry.

Awkward, yes—but oh, every moment had been pure heaven.

"Checkin' to make sure you haven't hooked up with a shoddy outfit, are ya?" The voice echoed in the open space.

With the quick pass of his palm over his face, Deke turned. "Not the Bar G, Jud. Everybody knew you'd send packing the cowboy who let one horse go untended or one cow without care."

"You got the right of it."

Leaning heavily on a cane, Jud Gentry shuffled forward to take Deke's hand and shake it. Deke pretended not to notice how weak the grip had become, how faltering and uneven his step.

Jud Gentry wasn't an old man, by any means. But

it had been clear enough ten years ago that his Parkinson's disease was progressing quickly. Anticipating the day when he'd need to turn over the bulk of managing the ranch to someone both he and his daughter could trust and depend upon, Jud had picked Deke's father to groom for that role.

The whole county had thought Jud crazy as a loon.

In true Gentry fashion, he cut to the chase. "Thought I'd come see for myself the cowboy my grandson said showed up and got his mama half riled."

"That would be me," Deke admitted.

"Figured." Jud sighed. "I wasn't expectin' you for another couple of weeks, so I guess you can understand why your appearance here was such a surprise—to everyone."

"Finished the job up north and didn't see the harm in coming on down early." Deke decided as long as they were taking their conversation neat, he'd give it a shot. "I'd've given you some warning, Jud, if you'd given me some."

The older man hobbled over to the rigging-filled wall. "T'weren't my news to tell. I'll admit I'm to blame, though, for putting off apprisin' Addie of the arrangement we'd made. I was waitin' for the right moment. But I guess there really ain't a good time to break the news to a daughter that the father of her son is returnin' after seven years away."

"Nope." Deke studied the slab floor underfoot, determined not to be put off by the hint of accusation in Jud's tone. "Nor tellin' a man he's been a father for about as long." He lifted his head. "Why, Jud? Sure, I'm to blame for bein' scarce, but why'd y'all stop lookin' for me after nine months?"

Jud's gaze was direct. "Because of Addie, of course.

Oh, she didn't want me looking for you from the first, but that was because she was sure you'd come back of your own accord."

"She was?" Another lightning-quick jab hit his vitals.

"Yup. But after the months wore on, with no sign of you and not one clue as to where you'd got to, somethin' changed in her." Turning, Jud straightened a halter one inch to the left. "As I said, though, that's her story to tell. And why, when I got that call from you about the troubleshootin' job I'd advertised, I didn't mention Jace to you. I figured, though, that since you'd made contact, you'd a right to know about him. 'Specially now."

"You mean with Addie marrying Connor Brody."

Deke's tone had been even, but Jud must have caught an edge, for he said, "I didn't expect that'd set well with you. But much as I don't blame you your reaction, I still won't have you puttin' Addie in the middle of settling an old score with the Brodys. I'm not fond of Mick myself, don't trust the man one lick, but Connor's a good sort. You hear?"

"I hear," Deke said. He wasn't exactly happy himself with his contentious and, yes, even jealous behavior earlier with Addie and Connor. Jud was right. Clearly, Connor Brody wasn't in the same league as his father, and Deke would be as bad as Mick to hold the guy to account for something he'd had nothing to do with. Moreover, Addie was moving on with her life; he'd no right to get in the way of her happiness.

Of course, this time he didn't have the choice of trying to prevent such a fate by leaving.

"So why did you bring me on as a consultant?" he asked.

Jud peered at him from under bushy eyebrows the color of steel and rust. "I'll be straight with you, son. We've never fully recovered from losin' that breeding facility to fire—" he held up a hand to arrest Deke's apology "—which is neither here nor there. But if we've survived at all, it's Addie's doing."

The craggy lines of Jud's face softened. "She's one top-notch rancher herself. Strugglin' to come back after the fire, though, it's made her pretty cautious. There's lots she wants to do here, but she's set on the Bar G not goin' another penny into debt."

Deke chewed the inside of his cheek. "I don't know your thinking on the subject, but ranching is by nature an occupation of risks. Too much caution'll kill you as much as too little."

Jud came back dryly. "Try tellin' Addie that. You know how headstrong she can be when she gets a notion 'bout something."

Deke nodded tersely. If he hadn't seen that determination just now with Addie, he'd certainly known it from before. Except then, the momentum had been the opposite way, forging through adversity—not digging her heels in to put on the brakes.

He supposed that was another sign of that legacy he'd left her with.

"That's why I'm thinking that once she marries the Brody boy," Jud continued, "it'll be the natural thing for the two ranches to share resources to complete some of the improvements on the Bar G that Addie's of a mind to make. Which, I'll be frank, don't set too well with me."

He at least looked apologetic as he slanted an enquiring look at Deke, meant to see if they were on the same page—although Deke sensed there was some information Jud was omitting.

"But you can't expect her not to take the Brodys' help without givin' her some options. Right?" Deke said.

Jud gave a terse nod.

Absently, Deke fingered into place the honda that made the loop of his catch rope. "Mind, I don't know what her plans are, but there're a number of ways to up a ranch's productivity and guard its assets without it costing a bushel, and I'd be happy to help you and Addie evaluate and implement any and all of them."

He shot Jud a telling glance. "That is, you, Addie— and Connor. I can see you have your doubts about me, but I'm here to tell you I'm a professional. Still…you may as well know, Jud—Addie's asked me not to tell Jace I'm his daddy, and I felt I owed it to her to give her my word."

He gave the loop a testing twirl, stirring the thick air in the stable. "But I'm not about to let any man try to be a father to my son without me getting a fair crack at it, too."

He held Jud's gaze steadily, and after a few moments came away with the feeling that, even if he might still have his issues with Deke, they understood each other as men who were doing what they had to do—as fathers.

Knowing he had at least that understanding from Jud helped to ease the wound-up tightness in Deke's chest. But then, Jud didn't know the whole story, either. Or, rather, not yet.

A trio of steps took Deke to the doorway of the stable. He scrutinized the scenery beyond, including that rise with the crumbling chimney beneath the towering cottonwood.

"Speakin' of dads…that fire never would've happened, y'know, if I'd been keeping an eye on mine," he said quietly.

"Now, Deke. The fire was purely accidental."

"But the accident happened on account of Dad's fallin' off the wagon." Doggedly, he made himself go on. "They found the empty whiskey bottles in his pickup."

"So they did. That don't mean any of D.K.'s drinkin' was your fault," Jud declared from behind him, then said with a sigh, "If only he hadn't lost your mama…"

Deke's jaw went rigid as he tried to swallow back the pain that crowded his throat. He'd known his return would call up all manner of feelings. He'd thought himself past this strong a reaction, however. Apparently he wasn't.

"I know better'n anyone the reason for my dad's undoing," he said. "You don't have to go into it for my edification."

"Well, now, maybe I do—for myself. 'Cause I understand how a man's grief can eat at him so much he'd need to numb the pain any way he can. I lost my wife, too, at a young age. And Addie a mother. That's why I encouraged your friendship with her."

Jud's words had Deke again seeking the scene on the slope. There were other words, though, that needed saying.

"And I betrayed your trust by takin' advantage of your daughter, then leaving her high and dry, didn't I."

The older man said nothing, which was answer enough. Then Jud heaved a heavy sigh. "Hell, I knew

why you had to go, Deke. T'wouldn't have been good
for you to stay, no matter what, with your daddy's mistake hangin' over your head.''

''For what it's worth, Jud,'' Deke said, gaze still
trained on the slope, ''I always intended to return and
make up for my dad's fatal mistake. And finally I've
got the training and experience I didn't have when I
left, to make a real difference to the Bar G.''

He turned. ''But I'd never've gone if I'd known
about Jace,'' he said with a low fierceness. ''No matter
what.''

''I know, son,'' Jud said, his blue eyes full of understanding.

Which made it more impossible than ever for Deke
to reveal his own fatal flaw, discovered that sundering
night, when it had occurred to him the reason D.K. had
sought the numbing oblivion of liquor on that particular
eve: He had needed to wipe from his mind that it was
the anniversary of his wife's death.

When the realization had hit Deke, the terrible fear
it had roused in him—and not any yearning to be his
own man—was what spurred him away from the
Bar G. Because he knew why he'd forgotten that date.

He'd forgotten because there'd simply been no room
in his own mind that evening for anyone or anything
but Addie Gentry.

And if he still felt so desperately betrayed by his
own will, could there be any hope on earth of *her* ever
forgiving him?

With that thought, something made Deke look
around.

There at the doorway stood Addie. And the answer
to his question. For in her face he glimpsed again that
legacy he'd left her—a loss of hope and trust, but most

of all, a loss in the belief of the redeeming power of a man's love for a woman.

Or was that the legacy that had been left to him?

Addie went still as the bottom dropped out of her world.

Oh, what a fool she was! A fool and a fraud, if only in her own heart. For she'd heard Deke's fervent words, quite obviously spoken from the bottom of his own heart: *I'd never've left if I'd known about Jace. No matter what.*

So he'd never have left—because of Jace. Would never have come back now—except for the debt he owed her father. Not for her. How could she have hoped or wished or believed differently?

Because…once upon a time, he'd made her believe his promise, so much that even when she'd discovered he'd gone, she'd refused to contemplate that she could be wrong about the man she loved. Even when she'd discovered she was pregnant.

And when her father had set out a search for Deke, he'd done so against her wishes as she faithfully clung to the belief that Deke would come back of his own accord—because of his promise to her.

Even when Jud's efforts had proved fruitless, indicating that Deke clearly hadn't wanted to be found. Even then, she'd held out hope with every fiber of her being.

It wasn't until the night she'd first held her son in her arms, and looked into eyes that were so like the father who hadn't given *any* of them the chance to prove their love, that she'd faced the truth: Deke Larrabie was not coming back.

She had thought him the kind who stayed, but obviously he wasn't the man she believed she'd fallen in love with.

Addie looked up to find Deke's cat-eyed gaze upon her, its intense focus as seductive as ever.

She lifted her chin, defiant.

"I thought you were goin' to town with Connor, darlin'," her father said, breaking the silence in the stable room.

"I changed my plans," she answered, stepping inside. She still wore her yellow suit and those infernal high-heel shoes, which she was of a mind to use as hole spacers in Opal's garden patch. That was all they were good for. "And I thought I'd better find out what's goin' on with the Bar G that I need to know about. Or am I consigned to fence-sitting when it comes to runnin' this ranch—and seeing to my son's welfare?"

She arched an eyebrow at her father, who gave back as good as he got. She still didn't know the whole story behind Deke's hiring, but trusted her father would never do anything to deliberately hurt either her or his grandson. Jud had stuck by her through the abyss of Deke's leaving, and it had been her one sustaining anchor. Of course, that didn't mean there weren't occasions when she could chew a railroad tie in two for sheer aggravation with him.

He no doubt felt the same way about her, too, sometimes.

"Believe me, darlin'," Jud said, "I surely intended to fill you in on my hirin' Deke. He wasn't supposed to get here for another couple of weeks." He leaned heavily on his stock saddle where it rested on its rack. "I'm sorry to have given you such a surprise. I never meant to."

"But why didn't you consult me *before* hiring him, Daddy?" Addie asked, crossing her arms. "You owed me that, I think."

"Now, darlin', we did talk about hiring a trouble-shooter—"

"And I felt then as I do now, that *I've* got the ability to bring the Bar G solidly back into the black."

She refused to look at Deke as he stood there, once again privy to a private family conversation and keeping her from asking her father the real questions she wanted to. *Why? Why, of all people, did you bring back Deke Larrabie, the man who broke your daughter's heart?*

But then, deep down, she already knew the answer to that one.

To his credit, Deke was at least making a pretense of not listening to their discussion as he ambled out the wide doorway of the stable, idly spinning his catch rope.

She couldn't help but watch as he swung a loop over his head, then to one side, then the other, as always his movements smooth, his technique flawless, his rhythm pure poetry. If truth be told, it had been his magic with a lariat that had won her heart, so much was it like the courtship between two lovers.

"Adeline."

Tearing her gaze away, Addie met her father's eyes, as keen as always.

"You're still the go-to man on all the decisions about the Bar G," he said. "That hasn't changed and won't. You know that, don't you?"

Exasperatedly—lovingly—she studied him as he stood there, hand upon his saddle, its horn still wrapped in inner tube rubber from his working days…days when *he'd* been in charge and in command himself, no dispute. She had always seen herself as being cut from the same cloth as Jud Gentry: fearless in carving out new territory in ranching, perhaps not literally but in the spirit of their ancestors who'd set down roots in these parts over a hundred years ago, hoping to build a future.

But she was also a woman who'd had some of the choices for her future taken away from her.

"Daddy," Addie said as gently as she could while still being completely honest, "I just don't think the Bar G can handle another Larrabie rainmaker coming in with big promises and taking big risks, then leaving everyone else to pick up the pieces."

"That won't happen, Addie."

This had come not from her father but from Deke, his attitude no longer casual as he stood in the dim light from the doorway. He was back to that intensity, again bent upon her.

"How do I know that, Deke?"

"It won't," he vowed. "You've got my word."

"But you made such a promise to me once before," Addie said, still without accusation, just speaking the truth she knew. "A promise to stay. Then you left."

"I came back, though," he responded with that maddening certainty. "Here I am. And this time, nothing'll make me leave."

He swung the loop around, the gesture automatic, she was sure, but did he have to do it at that moment? Did he know how mesmerizing, how seductive it was to her?

How it made her want to give in to more than just his will?

"Look at it this way—what could it hurt, Addie?"

Deke said. "I'm not charging y'all for my time. And you'd have the final say in anything that gets done."

What could it hurt? Oh, everything and everyone! Jace, for instance. The boy was searching right now. Searching hard. And who knew what he'd find if she let it happen? Or was she the only one who saw the danger on the horizon, coming at them all with the inevitability of a swarm of locusts?

Or was that still the danger within her? Because she'd seen the spark of challenge leap to Deke's eyes earlier today with Connor. Had seen the spark of desire there, too.

The mere prospect of it had Addie running scared, for she'd once held nothing back from this man, so much so that when he left, it felt like going from swimming in an ocean of emotion to being stranded on a parched, barren desert, where you'd have sold your soul to taste just one drop of those feelings again.

She simply would not—could not—risk taking one step in that direction again.

Yet once again she was being asked to give her trust. And once again she hadn't much choice but to give it, whether she wanted to or not.

For at that moment Jace rounded the corner of the doorway and stopped dead at the sight of three adults in the midst of one serious discussion.

"Hi there, hon," Addie said quickly, holding out her hand to him, needing literally to take him under her wing to try to protect him, one last time.

But it was too late. Something had caught Jace's attention. Fascinated, he came a few feet closer to where Deke stood on the threshold of the stable, on the threshold of their lives.

"Could you teach me how to rope, mister?" he asked, looking up at Deke.

And it was the way Jace said those words, soft and uncertain and more like the little boy he'd been a few months ago, that made Addie wonder if perhaps she was the one who was being shortsighted here.

Except, at the same time the sight of the two of them yearning toward each other almost without conscious thought drove that sense of danger in her even higher.

She was helpless to halt its progress, though, as Jace continued. "Y'see, mister, no one else around here can, but *you* could, 'cause…well, 'cause, you know, you're like *me*."

Deke's fingers clenched reflexively on the lariat in his hand. For a wild moment, he wondered if somehow he'd already unintentionally broken his promise to Addie.

His gaze flew to hers in question, in apology, and he saw fear within her blue eyes, too, but not for the same reason.

"What Jace is saying," she explained, her voice neutral, "is that Daddy and I, and the rest of the boys, have had the devil of a time tryin' to teach him to rope." She hesitated. "He's a southpaw, you see."

"Yeah." The boy nodded, his hat still screwed down on his head, Festus-style. "That's what I meant. I'm a southpaw."

"Well, fancy that, Slick. So'm I," Deke murmured, as first pride then regret filled him at discovering yet another trait his son shared with him. It drove home to him the loss of six vital years with Jace that he could never, ever get back. And brought back old insecurities that seemed to turn upon themselves like a snake swallowing its own tail.

No, he had no intention of betraying Addie's trust in him. Even so, he couldn't have made himself leave that stable right then if they'd made it a felony.

Lord, but it was a revelation to him, the look of his son. He saw so much of himself there that he'd never even realized belonged to him. The unbending tilt of his chin. The resolute set of his mouth. The vigilance in his eyes with which he gauged a changeable and uncertain world.

And since Jace had always had the constancy of home and other family, Deke knew there could only be one cause for that sort of measuring watchfulness in a boy.

The second hand governing his heartbeat sped up again.

"First say a proper hello to Mr. Larrabie, Jace," Jud said. "He's one of the best ranchin' troubleshooters around. We're lucky to have him come to work on the Bar G for a while."

Deke sent his silent thanks to Jud for his support. It helped, especially when Jace asked, "Is that your name?"

"Yup," he confirmed, trusting Addie would see no harm in revealing that much. "Deke Larrabie. You can call me Deke."

"So will ya teach me how to rope, Deke?" Jace asked with that mixture of hope warring with doubt in his eyes—and overriding them both a hunger that Deke was oh so familiar with.

He cut a glance at Addie. She stood with her arms crossed, one of those long legs of hers extended to the side as her weight rested upon the other. She evinced no reaction, and he guessed that was as much of a go-ahead as he could expect from her. Or as much trust as he could expect.

He had to come through for her.

"Got a piggin' string, Slick?" Deke asked.

The boy practically dove for the short, thin rope neatly coiled and hanging on one of the lowest pegs on the wall. He held it up for Deke's inspection. "Granddad already taught me how to take care of it proper."

"Well, that's the first thing a cowboy's got to learn—how to keep his gear in top condition. All right." He took a stance side by side with Jace. "The key to ropin' is startin' with a well-built loop, like so."

One at a time, he methodically measured an arm's length of rope, then laid it across his right palm, making uniform coils.

Tongue tip tucked over his top lip, Jace copied him. Deke approved with a nod. "Now, once you got a good loop in hand, you can practice your throwin' technique. You mind givin' us a target, Jud?"

"Not a'tall." The older man held his cane up like a sword.

Deke gave a few twirls above his head, then let the rope sail, laying out the loop in a perfect circle that slipped over the cane all the way to Jud's elbow before touching his arm.

Jace gave his rope a few shaky spins and let it fly, missing Jud's cane by a mile. His face fell to the cellar.

"Give it another go, Slick. 'Member, it's all in the wrist." Deke demonstrated, overdrawing his actions for Jace's benefit.

The boy's next try was better, and his next better still, as the loop of his rope caught the cane's tip.

It was all Deke could do not to give Jace's shoulder a squeeze of approval. He settled for a praiseful "Now you're getting it, Slick. I knew it wouldn't take you long to catch on."

The boy's smile at him from under the brim of his ten-gallons-too-big hat was heartrendingly naked in its yearning.

A lump the size of a melon crowded Deke's throat. He was almost ashamed to enjoy his son's regard, it had taken so little effort to win it.

"There's already a Larrabie here, y'know," Jace said out of the blue. "Out under the cottonwood. You know him?"

The watch spring in Deke's chest gave a tightening twist. "That was my daddy," he replied matter-of-factly.

He wondered what had compelled Jace to ask another of those surprising questions, but was fast learning that, much like his own interest, there was nothing aimless in Jace's, including the boy's next question, posed as he let sail with another try at heading Jud's cane.

"So you've been here to the Bar G before?"

"Yup." Deke dared not glance at Addie or Jud, rather than risk seeing their disapproval of this attempt, indirect as it was, to connect with his son. "Before you were born."

He was halfway to regretting his stab at getting to know Jace, when the boy said, "I know."

Perspiration broke out across Deke's forehead. "You do?"

"Yeah." Jace concentrated on hauling his rope in. "Mama tol' me about how your daddy got caught in that big ol' fire here on the Bar G. What'd you call it, Mama? A terrible, um…''

Deke's gaze connected with Addie's. She still wore a mask of neutrality, but her voice was soft as she answered, ''A terrible tragedy…for everyone.''

Deke supposed he should thank her for that, considering what she'd been going through, both then and now.

''That it was, Slick,'' he murmured as softly. ''That it was.''

''Why d'you keep callin' me Slick 'stead of my name?''

Deke tore his eyes from Addie. More than the others, this question seemed completely out of left field. He could only ask Jace in return, ''Why, do you mind it?''

''But a slick's a calf that ain't got a brand yet. I got a brand.'' Deke didn't miss the challenge in the boy's voice. ''I belong here at the Bar G—''

''Jace,'' Addie broke in. ''You've taken up enough of Mr. Larrabie's time for today—''

''I'll never be a Tanglewood man, no matter if Mama marries Connor Brody.'' Jace rushed on as if he'd never heard his mother, his attention focused on Deke. ''That won't make him my daddy, y'know!''

Deke set his catch rope carefully aside. ''I guess not, if you don't want it to,'' he answered Jace, trying for Addie's neutrality and obviously coming up short, for in the next instant he heard her warning ''Deke, please.''

It was Jace, however, who had no qualms about taking a stand. ''So did you know him?'' he demanded.

''Know Connor?'' Deke stalled.

The boy's own catch rope got tossed to the wayside. ''No—know *him,* from before.''

Deke shot Addie a glance of pure apology, which she returned, he saw, with one of regret—that she had let it go so far, that she had let him so far in. For at that moment, Jace, no longer either wary or hopeful but something in between, squared off in front of Deke. He had to admire the boy's gumption, even if he was suddenly disconcerted to find as sharp a scrutiny on him as he'd ever bent upon critter or human.

That's when something told Deke his son wasn't talking about either Connor Brody or D. K. Larrabie.

Still, he had to ask, "Did I know who, Jace?"

"My daddy!" Jace said impatiently. "Did you know my daddy?"

Chapter Four

Deke kept his poker face, but just barely, as the impact of the question pulsed through him, *tick-tick-tick*.

"What...what do you know about your dad, Jace?" he asked slowly, his mind going ninety miles a minute as he tried to sort through what Jace really wanted to know, and what he himself could say. Because even though he'd made a promise to Addie, he saw now that there was no way on earth he could lie to his son.

"That he left afore I was born," Jace answered. "That he din't want a hand in raisin' me."

"Is that... Do you think that's what he wanted?"

The question, which Deke had to allow was evasive as all get out, must have struck his son the same way, for Jace's expression shut down. "I don't care! It doesn't matter, anyhow. I don't want any daddy, ever. I sure don't need one."

Then, for some reason, the boy's anger turned on

Deke. "We don't need you, either. Mama and me can run the Bar G fine without anybody's help. So you can leave!"

Deke steeled himself against the rejection and the pain as his mind whirled madly. His promise bound him as surely as any straitjacket, but he had to come through here, had to give as good as he got.

He dropped to his haunches so he could face his son squarely, putting all the sincerity he had at his disposal into his gaze. "I don't doubt that you can, Jace. The thing is—"

He paused, torn. Yes, he'd given Addie his word, and just like the other, long-ago promise he'd made to her, he would keep it.

He had to, or he'd be lost forever.

"The thing is, Jace," he said slowly, "I'm not leavin'."

The youngster froze for half a second, then lunged at him, grabbing handfuls of his shirt and pulling furiously. "But we don't want you here!"

Deke was taken so off guard that he was drawn forward to his knees before he had a chance to catch his balance. When he did, though, it was by clasping his fingers around Jace's upper arms, just as he had earlier.

The contact seemed to send the boy into more of a frenzy. He released his hold on Deke's shirt, only to come at him with a flurry of fists.

"We don't want you here!" he cried. His hat flew off his head backward. "Just go, now!"

"Jace, please—"

A stray punch struck Deke in the Adam's apple. If he hadn't had any appreciation for what Addie had had to deal with earlier, he sure enough had it now, big time.

The boy was frantic, seemed himself pulled by two opposing needs. Oh, yes, Deke knew the feeling all too well. And it would eat you alive if you let it.

"Wait a minute." He tried again, fingers still clamped on Jace's arms. "What's this all about?"

He refused to be put off, even when Jace landed another blow, this time to the chin. "Tell me, Jace. Why're you so mad?"

The boy went still, gasping for breath. "'Cause...I just want to know! Why won't you tell me, if you know?"

"Know what?"

"How *he* could leave!"

Lord above, what he saw in his son's eyes at that moment! Yearning, anger, doubt. It crashed into Deke with the force of a raging bull. For he knew much of what showed in Jace's gaze was what Addie herself must have felt. Still must be feeling. To see it, know it in the flesh, was like laying open his gut with a filet knife; he felt exposed, vulnerable.

His own breathing came in spurts, his heart was beating so fast. So what was he to do—lie to his son? Or betray Addie's trust? It seemed another of those impossible choices, just like the other moment in time when his deepest vulnerability had been shown to him in vivid, absolute detail.

The emotion continued to radiate from Jace; it was like standing ten inches from the noonday sun, searing in its intensity. Deke couldn't turn away from it, though, no matter if it burned him to a crisp.

"Jace," he said hoarsely, "he...your daddy, that is...he didn't want to leave—"

"He didn't?" Jace interrupted. Abruptly, where seconds ago there'd been out-of-control anger, now tears of fearful hope sparkled in his son's eyes. Eyes that were so damn much like his own that it took all of Deke's strength not to glance away. Not to leave and never look back, rather than fail to live up to that hope.

"You *do* know why he left, don'tcha? You gotta tell me!"

Deke could only look back at him in mute agony. Lord, but he would have cut off his roping arm to know the right words to say at that moment.

Because how did a man tell his son that he'd never have left had he known about him—and that his mother bore part of the responsibility for depriving him of his father's love?

Oh, the naked longing in his voice! If Addie had never regretted before keeping her son from his father, she did now, unbearably so.

Why was she letting the exchange between Jace and Deke go on? What had she been thinking? She'd only wanted to let her son have the chance to be taught how to rope by an expert. To give him the experience of looking up to a man the way a boy looked up to his father, just for a little while.

But it was abundantly clear to her that Jace had not reconciled himself to his father's absence from his life. *That* was what the earlier scene in the ranch yard had been about. Jace would never be able to accept any man as his father until he'd confronted and laid to rest his anger and hurt about his real dad.

How could she have been so blind to her son's needs?

Except that she'd been trying to accommodate her own.

Deke still held Jace by his arms, his gaze glued to

his son's, but somehow she knew it was her that he was most aware of right now.

So what would he say, if she let him answer Jace? Would he tell him the truth—one in which neither of them came off looking too great, but would at least absolve him of the entire blame for his actions? And, she couldn't help thinking, would bring him a measure of retribution—for hers.

He'd made her a promise!

Oh, but he'd also vowed to take what was rightfully his without asking, and the consequences be damned.

"Jace," Addie said.

The boy turned his head, his look as desperate as she'd ever seen it, asking her, too, for answers that so far he'd been unable to get from her.

"I... Come here, hon—" Her voice cracked. "Please."

Without a second's hesitation, he tore himself from Deke's grasp and came to her, throwing his arms about her waist. Some of the ache eased in her as she pressed him close protectively, her fingers soothing his thick hair back from his forehead as over his head she met Deke's gaze.

He held it staunchly as he slowly drew himself up to his full six foot two. In that guarded glance she saw so little of the cowboy she'd lost her heart to—and so much of Jace—that she could barely keep her composure.

She couldn't lose her son, too.

Jace craned his head back to look at her. "He might know somethin' about what made my daddy leave." His forehead creased with apprehension as he caught the fear in her eyes. "But he doesn't, Mama. I know he doesn't. He's lying!"

He pulled away from her to face Deke again, standing between her and his father in that protective stance of earlier this morning, fists at his side. "You're lying!"

"Jace," Jud said sternly. "Show some respect for your elders."

The boy ignored him, even shook Addie's hand off his shoulder, and her stomach flipped over as she realized he wasn't about to back down, not this time. And as much as she wanted to keep Deke out of her son's life, she realized he already was.

She had to protect Jace, though!

"Jace," Addie said, "it doesn't matter, hon, not anymore—"

"But it does."

This, to her surprise, came from Deke.

"I'd like to answer the boy, if I might," he said with that infuriating self-possession and command. "I think he's got an explanation comin', don't you?"

You could have rolled her heart in cornmeal and fried it up, for all the good it was doing her in her chest. "Deke," Addie said warningly. "You made me a promise—"

"And I intend to keep it. I didn't lie, not just now—and not seven years ago," he said forcefully, then seemed to check himself. "I'd like to give the boy an explanation, Addie," he repeated more calmly, yet with as much conviction, "but the choice is yours."

Is it, though? she wanted to ask him. Sure, she'd told him she wanted the right to choose—rights he'd taken away from her when he left. Yet there had never been much choice where Deke Larrabie was concerned. It would have gone against her very nature not to fall in love with him, not to give herself to him so completely.

No, Addie realized, she had no one but herself to blame for many of the events in her life.

His gaze was a burning heat upon her, the message there loud and clear: *Trust me.*

Could she trust Deke, though? Trust him to put their son's emotional welfare above any of the conflicts between them?

Wondering if she were inviting the devil himself into her parlor, Addie nodded.

Deke settled into a squat so that he was on a level with the boy. "Jace, I do know why your daddy left and what caused him to stay away," he said calmly. "It's kind of, uh, complicated, but the gist of it is, he left not because he didn't care—about you…or about your mama—but because he *did* care, a lot."

"I—I don't get it," Jace stammered in confusion. "How could he care an' then leave?"

Addie ached to reach out and soothe his fears away. Yet some instinct told her any such gesture right now, no matter what Deke might have to say to their son, would do more damage than good.

"What I'm sayin', Jace," Deke said, "is that your daddy left because he was tryin' to do what he thought'd be right for everyone concerned. Making a clean break of it seemed the best way of doing that."

His chin dropped briefly, and to her amazement, she saw that in fact, he wasn't calm at all. Deke's Adam's apple bobbed as he fought to get a grip on himself. Yet when he lifted his head, Addie had never in her life seen a man look more rock-sure of himself.

"But here's something you can bank on, Jace, if nothin' else, 'cause I know your daddy like I know myself. And that is, if he'd known that you were here thinkin' he didn't care about you," he said, conviction filling his voice, "I promise you on my life that nothing on God's earth could have kept him away."

Addie froze, her ears ringing with his words. It didn't take a genius to know Deke's pledge was meant for her, too, almost more than for Jace.

Then Deke's gaze lifted and homed in on her. And this time it wasn't the polished and impenetrable cowboy who'd come back, but the one she'd fallen in love with all those years ago.

Immediately, the old familiar flame jetted up from her core as if fanned by a shot of pure oxygen, in that way that could make her forget all caution, forget the rest of the world, even. Forget how he *had* broken his promise to her, left her alone and pregnant at seventeen.

But then, he'd been no more than a kid himself, and dealing with so much.

She became aware of Jace trying to get her attention, nearly tugging her arm off. "Mama?"

She glanced down at him and saw what he wanted: He was looking to her for confirmation of Deke's vow.

Addie drew in a shuddering breath. "Deke Larrabie wouldn't lie to you, hon."

She experienced a small measure of peace as relief sprang to her father's eyes and hope to Jace's. Perhaps having Deke in her son's life would help Jace to resolve some of his feelings about the father he still technically never knew. On one hand, she was glad for Jace; a boy needed something to believe in. *Someone* to believe in.

But it was when she saw the question burning in

Deke's amber-green gaze, asking if she, too, could believe, that Addie knew she had to shore up her defenses.

The realization came to Deke about his fifth day on the Bar G that it was going to take more of his diplomacy skills than his ranch expertise to bring Addie Gentry around to even considering some of his ideas for the operation.

She'd been as hard to pin down as a butterfly's shadow over the past few days, as he'd tried to set up a time to go over the Bar G's situation so he could get an idea of the improvements to recommend.

But Addie had made it abundantly clear that she didn't want his help, thank you very much. Even more, Deke could tell she was making a point of showing him that the Bar G didn't need him.

There was no doubt, though, that Addie knew her ranching, Deke thought as he watched her stand in the bed of the ranch truck, pointing out to the cowboys with the flick of her wrist the heifers she wanted cut out of the herd and moved to the west pasture, where she'd turned the bulls out for breeding.

"Wes, you take tag numbers 2310, 3111, 2942, 1583 and 3523," she called out in rapid succession, barely consulting the computer printout in her hand. "Harley, looks like 3423, 2340, 1003 and 4039 are millin' around over there in a bunch. Whyn't you take them."

Her cow pony, a good-looking chestnut gelding called Keno, stood next to the pickup, lazily grazing while he waited for his mistress. Jud sat in the driver's seat of the pickup, but it was evident Addie was running the show today.

Deke waited until she'd finished handing out assignments, before lifting the reins on his own horse, a brown-and-white dappled paint named Nevada, and starting toward the pickup.

Jumping down from the truck's bed, Addie caught sight of him, a look of wariness immediately overtaking her face.

Well, she was just going to have to realize that when it came to avoidance tactics, he wrote the book, cover to cover. She didn't have a chance.

"Need a hand cutting some of those heifers out of the herd?" Deke asked.

"We've got it covered," she retorted, untying Keno from the side mirror.

From behind her, Jud gave an exasperated shake of his head that told Deke he'd gotten just about as far with his daughter.

Deke adjusted the brim of his Stetson a notch lower on his brow in silent acknowledgment.

"We're missin' a yearling heifer," Addie said to Jud, pulling on her leather work gloves. "One of the boys said he saw her over by the creek a few days ago. I'm going to go have a look."

Jud squinted an eye at the horizon. "Appears we got some weather comin' this way," he observed as he started the pickup. "You might keep an eye out for it."

"Will do."

She'd swung into the saddle and had started off without giving Deke a backward glance, when she noticed him trailing her.

Addie stopped dead. "And just what're you doin'?"

He graced her with his friendliest smile. "Thought I'd tag along, is all. I've got nothin' better to do—seeing as how you've got everything under control."

He thought she'd bust a molar, she had her jaw

screwed down so tight. "Suit yourself," she finally said.

Which he did, riding on her pony's right flank as she set off across the grassland.

Despite the overcast sky and muggy air, it was a fine day for being outside, especially on the Bar G, lying as it did along the Brazos River and jam-packed with rolling hills and eye-catching vistas. The spring had been a wet one so far, meaning the grass was coming up lush and green, making for good grazing. The sight was one to lift any rancher's spirits.

And today Deke found his heart further gladdened by the bumper crop of Texas wildflowers the rain had brought. Every now and again he and Addie came over a rise, and there they'd be in patches of every color— blue, orange, purple, yellow, white, pink, and one of the richest, deepest reds he'd ever seen—sprinkled cheerfully across the landscape like bits of confetti.

The sight of them sounded deeply in him, answering back with a haunting echo. He'd only spent a year here in Texas, but it had been the most intense, vivid time in all his life, so that the days and months since had paled in comparison.

It wasn't Texas, though, that had made him feel that way. It was Addie.

He ventured a covert glance her way. She was in her usual work clothes of faded jeans that hugged her shapely hips and long legs, and a blue-and-yellow plaid Western shirt that molded to her breasts when the wind blew.

Now it was he who was reduced to gritting his teeth. Would there *ever* be a time when he wouldn't ache at the mere sight of her?

He let the silence between them continue until they'd

reached the creek bank, where he decided the moment was prime to get down to business.

"Y'know, Addie," Deke said easily as their horses' loose-jointed walk carried them along the creek bank, "Jud had his chance to interview me about my experience, but I'm thinkin' that you might have some questions to ask about some of the things I've done."

He should have gotten a clue as to what was coming by the way her blue eyes narrowed assessingly under the brim of her straw Stetson. "Actually, Deke, I do have a question for you."

"Go ahead. Shoot."

"Why'd you leave seven years ago?"

He'd sure walked straight into that one. There was no way he couldn't not answer her, though. Not now.

Deke's heart skipped a beat, then raced ahead with that tick-tick-tick tempo.

"To answer your question," he said as truthfully as he could, "I thought my father had brought about the ruin of yours."

He paused, then went on. "And I honestly believed that if I stayed, I'd be the one to bring about your destruction."

Addie frowned. "That's what you said before. And I know I was only seventeen and couldn't have altogether appreciated what you were havin' to deal with, with how your daddy died."

She hit him with those laser-blue eyes. "But you could have talked to me about those things, Deke. About your father and how hard it was for you to see him struggle with…his problems."

Lord help him, her soft admonishment only brought home to him again his failure. He'd grasped it when he'd seen her with Jace and knew, in an instant, what fate his leaving had consigned her to. And he could see by the turning down of her mouth that she still was a long way from understanding that, even though he'd failed in his attempts to spare her pain, his intentions *had* been good.

Yet he was here to try to make her understand, wasn't he?

"There didn't seem much to talk about," he ventured. "Everybody knew Daddy was a drinker."

"They also knew he was kindhearted and loyal and always ready to help a friend however he could," she said softly. "It *was* a terrible tragedy, Deke, how he died."

Deke swallowed, hard. It was what she'd told Jace about his grandfather, even if the boy didn't know it. Her empathy—*her* loyalty—almost undid him.

He gave a nod toward an enormous live oak in the distance at the creek's edge. "There's your stray."

Again of one accord they turned their horses, taking it slowly down the steep grade. But that was all they seemed to share at this point, and Deke knew he had no one to blame but himself, as the gap between them widened, for shutting Addie out.

"Y'know, I don't remember ever tellin' you much what it was like before Dad and I came to the Bar G," he blurted out in a rush, fearing he'd lose his nerve if he gave himself too much time to think. "I guess it's no secret, though, that after Mom died, Dad had bounced from job to job for years before Jud hired both of us. It was quite a difference, after so long of living hand to mouth."

"You stuck by your father the whole time, though," Addie reminded him, "even after you were old enough to make your own way in the world."

She adjusted her weight in the saddle as Keno picked his way along the uneven creek bank. They were all choosing their steps and words with care, he realized.

He concentrated on the split-stitched seam of his glove as his hand clenched his reins, and made himself go on.

"That had been the hell of it." He gave Nevada his lead to do his own negotiating of the rocky incline. "Dad had been sober for almost a year, had had redemption practically in his grasp—right before he downed a quart of liquor, made his way to the new breeding building, and in some kind of alcoholic stupor set it on fire."

He wondered if his brutal painting of the scene would put her off. Then again, she'd asked for just such a heart-to-heart with him on the subject.

"But why," Addie asked beside him, "after he'd been sober for so long, and with things going so well, would he have…you know, taken a drink?"

Why indeed? Deke thought. How well he knew the answer.

He took a huge breath and revealed the most intimate information he'd ever shared with her, maybe with any other person on earth. "Y'see, it wasn't just that Mother had died that drove Dad to drink in the first place. He blamed himself for her death."

There was a beat in time, one in which Deke's pulse shot ahead like a cannonball.

Then "How, though?" came Addie's soft cry. "How could he have been responsible?"

"He'd taken her away from Texas, from her family and the support that'd always assured her of being taken care of, to go to Montana where he knew he could get work. But the ranch he was hired to manage was about as far from civilization as you could find.''

He noticed that his tone had gone flat, dead almost, but that was the only way he could tell this. "So when Mother came down with pneumonia during a killer blizzard, no doctor could make it through the snow to save her. She died in Dad's arms. After she did, I thought he'd go crazy.''

He fought to suppress a shiver, even though the back of his shirt was soaked with perspiration. "Anyway, I'd been my daddy's shadow my whole life practically, and I pretty much knew by heart all the signs that he was workin' up to a good drunk—first he'd rail at no one in particular, 'cept maybe God. Then it'd get quieter, more bitter. And finally'd come the… hopelessness. I think that was the worst of all.''

"But there were none of those signs the last time. It makes you wonder, doesn't it, if maybe something else was goin' on that night.'' Addie looked at him questioningly. "I mean, I know Mick Brody found the liquor bottles in your dad's truck, but who knew how old they were?''

Deke lifted his gaze and idly watched a black buzzard spiral slowly in the distance, its eye trained upon some carrion in the brush below.

"What else could have happened?'' He took another deep breath for courage. "That night'd been the tenth anniversary of my mother's death. I'd never known that date to pass without some kind of low hittin' Dad.''

He heard her sympathetic intake of breath. "Oh, Deke. How awful! I never knew!''

And once again her sympathy nearly undid him. It was harder to take, almost, than her anger and hurt, although he couldn't have said why.

"Sometimes...sometimes I'd give everything I own and then some to go back to that night and change what happened." He gave a rueful laugh. "Those kinds of thoughts were my major occupation for years. I pictured it so clearly—how I'd be there when Dad first got that desperate look about him that said he was fightin' taking a drink."

He held out his hand, palm downward. "I'd follow him to his truck, set my hand on his arm as he reached for the door handle, ready to drive to the nearest bar or honky-tonk or liquor store—wherever he could buy a bottle. And I'd convince him, however I had to, not to go."

Even now, the daydream was so real to him. Sometimes he awoke in the mornings and would believe it had happened as he hoped—before the truth hit him.

He let his hand fall to his thigh.

"When you're dreaming that dream, do you change the other part of what happened that night?" Addie asked quietly. "Because I've had the exact same fantasy—that I find you, set my hand on your arm and convince you, however I have to, to stay."

Deke turned his head and met her gaze, still direct but with a vulnerability he hadn't seen up to now lurking in the back of her eyes. Could it be he'd been wrong and she hadn't grown hard and cynical, at least not deep down? Or perhaps she'd only become more like he had: able to hide fears and doubts and hurts and weaknesses a whole lot better than she had seven years ago.

"I wish that I hadn't hurt you afterward by leaving," Deke said as quietly. "But can I regret what happened between us?" His own sense of vulnerability shot skyward, but again, he couldn't lie to her, even if he still couldn't yet give her the complete truth. "No, Addie. Not any more than I could regret the son that came from that night."

And that was the weakness *he* had fought for years to bring under control—that Larrabie way of losing himself in a woman, to the detriment of them both.

For he was backsliding at the slightest provocation of the naked emotion in Addie's eyes—fear, anger and hope, much like he'd seen in Jace's, in his own—that Deke felt himself tumbling, tumbling down....

Thank goodness they reached the stray at that moment, because he was very close to falling in love with Addie Gentry all over again. Ignoring her as best he could, Deke hefted his leg over his saddle and slid to the ground, looping his reins over a low-hanging branch of an oak tree to give Nevada enough slack so he could drink from the creek, aware the whole time of feeling as restless as a wildcat shut up in a zoo.

When he finally got up the nerve to turn around, he found Addie still a-horseback, watching him with the same pensive gaze she'd had when he'd given Jace an explanation of a different chain of events that held no fewer unanswered questions.

He held her gaze steadily, not giving ground—but not stepping forward to make up for the loss of any, either.

Finally, she sighed and dismounted.

The white-faced heifer eyed them both warily. Up to her belly in cool brown water, she was clearly not going anywhere without some none-too-gentle urging.

Addie stood looking at her with crossed arms. "You wanna flip for who wades in and takes hindside duty?" she asked.

Even as tense as he was, Deke suppressed a smile.

While game for just about any other ranch work need-ing done, Addie could be a regular pantywaist when it came to getting wet.

"I would, but I thought you had things perfectly under control," he drawled.

She treated him to a baleful glare.

"Well, it might be that neither of us'll have to wade into the creek," he said.

At the inquisitive lift of her eyebrow, he untied the rope from his saddle horn and built a loop to throw over the cow's neck, then sent it soaring through the air to hook the critter in one try. Digging in his heels, he tugged on the rope with a strong, steady pressure.

Fortunately, the soft-bottomed creek made it hard for the yearling to get any leverage herself. Apparently re-alizing she was outmuscled and outmaneuvered, she lurched forward and in a matter of seconds was climb-ing up the embankment and on her way.

"I sure didn't expect that'd be so easy," Addie ob-served, watching the heifer trudge off.

Deke coiled his lariat. "You mean getting a stubborn heifer to give in to the inevitable, or givin' me a little bit of rope to prove it," he drawled.

Her chin dropped, and she turned away from him to settle her rope back on her saddle. When she turned around, her expression was one of exasperation—and something he couldn't quite get a bead on.

"Look, Deke, I know you're wantin' to make it up to Daddy and me for what happened by comin' in and making an assessment of the operation, maybe play a part in turning some things around here, and I thank you for that, I really do."

She gave the slide on her hat's stampede strings an

unnecessary yank. "But I'm in charge of the Bar G now, and whatever gets done is on my say-so."

"And from the looks of it, you've got things well in hand. I'll say it myself—you're one helluva rancher, Addie."

He could tell his praise set her back. She wasn't expecting it. He pressed home the advantage.

"Can I ask you somethin' now, Addie?"

"I guess," she answered cautiously.

"How's your breeding program working for you?"

She frowned. "You know how we do things here. We calve year-round, although we do try to get our heifers bred within a thirty- to forty-five day period so the calves will be uniform in size and weight come fall market time."

"Which is a pretty sound strategy." He gave a nod in the direction of the folded computer printout peeking out of her shirt pocket. "And it looks like you've got fairly accurate records on the reproductive history of most of the herd."

"Of course. The rancher that doesn't keep track of his herd these days will get left behind for sure."

He made a show of mulling over her comment, until she became really curious.

"What's all this about, Deke?"

He scraped the pad of his thumb down his jawline. "We-ell, at the risk of getting accused of tryin' to shear you like a spring lamb, did you ever think about starting up an artificial insemination program on the Bar G again?"

She sent him a doleful look. "To tell the truth, I have. I'm with Daddy there, that the Bar G is going to keep playin' catch-up as long as we lack a comprehensive AI program."

"Then, why haven't you got one?"

"Are you obtuse or just plain mean?" She set her hands on her hips. "You know why. We can't afford it as things stand right now."

Then the stubborn set of her full lips eased, and she continued in soft admonishment. "You *know* how tough the ranching business is, Deke. The only thing we've got to spare is work needin' done. Anybody with a choice—and a brain—would rather sell sand in the Sahara than beat themselves up trying to make a living ranching."

And still, Deke understood that she wouldn't have it any other way.

"I don't see how you can afford not to implement an AI program," he said as tactfully as possible. "We're not talkin' about jumping feetfirst into a big program involvin' a huge investment in equipment and facilities."

"You mean like Daddy did," Addie said stiffly.

"I mean like *both* our fathers did." He held out one hand, palm up. "You're right, in that my dad came in and like a modern-day rainmaker sold Jud a bill of goods way bigger than was needed to get the job done. But your father also bought it lock, stock and cash on the barrelhead, with barely a thought for prudence."

The defensiveness leapt to her eyes like a blue flame. "Daddy knows he shares the blame for usin' up most of our cash and a good portion of our credit to build that breeding facility. He knows what happened was because of the choices he made."

Deke said nothing, letting her statement hang in the air between them until she admitted, "I know it, too."

Finally. It did him good to hear her say it out loud like that, even though he'd known her sense of fairness and justice would have come up with the verdict long ago. And her sense of compassion in a world where every day people let their fears or bad judgment or weaknesses get the better of them.

Yes, he knew that if he could find it in him to tell her the real reason he'd run out on her, chances were she'd understand. The thing was, he couldn't make himself believe that understanding would bring with it his reformation. That sure hadn't been the case with his father. And it sure wouldn't up Addie's trust in his staying power now.

So. It seemed a catch-22. He was damned if he did, damned if he didn't. Nope, he was just plain damned.

But he'd already figured out how that was his fate long ago, hadn't he?

A crow the size of an armadillo dropped down between them, gave them both a quelling look, like a teacher reminding a couple of schoolkids to play nice, and took off again.

"Look, all I'm sayin' is that there are ways to implement an AI program without a huge outlay," Deke said, falling back on the one subject he did know backward and forward. "It mostly takes sound herd management and a well-trained AI technician—which I am and can teach you to be."

"But, Deke—"

"And there are other ways to improve your balance sheet." He ticked them off on his fingers. "I'm talking about developing the Bar G's beef as a specialty product to get it out of the commodity market, and creating limited partnerships in the family to protect you and Jace from havin' to deal with huge inheritance taxes."

He'd registered about halfway through his speech how desperately he wanted to make it up to her and

Jud for the loss of their building, how much he wanted to help them through the straits they were in right now. And if only he could, maybe it would make up for what he could never compensate for.

But it seemed he wasn't going to get even that opportunity, for Addie said, "Actually, Deke, while I appreciate your input and insight, we really are doin' just fine on our own."

So she would still reject his support out of hand.

He couldn't help himself. "Damn it, Addie, anyone can see you're not! Not that you aren't maintaining, but it's going to take some serious strategizing in a bunch of different directions if we expect to hold on to this ranch for our son!"

She stared at him for a moment, and he wondered if he'd overshot his mark, trying to get through to her.

Then she blinked, dropping her gaze. "I hear what you're sayin', Deke. Believe me, I do. I don't know how much sleep I've lost, worrying about how to keep the Bar G going. But you can't expect to just barge into my life and start directing traffic, especially when I've made my own plans for the ranch. Which you didn't even ask about, or you'd know already that by the time fall breeding comes around, the Bar G will have the wherewithal to put a comprehensive AI program in place!"

She lifted her chin in challenge. "Connor and I have already worked out exactly how we'll do it, too."

Half a dozen years of screwing down the bolts on his emotions allowed Deke to bat not an eye at her barb. Instead, he concentrated on getting past Addie's own emotionality about this subject and helping her let go of her caution just enough to do the Bar G some good, as he'd been hired by Jud to do. He had to, or he'd sure enough find himself back where he was seven years ago, with as much control over what happened to him as a feather carried along on the breeze.

She had it out for him, though, that was plain to see. Even if she was willing to take a bit of a risk, she wasn't about to do it on his advice; otherwise, why would she want to wait till fall to put an AI program into place?

What, he wondered, was going to change between now and six months from now?

Then it hit him. Addie would be married—to Connor Brody, who'd be bringing with him the Brody ''where-withal.''

Deke went dead still as his mind churned with the evolution of another revelation. He *knew* Jud had been leaving something out! Sure, Addie's father had hired him because he felt Deke deserved a chance to be a father to Jace. But it dawned on Deke now, the real reason Jud had brought him in: To assure the Bar G's survival and protect his family's future and happiness, of course—but also to show Addie it could be done without an infusion of Brody capital.

And that could only mean one thing. Whatever the reasons Addie was marrying Connor Brody, it wasn't for love. Deke would bet his next year's salary on that.

His heart surged with a hope he had barely realized he harbored.

Or was this all just wishful thinking on his part? Was she still, deep down, the hopeful girl he'd left behind, or was she actually the sadder but wiser woman he'd spied within moments of seeing her again? Sure, she was more cautious, but would she really shortchange her own happiness so grievously for the sake of security—even Jace's?

All Deke knew was that if she would, then the blame for Addie feeling she had to make that choice rested squarely on his shoulders.

Chapter Five

Addie saw the obstinate set come to Deke's mouth—and the dangerous glint to his eye—the cause of which she'd come to recognize as being the mention of Connor.

"You—and Connor Brody," he said in the calm voice he used that made her feel anything but. "And just what, pray tell, did he have to contribute to your plans, since I hear he's so green at ranchin' that it wouldn't wash off after a month of scrubbing?"

She bristled. "He's learning, that's true. He didn't have the experience we did growin' up on the range because he was livin' mostly with his mother in Dallas after his folks divorced. But you won't find a harder worker or a more sincere heart than Connor's," she said loyally.

She could tell that didn't set well with Deke, as he

methodically adjusted the fit of his gloves, one finger at a time.

"Hard work and good intentions don't make a rancher out of a man," he said. "And they sure don't make him a father."

"Oh, don't even go there, Deke," she warned.

But it had become apparent to her these past few days how taken Jace was with Deke, how the boy was looking up to him more and more—and was less and less interested in forming a bond with Connor. And it was because Deke had the job of cowboy locked down and vacuum-sealed.

More than that, though, he had a world of patience for the boy, was never too busy to stop and make a gentle suggestion or even to go one better and give Jace the opportunity, with a bit of guidance, to figure out how to do something himself.

Our son. That's what he'd said. Deke wanted to help her protect the Bar G for their son. His words had nearly brought tears to her eyes, for it was her own heartfelt desire—one that every parent holds for their child.

So why did it hurt so much that Deke was so obviously as committed to that end?

Because much as he'd like to prove differently to her, he hadn't changed! Hadn't it been as clear as crystal to her just now in the way he'd gone back and forth between openness and shutting her out? The whole conversation had been agonizing to her, because it had been more evident than ever that this was a man who was still at war with his impulses. And as long as he was, she could never be sure of him. She'd have to be a fool to put her trust in him.

Yet, of all the burdens she'd borne over the past

seven years, this was the one Addie most wanted to lay down. She would give anything to be able to let go and trust again.

A drop of rain landed splat on the bridge of her nose. Addie stifled a groan. "Damn. I forgot to keep an eye on the sky."

This was just what she needed right now.

Deke peered into the distance. "Looks like an ugly one's on its way."

Of course she had her rain slicker with her, tied in a roll on the back of her saddle, but getting caught in a good gully-washer had never been her idea of fun.

Another drop hit her cheek, then another, as she squinted upward. The storm would be upon them in another few minutes. They'd get drenched.

Then her gaze collided with Deke's, and she knew what he was thinking.

"We could stay here like a couple of sittin' ducks," he mused, with a meandering turn to untie Nevada's reins. "After all, it's pretty far back to HQ. A body would have to have a real good incentive to take a shot at beating the storm back home."

As put out as she was with him, Addie couldn't help herself.

She lifted her eyebrows. "You mean, like a friendly competition of some kind?" Nonchalantly, she reached for her own reins, letting them slide over the palm of her leather glove. "Such as a race?"

It was an old game of theirs. The challenge was never overtly agreed to. Then the loser would have no way of saving face.

"A race? Hmm…now, there's an interesting idea," he allowed, as with a studied casualness he turned his nearside stirrup just so.

Addie grinned—and vaulted into her saddle.

Like lightning, within a split second they were both on their horses and lunging up the incline before taking off at a gallop, racing across the range, neck and neck with each other, whipped along even faster by a hefty tailwind carrying a gray curtain of rainfall.

Laughter bubbled up from inside her as she bent forward over the saddle horn, practically hugging Keno's neck, the air whistling past her ears and the pounding of the horse's hooves vibrating through her entire body.

And heavens, it felt good! How long had it been since she let loose like this in a full-out rush of exertion and sensation and action? She felt like she'd been struggling for so long now against an overwhelming tide, hampered by that weight that had to be borne. And making so little progress.

Addie shot a glance across at Deke and saw her own exhilaration reflected in the sharp lines of his jaw and the fierce set of his mouth, his Stetson pulled so low over his eyes as to render them pure shadow.

Her own hat, dangling behind her from its stampede strings, bounced between her shoulders. She felt the band holding her ponytail shake loose, which sent her hair streaming out to tangle with her hat and its strings and the glorious wind.

The ride ended far too soon. Addie and Deke pulled up in the ranch yard just as the downpour let loose in earnest with a shimmer of lightning and peal of thunder, drenching them instantly.

She slid from her mount to find him already on his feet and reaching to take Keno's reins. Sprinting for the stable, Addie lurched the door open, as Deke, head down, followed at a trot, leading the horses. She slammed it shut behind him, dulling the storm's roar only by a few decibels.

"Hoo-ee!" he exclaimed inside, shaking himself like a dog and sending water flying in every direction. They were all, horses included, sucking in air after the mad dash to get here. "I haven't had a good flat-out, run-like-the-devil's-on-your-tail ride like that in ages."

Addie sank back against the side of a stall, laughing helplessly. "I didn't know Keno had it in him." She gave a shake of her head. "I guess I didn't know I did, either."

"So much for not getting wet." His eyes made an appraising once-over of her. "Well, Boney, don't you just look like somethin' the cat couldn't be bothered to drag in?"

They both looked like drowned rats. Water dripped off the brim of his black Stetson, and his shirt and jeans were plastered to his body.

"Boney Gentry." She pulled a shirttail out of her jeans and daubed at her face with it. "I haven't heard that one in a while."

His next once-over was much more thorough. And much more disturbing.

"Of course, your old nickname doesn't exactly fit you anymore, does it?"

Addie flushed hotly, despite the chill of her wet clothes that clung to her, she realized, like the shrink-wrap on a package of hot dogs.

"You were the only one who ever called me that," she said almost breathlessly. She wondered if he remembered the other name he'd called her. Wondered how it would sound to hear it again in that low, rough, passion-filled voice of his.

His respiration seemed a little limited, too, as his

chest rose and fell with the deepness of his breathing. It drew her attention to the way his shirt molded to his broad shoulders and flat stomach, his jeans to those long, lean legs of his.

Her gaze jerked back to his, and they stared at each other, the tension so thick between them it was about to spontaneously combust.

Then Deke did speak in those husky tones she remembered, although the words were angry rather than passionate. "Damn it, Addie, of all people, why'd you hook up with a Brody?"

The question took her aback. Not *why did you fall in love with a Brody?* It got Addie's defenses up.

"You're gonna have to get right straight over that, Deke," she ordered. "Connor is not Mick."

"But he's all set to inherit the Brody ranch and money, isn't he? What's the sayin' these days? 'How *convenient.*'"

Shock rippled through her. How dare Deke insinuate she was only marrying Connor for the material advantages he brought with him. How *dare* Deke!

He was wrong, that was all there was to it. Dead wrong.

Then, how come she couldn't face him down and tell him so?

"I don't have to stay here and listen to this!" Addie exclaimed.

She started to stalk past him, but damn if she didn't catch the heel of her boot in a drainage trough in the concrete floor, which sent her stumbling.

Deke's hand shot out to catch her arm. Addie gasped, her head rearing back automatically, bringing her nose to nose with him. Even with his hair plastered to his temples and the smell of horse sweat steaming up around him, she experienced a lightning-quick jolt of desire at his grip above her elbow.

What was it about this man that made her feel she walked on stilts, even when her feet were planted firmly on the ground?

Or were they?

His gaze dropped to her mouth.

He was going to kiss her any second now, she just knew it. And when he did, what would she do? Addie wondered as the thought sent fear blazing up in her like a match set to kindling.

Yet spreading through her as quickly was that desire that couldn't be beaten back or doused, it seemed, even with the flood of an ocean.

She couldn't give in to it. She couldn't give in to him.

"Damn you, Deke, you can't barge back into my life like this! You just can't!"

Was it simply her, or did she sound desperate instead of resolute?

Something of her determination must have come through, however, for his lips thinned abruptly into a line mirroring his own struggle for control. He uttered raggedly, "But you've gotta see there's no way I can leave, either."

The hell of it was, his action drew her attention to *his* lips, and, unbidden, just the whiff of a remembrance of that mouth upon hers brought the memories charging back in vivid, spine-tingling detail.

Addie swallowed, audibly.

Those cat eyes of his grew dark, predatory, and in an instant he had swung her around, bringing her solidly against his chest—and his mouth hard upon hers in a kiss of such naked hunger it took her breath away.

And heaven help her, she didn't care. Didn't care if she ever took another lungful of air in her life as his tongue thrust into her mouth with even less finesse. But she didn't care; she took him with shameless eagerness as she displaced his hat with the force of her fingers driving into his thick, damp hair. Damp not from rain but from striving—to push her, push himself, harder and farther than either of them could go on their own.

Because suddenly all that mattered was this consuming need in Deke that her soul was called to answer without reservation.

"God, Addie, it's been so long," he muttered against her mouth, almost bruising her lips. His eyes were dark and burning, so close to hers. "Too long."

"I thought I'd die when you left," she whispered fiercely, suddenly needing him to know the depth of her anguish, when moments before she'd have done anything to hide it from him. But that was the nature of the emotion between them. They had always been nakedly honest with each other. There was simply no room for pulling back or evasiveness. There'd been no ability to be so. "I wished with all my heart that I could die. And maybe, if it hadn't been for the child you left inside me, I might have had a chance of letting go...."

To his credit, he didn't glance away, didn't loosen his hold on her one bit, even if a war of regret raged in his eyes. It gave her the courage to go on, as vulnerable as she'd ever been in her life.

"But I didn't forget you, Deke," Addie said with a catch in her voice. "And I didn't forgive you—and that's got nothing, *nothing* to do with Jace."

He didn't respond, at least not in words. Deke crushed her to him, taking her lips even more roughly than before, as if he couldn't help himself. Addie didn't pull away from him, either, but opened wider to him, her heart curiously soaring.

This was what she needed from him—for him not to turn away when she reached out to him. For it to be as impossible for him to make that choice as it had been for her seven years ago, and still was.

With a guttural groan he took the kiss even deeper in a mating of plunging tongues and bruising of tender tissues. With hungry hands, he cupped her bottom, lifting her against the cradle of his pelvis and the long hard length of him. It sent a hot rush of passion up from deep in her vitals, surging in a lava flow through the rest of her body.

Deke seemed attuned to it, so much so that that he dragged his mouth from hers to demand "Tell me."

"Tell you what?" Addie whispered hoarsely, starved for his lips upon hers again after only a second of their separation.

"Tell me he makes you feel like this, that you would marry him even if the devil himself were his father," he rasped. "And I swear I'll leave here in the next instant and never come back."

In a daze, Addie almost damned herself by asking "Who?" But then, who Deke meant dropped on her like an anvil, bringing her back to her senses.

With all her might, she shoved herself away from him.

"Is that what this is about?" she choked out. The front of her soaked shirt, warmed by his body, grew instantly cold again, making her shiver. "You showing up a Brody? *Is it?*"

Again he said nothing, only wiped the back of his index finger along the length of his lower lip, amber-green eyes watchful.

It was all she could do not to break down in tears. Instead, she said with the deadly calm that was his trademark rather than hers, "Not that I'd be surprised if it was. Oh, not about your wanting to get back at the Brodys. After all, that's the Larrabie way."

She hit him with a laser-straight glare. "Just like it's the Larrabie way to promise to stay in one breath— and then admit what it'd take to make you leave in the next. *That's* why I stopped looking for you after nine months. The first time I held our son and looked into eyes that were so like those of the father who hadn't given either of us the chance to ease his burden with our love, I faced the truth about you—" Her voice broke. "Y-you were not the kind that stayed."

She couldn't keep it up, it seemed—the nerves-of-steel, ice-water-for-blood facade he had down to a science. She had to go on, though. "So don't go blaming me for cheating you out of six years with your son. You cheated *yourself* out of the love and support that comes from sticking by each other through the tough times."

He registered her words with barely the twitch of a muscle, but she knew she'd hit home. It seemed a small victory that she'd been able to retain the same emotional honesty they found when in each other's arms, now while standing apart from him.

Yes, it was a victory, she realized—and a defeat. It was like that wild ride just now. With one look they'd both thrown caution, decorum, everything to the wind, and laid themselves out there without restraint, just as it had always been with the two of them.

That was the hell of it. It *was* more than a physical connection that drew them together, both years ago and now.

With that thought, the words he had spoken to Jace came roaring back to her: *If I'd known that you were here wondering if I'd deserted you, or didn't care about you, nothing could have kept me away.*

Those words had been for Jace, not her. He wasn't walking away from her now, though, even with her anger at him so fresh, the hurt in her so evident—still.

Of course, she hadn't answered the one question that would send him on his way.

Addie stared at Deke, her breathing speeding up again despite herself. And despite herself, letting every bit of her hurt show—raw—on her face.

Like before when they'd stood in the ranch yard with Connor, Deke finally seemed to register the anguish he was causing her, for he said, "You're right, Addie. Not that it's all about Brody, but that I've got no right to blame you for anything that's happened in the past. And that I've got no right to barge into your life. I won't touch you again. I know my word doesn't hold a lot of weight with you right now. But you can take that, if nothing else, to the bank."

His lashes flickered above those glowing eyes before he turned to tend to their horses, his mouth resolute as ever, but this time for a different reason.

And as she watched him lead the two exhausted animals away, it did Addie no good to realize she wanted him more than she ever had.

It was difficult for Deke not to be sour as an old wet rooster as he pitched rocks at a row of pop cans perched on a fence railing in back of the Bar G's HQ.

The ranch yard was pretty much deserted. Addie and Jud had taken off for somewhere, and the ranch hands were either making their Saturday rounds or taking advantage of a day off to spend time with their families or best girl.

And here he was, exactly two weeks since he'd first stepped foot on the Bar G, still spinning his wheels in a cow pen gumbo of Addie Gentry's making.

Sure, he'd been able to make a little headway, despite her resistance: He'd gotten a cattle reproductive history software package installed on the ranch computer and had started converting some of the information about the herd Addie had already collected to the new system, with Jud's help. Deke had also developed a general sorting scheme for the herd, which would help cut down on the economic losses that could result from either over- or under-feeding cows, depending upon their reproductive status.

But it was all still a far cry from what could be done that would put the Bar G into a more secure position—without any outside funding…Brody or otherwise.

He wished to hell he knew how much time he had left before that particular deal was sealed.

Deke scowled and slung a rock so hard and with such deadly aim that it hit one of the cans with a sharp *clang* and sent it flying backward off the railing a good ten feet.

"That was neat!"

Turning, Deke spied Jace a few yards away.

"Hey there, Slick," he said, surprised. "You at loose ends today, too?"

The boy nodded, scuffing the toe of his dusty brown cowboy boot in the dirt and raising more dust. He was wearing his usual T-shirt and Wranglers with the cuffs turned up. And the hat that made him look like the cowboy version of the Flying Nun.

"Mama and Granddad hadda go all the way to Houston for the afternoon,'' he revealed, picking up a rock. ''They said they had some things to get done that wouldn't 'specially interest kids.''

He took a stance just like Deke's, right foot forward and left arm cocked, and let the rock fly. It whizzed between two of the cans and plunked to the ground.

''Hey, nice try,'' Deke said, but the boy's disappointment was written all over his freckled face, causing a tug at Deke's heart. He'd discovered in the past few weeks that he had a mammoth-size soft spot for his son.

He often found himself wondering if the boy recognized himself in the cowboy who'd come to stay on his granddad's ranch, and whether it was just a matter of time before his son would figure out who Deke Larrabie really was to him. Every now and again, Deke would catch Jace watching him, especially when Addie was around, too. For that reason, he tried to keep his frustration with her to himself.

The last thing he needed was for Jace to pick up on the tension between him and Addie—because he knew the day would come when his connection with Jace would be revealed, and the boy would know who his real father was.

It was inevitable—even if Addie liked to believe there was some element of choice in the matter.

''I was thinking of takin' a drive myself, get some ice cream at the D.Q. in Bridgewater,'' he asked Jace to distract them both from their frustration. ''You wanna come?''

Jace lit up like a Christmas tree. ''Sure! Oh, wait. Maybe I better not, since Opal's baking cookies. My fav'rite kind, too—chonc-late chip. She said she'd have a batch comin' out of the oven for me any minute now."

Just as quickly as his face had fallen, he perked up again. "I bet there'll be enough for you, too, if you want."

Deke cocked his head, one eye closed. "Am I remembering right that Opal used to win just about every blue ribbon at the county fair for her bakin'?"

The boy nodded enthusiastically. "She still does!"

Ten minutes later, they were sitting in the wooden seat in the gazebo with a plate of warm, gooey chocolate chip cookies and two perspiring glasses of cold lemonade between them.

The day was hot, as usual, but a brisk breeze had cleared away the moisture in the air, which sharpened the color and detail of everything in sight.

And the view was Texas at its best. The old Bar G homestead, built a century ago of durable Austin stone, glowed like old gold under its corrugated metal roof, which itself shone blindingly in the bright sun. In the distance a bunch of Herefords grazed in a patchwork of white and rust against the deep green landscape.

"So what do you want to do now?" Deke asked once the last cookie had been dispatched.

"I dunno," Jace answered. He was licking chocolate off his fingers with such relish, Deke didn't have the heart to correct his manners. "Did y'know it was Mother's Day tomorrow?"

"Actually, I plain forgot." He settled back against the railing, stretching his arm along it, only inches from Jace. He still ached to touch his son whenever he could, the experience was so novel to him, and had to force himself to not fabricate opportunities to do so. He'd been fairly successful, given how he'd been getting tons of practice doing the same with Addie.

He'd been mentally kicking himself ever since that day he'd kissed her in the stable—while simultaneously glad he'd done so. Which was pretty much the problem. It drove home to him once again that when it came to Addie Gentry, he'd never be able to control his actions completely. She raised in him a powerful craving he simply couldn't deny. And if that wasn't the definition of an addiction—like his father's alcoholism—then Deke didn't know what was.

Addie would never see it that way, though, just as she'd never see in his leaving seven years ago the strength it had taken for him to go—and to stay away.

He sighed. "I don't tend to mark the day, I guess because my mother's been gone now for some eighteen years."

"Eighteen years?"

The span of time clearly seemed an aeon to the little boy, especially one in which to be without a mother.

"Yup." He chewed on the corner of his mouth for a second, wondering if he should get much further into this subject with Jace, then decided there was no harm. "Your own mom's mom, who would've been your grandma, hasn't been gone much less."

The youngster gazed up at him solemnly. "Did you know her? My grandma, I mean?"

Deke gave a brief shake of his head. "She'd passed away before I came to the Bar G." He ran his palm over the rough surface of the peeling railing. "This gazebo used to be her pride and joy, though, I know that. I don't know if she likes to anymore, but your mama used to sit here when she wanted to feel close to her mom."

Jace screwed up his face in contemplation. "I don't think I've ever seen Mama just sit anywhere. She's awful busy."

The stab of guilt Deke experienced couldn't have gone any deeper if he'd driven it in with a sledgehammer. He knew if Addie felt she had to keep going all the time just to keep up, he was partly responsible.

But damn it, here he was now, ready and willing to lend a hand, and she continually rejected it outright!

Scowling to himself, he flicked away a scab of paint he'd picked loose. Somebody really ought to give this gazebo a good once-over with a scraper, a layer of primer and a couple of coats of paint.

"So have you gotten a gift for your mom for Mother's Day?" he asked in a half-assed change of subject.

"I made a clay handprint in school to give her." Jace drummed his heels against the wood seat. "It's not very fancy, though. I'd kinda like to do something else for her, but what?"

He peered up at Deke, obviously looking to him for an idea.

"That would be the question, wouldn't it," Deke muttered ruefully. But it did him some good to know at least someone on the Bar G would trust him, even though he couldn't imagine how he could come through for his son in this instance.

Then Deke straightened, for it had just occurred to him how he could do so this time for Addie, too.

"So you're lookin' for what else you can do for your mama, are you, Slick?" he said with a slap of his palms on his thighs. "Well, as luck would have it, you've come to the right man."

* * *

Two hours later, Deke and Jace had returned from their dash to the nearest hardware store for paint, primer, brushes and scrapers, and were making slow but steady headway in sprucing up Addie's gazebo.

Mostly Deke was trying to get the exterior scraped down and sanded while simultaneously steering his son's shaky technique with a brush. The boy seemed to get more of the latex primer on himself and the grass than on the gazebo.

Deke eyed the inch-wide swath of white across the front of Jace's shirt and hoped to heaven the manufacturer's claim that the paint would wash up with warm water and soap held true. At least Opal had recognized his plight and had contributed a few old sheets as drop cloths, as well as kept the snacks and cold drinks coming.

There was no way they'd finish the job today—it was already coming up on suppertime—but thanks to the dry air and good strong breeze, the primer had dried nicely. The two of them would at least be able to apply a topcoat of the gunmetal-blue paint that nearly matched the current color on the gazebo's exterior, and maybe even have time to start on trimming the gingerbread cutwork in ivory.

Taking a step back, Deke gave their work so far a slow appraisal and pronounced, "Looks pretty good, doesn't it, Slick?"

Jace imitated his stance down to holding his paintbrush in his left hand, right thumb hooked in his belt loop. "Sure does. Ya think Mama'll be surprised?"

"I guarantee it."

The youngster bent to dip his brush into the paint can just as Deke had showed him, coating the bristles about halfway and letting the excess drip off before applying it to the wood.

Deke's chest swelled with pride—and a certain grim satisfaction. Yup, he and Jace were only growing closer every day. There was no way Connor Brody could be the father that Jace wanted and needed.

"I wish I'da had the chance to know my grandma," Jace said, bringing Deke out of his thoughts. They were painting side by side, Huck Finn and Tom Sawyer-like. "Both my grandmas. And my other granddad, too."

He swiped at a fly and effectively daubed his cheek with a smear of blue paint. "Y'think they're still alive somewhere, and just don't know about me?"

Deke was sharply aware of the cottonwood tree in the distance with the headstone beneath it. Yes, there was just such a yearning in the boy, too, for a connection, for roots, even though he had grown up with the stable foundation of a Bar G heritage.

But would he want the kind of roots that came from the Larrabie family tree?

Deke shook such doubts from his head. "No. I know for a fact they're not, Slick. But I think I can safely say they'd have loved to've known you, too."

"Really?" Jace said, clearly disbelieving. "How d'ya know?"

He wasn't going to lie to the boy, but he knew he was going to have to be careful. "Because I knew 'em both—your grandma and granddad on your father's side—same way I...same way I know your father."

This news was evidently ponderable enough to absorb Jace's thoughts for the next several minutes. And just when Deke was sweating a river, wondering if he'd said too much, his son let loose with a bombshell of his own.

"I figure my daddy must be dead, too," he said matter-of-factly.

Deke went cold. Stone cold. A hundred and one questions and possibilities raced through his mind. Finally he croaked, "Why would you think that, Slick?"

"'Cause. You said he cared—y'know, 'bout me and Mama. So I got to thinkin' that something must be keeping him from comin' back to see us. Something big."

Jace sounded so matter-of-fact, as if he'd puzzled out all by himself how to put a fiador tie in a headstall, and Deke instantly realized the legacy—again, of his own making—that he had left his son. It was a legacy that might forever prevent him from having the relationship he so wanted with Jace, for the same reason he'd never have Addie's trust again.

Still, he had to ask. "Like…like what, Jace?"

He shrugged his small shoulders. "Well, the only thing I could figure that was big enough to keep my daddy from comin' back after all this time was he's dead."

Chapter Six

Addie took the hand Connor proffered as she got out of the passenger seat of Mick Brody's Lincoln Town-car.

"You look tired, darlin'," Connor said, putting his arm around her and giving her a squeeze.

She gave him a wan smile in return and leaned gratefully against him. It had to be almost midnight. What a long day! And an even longer evening, as she, Connor, her father and Mick Brody had gone out to dinner, at Mick's insistence, to "celebrate" successfully hashing out the particulars of a prenuptial agreement at the attorney's office.

The whole process had been about as conducive to a sense of real partnership between her and Connor's families as one of them shooting the other's purebred hunting dog. She'd hated each second. It went against every instinct in her of how a marriage and a relationship should work, where two people committed themselves to each other with the knowledge that they'd have their concerns and their differences, but that their love and trust would see them through the rough spots. And family differences be damned.

Of course, having that sort of bond wasn't where she was at with Connor.

Just not yet, she reminded herself.

"Looks like your dad's going to be talking to mine in the car for a few more minutes," Connor said. He pressed his lips to her temple, then whispered against it, "Which gives us a chance for a little alone time."

Taking her hand, he tugged her across the springy turf and out of the glow of the yard light, until they had reached the darkened gazebo and climbed its steps.

Once they were inside, Connor swung her around, wrapping his arms about her waist and nuzzling her ear.

"Damn, I've been dying to get close to you like this all day," he murmured. "I thought that meeting would go on clear into next Tuesday."

Linking her hands behind his neck, Addie wrinkled her nose at the whiff of what smelled almost like paint. But then the breeze floating through the gazebo whisked it away.

Ah, how glorious the cool air felt on her skin! Especially after she'd been cooped up all day.

"It was pretty grueling, wasn't it," she admitted.

"No more than a root canal during a migraine the day after your dog's gone missing."

Addie chuckled, amazed at how their thoughts jibed.

"I thought Dad would ruin everything today with all his hard-lining every detail." Connor sighed and went on. "I know he hasn't gotten to where he is today for bein' the shy, retiring type. But Good Lord, it's not like he hasn't known your dad for all his life.''

Again, she thought it amazing—and endearing—that the worst Connor could say about his father was that he looked out for his interests a little too zealously.

''You're so sweet,'' she said impulsively but with all sincerity.

''Just sweet?'' His expression was difficult to make out. ''Not…I don't know—irresistible, or dangerous to your equilibrium, or—'' he gave a nervous laugh ''—sexy as hell?''

Now she sighed. ''Connor—''

But he wouldn't let her go on. His mouth was on hers, kissing her, needing her that way, needing her to need him that way, as he backed up slowly toward the wooden seat and sank down on it, pulling her down on his lap.

And heaven help her, all Addie could think about was not the man who held her tenderly and who was, would be, so good for her, but another man who'd only make her crazy. Or drive her wild with his kiss, so potent and powerful—

''I wouldn't do that if I were you.''

Both Addie and Connor jumped apart like two teenagers caught necking on the living room sofa. Suddenly, they were caught in the crosshatched beam of an industrial-size flashlight.

And even though the person who held it was a mere shadow, there was no mistaking his identity.

Raising a hand to block the glare, Addie squinted, furious, as both she and Connor scrambled to their feet.

''Deke, honestly! What do you mean, scaring the life half out of Connor and me!''

"I purely didn't want either of you doin' something you'd regret in the next instant," he drawled, rising from the opposite bench.

Her face flamed, despite herself, as she recalled the kiss she'd shared with him—and how it had overrun her thoughts while she kissed Connor.

"I don't see how it's any of your business what Addie and I do, Larrabie," Connor said levelly from behind her.

Deke averted the light slightly so that it cast an eerie glow.

Especially on himself. He looked positively forbidding.

"We-ell, now, I think you'll agree that it is, once I tell you that you were about two seconds from that fancy Neiman Marcus sport coat of yours gettin' a nice, big strip of wet paint across the back of it."

"I *thought* I smelled paint," Addie said, turning to peer at the spot where Connor had been sitting.

Then she crossed to take the flashlight from Deke and slowly rotated in the middle of the wood floor, her mouth drifting open.

For what she saw was how her mother's gazebo gleamed with fresh blue and creamy-white paint.

At least the railings, posts and fretwork did. The unpainted inside of the gazebo presented a dull contrast that made the new paint that much more impressive.

Finally, she turned back to Deke, realizing only then that he held a sleeping Jace, obviously passed out cold as a wedge, against his chest.

"It's your Mother's Day present—from Jace," Deke explained, inclining his head slightly to indicate the boy.

Her anger and embarrassment were surprised right

out of her. She descended the steps to shine the beam on the exterior, as Deke and Connor followed.

She squinted in momentary disappointment.

Even in the dim light, Deke must have detected her expression. "What is it? Did we paint it the wrong color?"

"No!" she answered hastily. "Not at all. I just… Connor, would you be a dear and go flick the switch to the floodlight that's just inside the back door?"

She could tell he was miffed at being sent off like a schoolboy, but Addie couldn't be bothered at the moment. Within seconds, the floodlight came on, bathing the gazebo in a white light that made the new paint literally glow.

It took her breath away.

"Why, Deke! It must have taken you all day!" Addie exclaimed, marveling at how the paint made the whole structure look like new…like it had years ago.

"Just about—" he allowed, hitching the boy up a fraction.

Jace, his cheek pressed against Deke's shoulder and arms locked about his neck, didn't rouse a bit.

"He tried with all his might to stay awake so's he could see your reaction when you got home, but all the activity did him in."

Addie detected just a hint of accusation in his voice about the lateness of the hour, with which she couldn't be bothered to take issue. She was simply too thrilled. And touched.

Brushing Jace's unruly forelock off his forehead, she murmured, "I wonder how he came up with the idea in the first place."

"We got to talkin'—about mothers." He paused. "And fathers. I told him how important the gazebo was to you, how it puts you in mind of your own mother, makes you feel close to her, even though she's gone.''

There was another pause before Deke went on quietly. ''I also told him about…his father.''

''You did?'' Her stomach somersaulted. ''But, Deke, you prom—''

''And I kept my promise.'' He broke in softly but forcefully. ''I told Jace about the kind of man his father had been, some of the things I knew about him that he'd want passed on to his son.''

Addie shook her head in confusion. ''Why would you make it sound as if you—'' she shot a quick glance at Jace, who was still out for the count ''—as if you're dead?''

''Because that's what Jace believes.'' Deke's gaze met hers over their son's head, eyes as inscrutable as ever. ''It seemed easiest—it seemed best for him—to go along with the idea.''

''But that means…that means you won't be able to be the father to him you want to be,'' Addie said, still confused. It was the opposite of the intention he had voiced all along.

He still gazed at her with that unfathomable expression in his eyes.

''No, I won't be able to be a father to him. But I can be the man who knew his father. And maybe through telling Jace about that man, I can help the boy set to rest some of the hard feelings he has—so he can learn to accept the new father in his life.''

To her dismay, Addie felt instant tears spring to her eyes. Much as she wanted her son to accept Connor as a father, it wasn't right that Deke give up all rights to that role. She could see now that it was wrong for her to have made him promise, even for a while, not to tell Jace the truth.

She'd simply been so afraid, though! Afraid that Deke wouldn't stay in Jace's life or hers, and that the pain would be doubly difficult when he left again.

Yet his leaving hadn't broken the bond between the two of them. She saw that now. Even if Deke hadn't left her with Jace, there was still something strong and deep and sure between them.

Addie madly batted her eyes. "I—I don't know what to say, Deke," she stammered.

"Don't say anything, Addie," he said, low. "I'm not one-hundred-percent sure how I'm gonna be able to keep this up for the rest of my life. I only know I don't want my son feelin' about me the way I felt about my dad."

His voice dropped even lower. "And I don't want you feelin' about me the way you have for seven years—not if I can help it—that you can't forgive and move on."

Oh, how mixed up things had become! How was she to marry one man when there was another who still held a large piece of her heart, and always would?

She squeezed her eyes shut, trying to focus her thoughts. What if Jace was told the truth about Deke now? How would it affect the boy's feelings for Connor?

Or, for that matter, it struck Addie, for her? Once Jace realized she was responsible for keeping his father from him—not only now, but for the past six years—how would the news affect *their* relationship?

Yet, she was his mother, and despite the problems between them, Jace knew she loved him more than life. Sure, she'd kept his father from him and that was wrong, but she'd never represented herself to her son as being perfect. Yes, he did know: People made mistakes. And she was only human.

And so was Deke. So was Deke.

She lifted her head. "Deke, I—"

"Well, if it isn't Deke Larrabie."

With a heavy step, Mick Brody came forward out of the gloom, his black eyes wary despite the smile pasted on his face.

Addie stifled a groan. She'd forgotten all about Mick being here—for that matter, had forgotten, too, about Connor, who returned to the yard and stood to one side of his father with a bemused look on his face.

"Mick" was all Deke said in return.

Her future father-in-law was a big man, had most likely been quite handsome in his earlier days; that could be seen in Connor. But while he still had a firm jawline, his skin a healthy tan and his dark hair only a dusting of gray at the sides, there was something of a look of decay about Mick Brody.

For some reason, the impression was even more evident right now, as the two men assessed each other like a couple of gunslingers at high noon.

Addie suppressed a shiver.

"What's Jace doin' out here so late?" asked Jud, who'd followed Mick at a slower pace.

She indicated the gazebo. "He and Deke spent most of the day paintin' Mama's gazebo." She avoided Deke's gaze. "S-sort of a Mother's Day present."

"Y'don't say!"

She could tell her father was as touched as she'd been.

"I've been meanin' to get to that since heaven knows when."

"Well, there's plenty of painting left to do on the inside, if you're of a mind," Deke told him, adding, "I'll bet anything, Jace here'd be tickled to have his granddad give him a hand with the job."

As Jud beamed fondly at his sleeping grandson, Addie noticed how once again a circle of intimacy had been created that effectively excluded the Brody men—especially when Deke placed a palm on his son's back in a gesture of tenderness that brought yet another lump to her throat.

But it was when Jace stirred, and Deke slid his hand up to cup the back of his son's head and press his cheek to Jace's crown, that she had to turn away, or betray herself to Connor and Mick.

And perhaps most of all to Deke.

"Goodness, I'm tired," she offered as an excuse, but it was pretty evident she hadn't been the only one to mark the homey little tableau they'd made—and her reaction to it.

"Connor, where're your manners?" Mick said. "Give Addie a hand gettin' the kid there inside and in to bed. He looks just about as tuckered as a boy can be."

The last thing she wanted was for Deke to have to relinquish his son to Connor in front of Mick Brody. *That* situation would be too packed with veiled symbolism.

"Here, let me take him," Addie volunteered quickly, holding out her arms.

But Deke had ideas of his own on that score. "I can take him in and get him to bed. There's no need to wake him." His eyes met hers. "No need to leave your guests."

"A-all right," she stuttered, thinking that perhaps it

would be best if Deke did take Jace inside. Something had to give, or the tension in the group was going to unhinge her.

Yet relief wasn't to be hers, for as Deke turned to go, Mick spoke up. "Say, Deke. Now that you're back, I'm thinkin' that calls for a celebration."

The older man cocked an eyebrow at her. "Addie, weren't we just talkin' about having an engagement barbecue at Tanglewood for you and Connor here?"

"Y-yes," she answered, the tension in her escalating.

"T'ain't no reason we can't make the party do double duty by having a welcome back party for Deke, is there—?"

He turned to her, the light glinting off one of the dinner-plate-size handcrafted belt buckles that were Mick's signature and that fairly shouted his prosperity.

"Sorta to show there're no hard feelings?" He paused, then went on smoothly. "You know—about Connor here sorta repeating history in reverse by stealin' away a Larrabie woman."

Addie's breath stopped in her chest. Deke, still holding Jace, stopped dead, and she knew it was taking every bit of his control to keep from giving Mick Brody a sizeable piece of his mind…at the very least.

And she could hardly blame him. How *could* Mick? She'd known he had a bone to pick with Deke's father, but this sort of thing was uncalled for, so far as Deke was concerned.

Yet now wasn't the time to make a stand—not with the possibility of Jace waking up any moment and hearing something he shouldn't.

Let it go, please. Addie sent a silent appeal to Deke, knowing she was asking a lot of him after he'd already given so much. Still, he seemed willing to adhere to her wishes—until Addie brushed back a tendril of her hair that had blown into her eyes and the treacherous light caught the shimmer of something on her hand that puzzled even her, at first. Then she remembered: it was her diamond engagement ring, newly presented to her just this afternoon by Connor.

Deke's eyes homed in on it like those of an eagle spotting its prey, then lifted to hers in a gaze so direct and piercing that she felt as helplessly pinned under it as some hapless quarry in the clutch of razor-sharp talons.

She wondered if she were the only one to glimpse the disgust that hardened Deke's jaw.

Oh, she knew he had no right to make her feel defensive or guilty or ashamed or a thousand other emotions, including the underlying feeling that, indeed, there was some unfinished business somewhere. Whether it was between her and Deke, or with the Brodys or whomever, though, now was not the time to take care of it.

Please, she begged Deke silently with her eyes. *For…for Jace's sake.*

Finally, with an imperceptible nod, he said, "That sounds like a fine idea, Mick." His voice was all pleasantness. "Just let me know when, and I'll be there with spurs on."

Relief nearly cut her off at the knees.

"Now, if you don't mind, I've got a boy here that needs tending to."

But as he disappeared with Jace into the shadows, Addie wondered if they had yet again delayed the inevitable.

*   *   *

Deke paused at the entrance to Tanglewood Ranch. If the number of cars and trucks lining the long driveway and down the ranch road a good half mile in either direction were any indication, Mick's bash for Connor and Addie was already an unqualified success.

Which was, no doubt, why he'd wanted to ensure Deke had a ringside seat.

He would rather have pulled a rattler from its hole bare-handed than attend Mick Brody's shindig, but he didn't see much way of getting out of it without looking like a poor sport.

And he sure as hell wasn't planning to look like any kind of loser in this game—even if he had yet to figure out just how he might win it.

Adjusting his Stetson over his eyes, he started up the drive toward the Brody homestead.

Once he reached it, Deke simply had to take a moment on the edge of the crowd, which spilled out the back of the sprawling ranch house, onto the patio and across the acre of lawn, to marvel at that force of nature and eighth wonder of the world called an old-fashioned Texas barbecue.

It appeared Mick had gone all out, making sure the party had every trimming and then some, with three bars and two buffet lines. Along one side were no less than three industrial-size smokers big enough to hold a side of beef each, as well as a grill manned by three cooks. The local buzz was that Mick had called in a caterer from Houston who'd provided Tex-Mex barbecue for the likes of such notables as the Bushes and a U.S. senator or two. He'd even hired two bands: a mariachi foursome that strolled from group to group scattered under the towering live oak and pecan trees. The other band was, of course, country and western.

They were keeping things lively under a huge canopy that provided shade from the setting but still sizzling sun.

With a glance around, Deke could see in an instant he'd made a tactical error by planning to arrive after the party was in full swing. First, most everyone was well on their way to getting tanked, which tended to put people into a rowdy mood. And which tended to put him on edge, after his experiences dealing with his father in such a state.

More than that, though, Deke knew he'd been fooling himself thinking Mick wouldn't be waiting for him to show up, no matter how inconspicuously, so he could make a big deal out of it.

"Here he is!" the big man exclaimed, as if Deke were the prodigal son.

He pushed his way through the crowd, jostling elbows so that one woman nearly lost her drink. Yup, judging from his bloodshot eyes, Deke knew Mick had more than a few drinks under his belt.

For some reason, that, in particular, set Deke's teeth on edge. He hoped he'd be able to get through this evening without losing his cool.

Because he really didn't want to make things more difficult for Addie. Sure, he still had some problems with how she was managing things—including marrying a man she wasn't completely in love with—but Deke could see that she considered him a loose cannon on deck, which only put more pressure on her.

And he wasn't going to make anyone's life easier that way.

Still, when Mick clapped a hand on his shoulder, it was all Deke could do not to throw it off. Luckily, Jace came running up at that moment, giving him an excuse to bend down to greet the boy.

"What kept ya, Deke?" he asked, latching on to Deke's hand like it was a lifeline. He shot a strangely defiant look at Mick. "All I been doin' is waiting for you ta get here."

"Really?" Deke's chest puffed with pleasure—especially since he knew Mick looked on. "Well, it looks like you've at least been keepin' company with a rib or two, if the amount of barbecue sauce on your shirtfront is any clue."

Jace tucked his chin, trying to get a look at the damage. For once he'd forgone that hat of his that made him look like he was hiding a mother cat and ten of her kittens under it. Without it, though, the boy's resemblance to Deke was even more apparent.

"I guess I did have somethin' to eat already," Jace admitted.

"And there's plenty more, Jace," Mick interjected expansively. "We got enough food and drink to last clear through to next Tuesday, so don't stint yourself, boy."

Jace's brow puckered. "Only thing is, Mama says I gotta go home pretty soon, 'fore things start buckin' in eight directions at once. Whatever that means."

Deke hid a smile. "It means you better show me where the line is for the pulled pork and pinto beans, while we still got time."

"Sure, let's go!"

Deke couldn't resist throwing Mick an inculpable shrug as Jace grabbed his hand to drag him across the lawn to the buffet.

"Wait, Slick," he said halfway there. "Before we

load up our plates, would you come with me while I talk to your mama…and Connor?''

The boy stopped cold in his tracks. "Do I haveta?"

Deke bent down, close to his son's ear. "What, so it's all right to fill up on Tanglewood chow, but it's not all right to pay your respects to one of your hosts?"

His no-nonsense tone clearly hit home with Jace. His son made a face, but didn't protest any further as Deke steered him toward the edge of the crowd, where Addie and Connor Brody were standing next to one of the bars.

Addie saw him coming and immediately went on alert, he noticed.

She looked just about good enough to eat, in a mint green-and-pink plaid sundress that hugged her body like a custom-made glove. Her flame-red hair was pulled into some kind of updo that made those big blue eyes of hers look about ten times bigger. And made her every bit as irresistible to him as ever.

He gritted his teeth. While not much of a praying man, Deke wasn't beyond sending a request skyward for a little help to get through the next few minutes.

"Addie, Connor." He stopped in front of them, Jace at his side, and from the corner of his eye alone, Deke could count fifteen heads turn their way. Well, he may as well get this over with.

"Just wanted to give you my best and wish y'all good luck." He stuck his hand out to Connor. "You're a lucky man, Brody."

For a moment, Connor just stared at his extended hand in complete astonishment. Then he recovered himself and reached out to shake it heartily. "Thanks, Deke. I appreciate your good thoughts for us."

Deke gave a curt nod and got on to the hardest part. He turned to Addie. "My best to you, too."

She looked half bowled-over herself. "Th-thank you, Deke."

It seemed ridiculous to shake her hand, as well. So he leaned in to give her a quick peck on the cheek, his lips barely brushing her soft skin. Then he pulled back so she wouldn't hear his heart pounding at the closeness of her. He didn't think that pounding would ever diminish.

But he'd had his chance with her.

Which brought Deke to the most difficult moment yet. He glanced down at Jace, who'd been taking the conversation in with interest. He squeezed the boy's shoulder. "So, Slick. I guess you'll be getting a new dad in Connor here, eh?"

"I guess so," he mumbled, but his lower lip was gearing up to do its rebellious thing, which Deke knew he had to nip in the bud.

"Now, I know it'll seem strange at first, but all change is. That doesn't necessarily make it bad." He swallowed and managed to go on. "The important thing is that you hang in there, give things a chance. Give people a chance."

The youngster stared at him, his eyes disconcerting in their focus, as if he were trying to figure out an intricate puzzle—and Deke held the key.

But Deke didn't have all the answers, as he well knew. Hell, he wasn't at all sure this was the right way to proceed: encouraging his son to make an alliance with another man—and a Brody, no less.

Yet he had to look out for Jace's best interests, as much as he could look out for a son who would rather believe his father dead than human and flawed.

Finally, Jace said, "'Kay. If you say so, Deke."

Deke couldn't resist reaching out and ruffling the boy's pecan-brown hair. "Now, how about some of that barbecue?" he said around the lump, thick as a brick, lodged in his throat. "I'd be obliged if you'd fetch me a plate."

After Jace left, the three adults stood for an awkward moment, until Connor reached for his drink and Deke spied the college ring on his hand.

"So what was your area of study at UT?" he asked with a nod toward it.

"Got my undergrad in finance and an MBA in mergers and acquisitions," Connor answered readily enough, then added ruefully, "Good knowledge to have, but it doesn't help much in figurin' out which way a cow's going to cut when he's of a mind to lose you."

Deke had to laugh. "See, now, I took the opposite route—got the cowboyin' down pat and had to get the schoolin' to learn the business side."

"Which you've done in spades. From what I hear tell, you're your father's son in that respect."

And in others? was the retort on the tip of Deke's tongue. Yet he could tell Brody's comment was in earnest—and that it had to have been Addie who'd told Connor of D.K.

Dropping his gaze, Deke fiddled with the cocktail napkin the bartender had set in front of him. He was amazed to find himself liking Connor, which seemed to produce a mingling of resistance and acceptance in his chest.

Maybe…maybe marrying Connor *would* be best for Addie, too, although in Deke's mind the idea met with even more resistance.

Looking up, Deke found Addie's gaze upon him. It was filled with an impossibly strange mixture of regret and appreciation for him, and the bittersweet irony of it nearly closed off his windpipe.

Because if anyone had told him that the way to win Addie Gentry's regard would be to make peace with the man she was to marry, he'd have told them there must be some pretty fine ice-skating available in hell.

"So, Deke, what'll be your pleasure?"

Deke came out of his thoughts with a start, to find Mick Brody leaning his meaty fists on the padded armrest next to him.

Damn. Dealing with Mick was definitely what he didn't need right now.

"Coke, please," he told the bartender.

"A Coke!" Mick gave him another of those hail-fellow-well-met claps on the back that grated a raw patch along Deke's nerves like fingernails across a blackboard. "How about a *real* drink, like your daddy used to have?"

Deke went still. Beside him, he heard Addie gasp, even heard Connor's shocked intake of breath. Deke had no doubt the surrounding people were as much on pins and needles.

"No thanks, Mick," he answered evenly, taking a stab at deflecting the inevitable. "I don't touch the stuff."

It was a futile aim, to be sure. Oh, he had done the right thing in demonstrating to Addie and Jace that he could come through for them. And he had no doubt his soul could do with some more improving. But Deke hadn't a clue what he'd done in his life to deserve this kind of trial.

For that's when Mick sloshed two fingers of whiskey

into a tumbler and shoved it toward him, his florid face inches from Deke's as he taunted ''Aw, c'mon. Surely one drink can't hurt. Or can it?''

Mick lifted his black eyebrows—making Deke wonder if, indeed, he would have to wrestle with the devil himself before this was over—and went on. ''I mean, you *are* D. K. Larrabie's son.''

Chapter Seven

Addie's heart stopped.

She could see in an instant that Deke's thoughts had gone to the same moment hers had.

Your dad never was anything but a low-life drunk! And now he's gone and overstepped his bounds again, thinkin' he could be anything more than the shiftless cowboy he was born to be. Well, I'm bettin' the apple hasn't fallen far from the tree. Not at all.

In her mind's eye, she could see Mick Brody's face so clearly, painted blood-red by the glow from the fire, looking like pure…hate. She realized she'd resisted putting such a strong label on it before, but that had been the emotion radiating from him: undiluted, unmitigated hatred for Deke.

What *was* it about Deke that Mick couldn't let go of? It couldn't still be D. K. Larrabie's transgression against Mick that he was making Deke pay for. And if so, it was unconscionable of him, especially when Deke had come here to make peace.

Oh, what his forgiving gesture had done to her! Mixed her up, stirred her up, more than ever.

Deke had moved not a muscle at Mick's barb, and even now his movements were deliberate as he lifted the glass of cola the bartender had served him to his lips and took a long, unhurried draught.

"To tell the truth, Mick—" he finally said matter-of-factly—and loud enough for at least the nearby crowd to hear "—it surprises me you'd think I wouldn't already know one drink *can* hurt." He shrugged. "Of course, it was never one drink that got my dad into trouble. More like he was on a one-man mission for years to keep the distillers of Jack Daniel's from goin' out of the whiskey-making business."

At this, Mick's jaw went slack in bafflement—which Addie was sure had been Deke's aim. Deke's candidness had taken the wind right out of Mick's mean-spirited attempt to humiliate him.

And it got Deke a bit of his own pride back.

The problem was, the move only seemed to get Mick's back up. In one gulp he angrily downed the whiskey he'd poured.

Addie frowned. Something about the gesture nettled. What had Deke just said? That his father had been a drinker of Jack Daniel's? Except…she could have sworn the label on the bottle Mick Brody found in D.K.'s pickup those years ago had been Jim Beam.

Why that stuck in her mind, she couldn't have said for the world—except, perhaps, that there was little of that night that wasn't seared into her memory.

She watched as Mick poured himself another shot— of Jim Beam.

Lifting it, he glanced around and found himself surrounded by a bunch of somber faces. Mick scowled. "Damn, this party got dull of a sudden. We can't have that, not at the Tanglewood."

His gaze lit on his son. "Say, Connor, how about getting up a friendly little competition shooting beer bottles off the fence over yonder. I'll even take wagers, for anybody whose blood is rich enough."

It was yet another dig at Deke, Addie realized.

Next to her, Connor shifted on his feet. "Uh, Dad, I don't know that bringing guns out is a very good idea. You know, given all the people around."

"Hell, shootin' off guns at a backyard barbecue is about as close as you can come to a time-honored Texas tradition, next to visitin' the Alamo." He leveled a bloodshot eye on his son. "Now quit bein' so damn squeamish and go get my pistol."

"Really, Dad, is this a good idea?" Connor hedged, shooting an embarrassed look at Deke, whom Addie could see had gone as impassive as ever.

"Oh, for the love of…why wouldn't it be?" Mick nearly shouted. "Aiming with a gun is just about the only thing worth doin' that you're good at."

Addie wondered if Mick had any idea how his comment hurt Connor, but he had already turned to Deke with a sneer.

"Not like Deke here, I'm bettin'," he said. "D.K. was never much of a shot, as I recall. Couldn't hit a target if it was ten foot wide and within arm's reach."

"Yes, he can!"

This, to everyone's surprise, had come from Jace. He stood a few feet away, a plate piled high with barbecue clutched in his hands, Granddad Jud behind him with the fixings.

"I saw Deke chunkin' rocks at pop cans," he exclaimed, his face pale enough that the freckles stood out across the bridge of his nose like leopard's spots. "He could hit 'em even if they wasn't ten foot wide, and they were plenty far away, too!"

Bless his little heart, but for some reason his defense of Deke just about put Mick into orbit.

"Line 'em up, Merle," he ordered one of the other guests. Then he stormed off, as everyone stood in uncomfortable silence.

Addie started to move to her son, but Deke had already bent to distract Jace by instructing him to help his grandfather find a place for them at a nearby table.

Straightening, his back to the boy, he said to her, "Get him out of here."

Yes, they clearly needed to get Jace gone as soon as possible. With all the covert messages being thrown around, he was bound to catch the whiff of something he shouldn't—at least, not yet and not in this public setting.

"I was going to take him back to the Bar G in just a few minutes," she answered.

"The sooner the better." His mouth thinned. "I'm surprised you'd bring him to this kind of thing in the first place."

Addie took exception to Deke's tone. "It's only a barbecue, Deke!" she whispered fiercely.

"No, it's not," he contradicted. His gaze went past her to Connor, who stood on her other side. "It's a damn command performance for everyone in the county, meant to show up the Larrabie name once and for all."

He leveled that eagle-eyed scrutiny at her again. "Now, I'll thank you to get Jace home, soon as you can. 'Cause I'm not gonna have him watch me walk away from a confrontation that's been a long time comin', which is what I'll be forced to do in order to protect him—''

She had never seen him look so implacable.

''And if I have to back down again to Mick Brody's accusations, I'll never forgive you for it, Addie. Never.''

She flushed, but it was in shame rather than in anger. Of course, he was right. Why Mick had it out for Deke still wasn't clear to her, but the fact was, he did.

And it was because of her relationship with Connor that Deke had been put in this position.

Connor seemed to realize the situation, too, for he said, ''Let's take Jace back to the Bar G, Addie,'' giving Deke a grim nod.

But it was too late. A low murmur filtered through the gathering as Mick, a thunderous look on his face, returned with a revolver. Addie was stunned when he strode up to Jace, of all people.

''Lookie here at this, Jace—a mint-condition Remington army revolver. Been in the Brody family for over a hundred-thirty years.''

''Really?'' Jace asked, immediately absorbed. ''Can I touch it?''

''Why, sure!''

As Addie's apprehension mounted, a fascinated Jace ran the pads of his fingers over the deep brown patina of the gun's hardwood grip.

''Jace, hon, actually, it's time to go home,'' she said, moving to grasp him by the shoulders from behind. Having a loaded weapon so close to her son was unnerving enough, but somehow, having Mick Brody in such proximity to Jace was worse. The fine hairs actually stood up on the back of her neck.

Especially when Mick ignored her, turning the revolver over in his large hands.

"In fact, my great-great-granddad Johnse Brody used this very gun to settle this part of Texas. No rancher was without one of these guns. And no son of a rancher grew up not knowin' how to use one."

"Yeah?" Jace breathed. "I don't know about my daddy, but Granddad's a rancher, and my mama's a rancher, too. So that makes me the son of a rancher, right?"

He'd looked to Jud for confirmation, but it was Mick who answered him. "Sure does," he said, throwing Deke a smile that was unmistakable in its gloating.

He pulled himself up straight. "Here, Connor, give the boy an idea of what can be done with this here Remington."

But this time Connor shook his head firmly. "No, Dad."

"Connor…" Mick warned.

"No. This isn't right."

"What's not right about it? Just shoot the gun!"

"Look, Dad, with all the drinking that's been goin' on, someone could get hurt." He held out a hand in appeal. "I mean, you've been drinking—"

"Nobody's gonna get hurt, damn it!" Mick bellowed.

Marching to the spot that had been cleared, he aimed and let fire with six shots, one right after another, picking off a line of beer bottles like firecrackers on a string.

Each shot made Addie jump, her nerves strung taut as she clutched Jace's shoulders. She had a terrible sense of foreboding, not unlike that of the night D. K. Larrabie had died in the fire.

Mick swung around to a smattering of nervous applause, clearly pleased with himself.

"Care to take a turn?" he asked Deke, digging into his jeans pocket for a handful of cartridges to reload the gun. "Or did you inherit your daddy's lousy aim—along with his other failings?"

Shock rippled through her. What had Deke ever done to Mick to deserve this kind of retribution? Sure, D.K. had stolen Mick's fiancée, had practically run off with her in the middle of the night, or so the story went—but that was before Deke was even born! And Deke couldn't be blamed for his father's actions.

Then Mick said, "Of course, once Jace is officially a Brody, he'll be able to practice his aim with a gun anytime he wants."

She wished to heaven she knew what was going on here! It was more than Mick having a little too much to drink; more, even, than having a bone to pick with D.K.'s son, for lack of having D.K. himself to get back at.

Something made Addie glance down. Jace was staring up at her, worry etched in his amber-green eyes, so like his father's....

And that's when it hit her. This wasn't about D.K., or even about Deke. *It was about Jace!*

Shoving her son behind her, Addie stepped forward, not knowing how she would put a stop to things, only that she had to, whatever it took.

But she stopped in mid-gesture as she caught sight of Deke. He still stood by the bar, and everyone around him had faded away, as if this truly were an Old West showdown. His whole being seemed stretched to the breaking point, torn between two opposite forces, and she had a sudden perception that were she to place her hand on his arm, as she had on that long-ago tragic night, he would bestow upon her the same look of utter forsakenness—of having his choice in this matter of life and death snatched away from him.

In the next instant Addie felt something happen within her she'd never have believed possible, for just as it had that tragic evening, her whole heart went out to Deke Larrabie and became his—against her better judgment, against her very will—even as it raced in fear.

For she dreaded how he would respond to Mick's insult, so like the one that had sent him away from here years ago. Dreaded, with the clenching of her very soul, how it might send him away from her again—and take away her own choice in this matter.

And this time, she would have no one to blame but herself for putting them both into this position.

That's when Mick, locking gazes with Deke, added deliberately, "Yup, all it'll take is a little target practice with Connor and me, and the boy'll soon prove himself better than the cowboy blood he got from his Larrabie daddy."

To Deke, it felt like the earth had stopped turning on its axis right then and there.

Damn Mick Brody to hell and back! He truly didn't consider himself a vengeful man, but at that moment Deke would have sold his soul to the devil, cash on the barrelhead, to have the satisfaction of being able to take swift and immediate retaliation against this man.

For when he dropped his gaze, it was to find Jace

staring at him in complete and utter disbelief—and betrayal.

He should never have come here today, Deke thought wildly, should have left as soon as he saw the mood Mick was in, should have whisked Jace—and Addie, for that matter—away from here himself.

All the should-haves in the world weren't going to change things, though. How could they, when he seemed doomed to be endlessly caught in one of these impossible situations after another, with impossible choices?

It tore the heart right out of him.

"*You're* my dad?" the boy asked, incredulous.

Deke swallowed, painfully aware that every eye and ear in the place was trained upon him and his son.

"Jace, let's go find someplace where I can explain—"

"No, tell me!" He stumbled forward, taking a solid stance before him. "Are you my dad?"

There was no way to get around it. None in the world. Addie stood behind Jace, her palm pressed to her mouth, her face stricken.

"I am," Deke answered.

Tears filled the boy's eyes, so much like his own. *So much.*

He whirled on his mother. "Why didn't you tell me? Why?"

"Oh, Jace!" She bent to enfold him in her arms, but he fought her off.

"No! I gotta know!" He turned back to Deke. "Why'd you tell me he was dead? Didn't you *want* to be my daddy?" he cried.

Deke wondered if it were possible to develop a spontaneous ulcer, he was so angry with Mick, so torn by the gut-wrenching abandonment he heard in Jace's voice.

But he had to come through here.

Without a thought for himself, Deke dropped to his knees in front of the boy and grasped him gently by the shoulders. Jace struggled against the restraint for a moment, but Deke held on, refusing to be thrown off or shoved away.

"Jace," he said, once the boy had quieted and stood before him in the same rebel stance as he had that first day in the stable. And as he'd been then, the boy was searching for answers.

Aren't we all? Deke asked himself ruefully. Yet, he'd left here seven years ago without pursuing any answers. Had left before he could provide them to those who deserved better.

"Jace," Deke repeated more strongly. "Of course I want to be your dad. From the moment I first knew about you, I wanted to," he said in complete honesty, glad he could be so. "And if I didn't tell you who I was, it was because I made a promise that I wouldn't— a promise I intended to keep."

Jace blinked. "A promise? Like, who to? And why wouldja make a promise like that, anyway? Why?"

Out of the corner of his eye, he saw Addie pale. But then she dropped down to a level with their son, too.

"Hon, the reason Deke made that promise was because—"

"Because I was doin' what I thought would be best for everyone, at the time," Deke broke in, avoiding Addie's gaze. "It's what both your mom and I have always tried to do, where you're concerned. You'll just have to trust us on that one, son. And as me for wanting to be your father…"

His voice roughened, and his fingers tensed around Jace's small arms. Lord, how he'd come to love this boy in such a short time, he realized all of a sudden. Actually, as impossible as it seemed, he knew he'd loved Jace with all his heart—from the first moment he'd set eyes upon him.

Deke cleared his throat and went on more strongly. "As for wanting to be your father, well, I wouldn't for the world be anything else, and to prove it, you can count on me doin' my utmost best to fill that role for the rest of your life."

Jace stood completely still, and while Deke could see that his son badly wanted to believe him—sorely needed to, in fact—Jace was still a long, long way from doing so. If he ever would.

Rising, Deke took the Remington from Mick. He weighed it in his hand for a moment. It was as fine a piece of craftsmanship as he'd ever seen. Just from the heft, he could tell how it would feel to aim and fire, how it would feel to shatter, one after another, each of those bottles. How he would feel turning to see the regard in his son's eyes as he'd seen it so clearly in Addie's....

On that thought, Deke flipped open the Remington's chamber and swiftly unloaded the six cartridges, before dropping the loading lever and pulling out the cylinder pin to disassemble the revolver.

He handed its pieces back to Mick. "Time-honored Texas tradition or not, Mick, guns've got no place in a gathering, especially when there're impressionable young'uns about who're bound to pick up the adults' casual attitude about the handling of firearms, prized or otherwise. Which, I trust, you won't be giving Jace access to once my son is living on the Brody ranch.

Because if you do, rest assured you'll find yourself standing before a judge and facin' child endangerment charges.

"And if you think this Larrabie doesn't have it in him to find whatever means needed to put you there," he went on softly, but with a ton of galvanized steel weighting his words, "then, you'd best be thinkin' again, Brody."

Mick's expression verged on rabid, but he said not a word in reply.

Deke couldn't have cared less if Mick *had* wanted to carry this scene out to the stony end, for he turned and caught Addie's eye, and it did him a measure of good to see that newly won regard still shining in her blue eyes.

The problem was, he wasn't sure how he felt about her right now. Wasn't sure what *he* believed, or who had to do the proving. Wasn't sure what it would take to bring *himself* back to the point of trusting again.

Especially since they'd both made their choices. Had both had their chances.

Regardless, he experienced a pang at the hurt that leapt to her gaze when he said to her, "It's definitely time now for Jace to go home, in my opinion. So if you don't intend to take him, I will."

But in the next instant the expression had disappeared. She lifted her chin.

"I'll take him."

He gave a short nod and turned. As he walked through the crowd that parted for him the way it would for the most feared and revered of gunslingers, Deke wondered what it *would* take to soothe a soul that continued to be as restless as that of any cowboy who'd ever ridden off in search of a peace that would always elude him.

Addie climbed the steps to the gazebo, her footsteps echoing hollowly in the dark.

Her heart, however, was banging like a bass drum in a way that exhausted her.

In the distance, she heard the hoot of an owl and the intermittent lowing of a cow as the herd settled down for the night. Closer by, she heard the skitter of some small animal she'd disturbed with her unexpected wanderings about the yard, usually long-deserted by this hour of the night.

Well, it was past midnight, long after the whole ranch was normally put to bed. There was no way she'd be able to get to sleep herself right now, however. At least, not until she'd taken care of a bit of business.

That was why she'd come here, in need of comfort and knowing of nowhere else to find it.

Oh, Mama. How I miss you!

She dropped onto one of the bench seats. Beyond the toes of her shoes, the newly painted wood floor gleamed in the light of the full moon. The whole structure shone, in fact. Jace and her father had only finished painting it a few days ago.

And Deke.

At the thought of him, her heartbeat boomed louder in her ears. After leaving Jace's bedside, she'd looked for him practically all over the ranch, through every building and corral. She'd even ventured out to the ruins beneath the towering cottonwood. But he was nowhere to be found.

It had started up in her a panic, the situation was so

close to that of seven years ago when she'd discovered him gone.

He would not do this to her again!

"Damn it, Deke, where are you?" Addie whispered angrily.

There was no answer—not that she'd expected one—just the gentle sigh of the wind. Just the lonely beat of her heart.

Then a shadow detached itself from the trunk of a nearby live oak tree and moved toward the gazebo.

"I'm right here, Addie," Deke said, stepping into the bluish beam of moonlight streaming down.

"Where have you been?" she demanded, her voice sounding breathless even to her own ears. "I looked all over the Bar G for you!"

He gave a nod, indicating the gazebo. "I've been right here the whole time. Why—did you think I'd head for parts unknown again after that ugly scene at Tanglewood today? I'm sure as shootin' that's what Mick was aiming for."

Addie flushed in shame.

"Come to speak of it, you're back early," he observed blandly, climbing the steps across from her. "I'd've thought any party thrown at Tanglewood wouldn't break up till the skinny hours of the day, and then only because people had to get home in time to do the mornin' chores."

"Actually, I didn't go back to the party after bringing Jace home," Addie said, rising to face him. "H-he seemed pretty upset by today's happenings."

She linked her hands behind her back to hide their trembling. "It took quite a while for him to fall asleep."

"I can believe it. Jace received a real blow today,

with Mick springin' the news on him that I'm his daddy.'' He made the statement without accusation, as fact.

"Yes, he did." Her fingers were practically tied in knots. "That's what I've been thinking. And why I wanted to find you. To…to thank you, Deke, for taking such good care of Jace. The way you handled that situation today with Mick…well, you surprised me, that's all,'' she said candidly. "Surprised a lot of people, I think."

"Somethin' tells me there was a compliment buried in there, so I'll take it,'' he drawled dryly.

She had to smile. "If it helps, too, you might like to know that I gave Mick Brody a piece of my mind."

He took a step forward, bringing him back into the pale light, and she could see he held his lariat in his left hand.

"And just what piece would that be?'' he asked in that rough, provocative voice of his that sent a quiver through her.

"I told him that if he ever even thinks of pulling such a stunt again at the expense of my son, h-he'd answer not only to you but to me, too,'' Addie answered, aware that the breathless quality of her voice made her sound anything but resolute.

"I bet that went over big."

"Oh, Mick was mad as a hornet, to be sure. I don't care if he is, though. What he did today was inexcusable."

"And Connor?"

He took another step forward as he unwound his lariat, spinning it idly in a flat loop that instantly mesmerized her, as it always did. His skill with a lasso, the very rope itself, was to her as Deke himself: ever changing, ever moving, ever elusive, while at the same time conveying a sense of constancy in the smoothness of the spinning loop, in the magic of the unbroken circle formed from a simple piece of rope. Why did Deke have to do that now?

"Connor?" She frowned. "Connor didn't do anything."

He let her statement hang between them, his only reaction the quickening of the rope's twirl, until she got his implication.

"Come on, Deke!" she protested. She wrested her gaze away from the lariat, only to have it land on his watchful gaze. "You saw how it was today. He was as interested in stopping that scene as I was!"

"Oh, you *were,* were you?"

Addie felt her face turn hot again. "Yes, I was, although you're right in that I could have done more. That's the other reason I came—to apologize."

Unable to remain facing him without succumbing to the rope's slow undulations, Addie crossed to the opposite entrance to the gazebo, where she hoped to heaven she'd find some distraction.

"You've got to believe I had no idea that Mick would ever take things so far," she said, gripping the smooth post. "Or that he even held the kind of grudge he seems to have against you, so that he'd put an innocent little boy in the middle."

The breeze started up again, rustling the rose of Sharon bushes that her mother had lovingly planted on either side of the steps. She drew comfort from the thought. They were on *her* turf this time, instead of in the stable, where the vibrations were undeniably about the two of them and what they'd shared there.

"That's some of what I've been thinkin' on, the past

few hours.'' She made herself go on. ''I honestly don't understand it, Deke. Until you came back again, Mick really was fine—still Mick, of course. But not the way you saw him today. I'd never have put Jace into that situation if I'd had a clue what would happen.''

''And now—?''

At the edge of her vision, she saw him come closer.

''Now that you've seen the grudge Mick's got against the Larrabies, you'd still move Jace to Tanglewood and put him in proximity to Mick Brody on a daily basis?''

''And just how do you see that I could get around it?''

She felt rather than saw the slow, lazy loop his rope made, sending the whisper of a different kind of breeze over her bare arm, making her stifle a shiver.

''If you don't know, Addie, I sure as shootin' ain't gonna tell you.''

She got his drift. ''You mean, not marry Connor?'' She whirled to face him. ''I thought you were just fine and dandy with me marrying him, or was that all just an act today?''

''It was no act, and you know it.'' In the dim light, he looked as forbidding as ever. ''I'm talkin' about doing what's best for Jace. The boy's had a shock today, and at the hands of two people he trusts. It's gonna take time to sort things out and build that trust back up. 'Cause if you don't take the time to do that,'' he added significantly, ''I guarantee it'll haunt him for the rest of his natural life.''

Addie slumped against the post, not happy that he might be right. Oh, she'd already realized Jace was going to have issues with her. But she'd have an easier time of it than Deke. She had a six-year history with her son, and while their relationship might be rocky for a while, it would survive.

She knew Deke didn't have the same assurance. And if he didn't, part of the reason was that he'd taken the hit today for her by keeping her secret.

He hadn't betrayed *that* promise to her, had he.

"I agree there're some important fences to be mended, Deke," Addie admitted slowly. "But how does that change my marrying Connor?"

His expression became positively ominous. There'd be bolts of lightning shooting from his eyes next, she was sure. At least he'd stopped spinning that infernal rope of his.

"Because this time I'm not backin' down and leaving town," he answered. "Now that Jace knows, I intend to stay right here and be the father he needs me to be, no matter how big a monkey wrench that throws into Mick Brody's plans."

"But it's not Mick's plans that matter! I've got plans, too. I mean, Connor and I do!"

She should have known Deke would jump on her slip.

"All right, since you brought it up, let's take a look at that whole situation," he said.

"What do you mean?"

He moved closer, so that he was nearly hovering over her. "Why aren't you with Connor now, Addie? Why aren't you with the man you're supposed to marry, talkin' things out with him?"

"Because." Blindly, she felt for the handhold of the railing as she retreated down one step. "Because, as Jace's parents, we need to discuss how to proceed with him, now that he knows you're his father."

"But you just told me I don't have a lot of choice in the matter, since your future's with Brody."

His gaze made a tour around the interior of the gazebo. "Come to speak of it, that was one of the subjects *I* was thinkin' on here—about how it still seems pretty damn convenient that right when you're feeling kind of desperate about how the Bar G is going to survive, Connor Brody comes along and you two fall madly in love."

Oh, how dare he! "So maybe the feelings between Connor and me aren't as strong as they might be—yet. You tell me what choice I had, runnin' a ranch that wouldn't be able to survive a down year, dealing with a parent whose health is failing and trying to raise a boy whose father I had no hope would ever come back!" Addie retorted.

His coiled rope skidded across the plank floor as he flung it aside in disgust. "Damn it, Addie. You had a lot of choices and still do, if you'd only quit bein' so blamed stubborn, quit bein' so blamed scared to take a risk!"

"A risk on what? The pie-in-the-sky plans you rode in with, just like your father did!"

He took an angry step toward her. "That was low, Addie. You know I'm not suggesting you do anything that drastic."

"Aren't you?" she cried, taking yet another step down and losing even more ground against him, both literally and figuratively. "Aren't you asking me to put my trust in you again, when I spent seven years trying to put behind me how you betrayed it?"

"That's just it. I *didn't* betray your trust. I've kept the promise I made to you."

"But you said you wouldn't leave!"

Deke took away the space between them, causing her to retreat further.

"Yes, but I came back! I came back, Addie, because I'd always kept the other part of my promise to you—"

"Oh!" She gasped in pain.

He was instantly solicitous. "What? What is it?"

Awkwardly, Addie turned and sat down on the floor of the gazebo, clutching her ankle, which she'd come down hard on with that last step. "I think I sprained my ankle. It's not bad. Just me bein' clumsy again."

He squatted beside her. "Let me see."

"No!" she protested on reflex, even jerking away from his outstretched hand. She registered the hurt in Deke's eyes, but she simply couldn't let him touch her right now.

"It's not a bad sprain," she snapped, sure she'd jump out of her skin any second with his closeness. "Just a two-bit owie, really."

She tried to stand, and winced at the effort before deciding she'd better sit tight for a few minutes more. She slid her sandal off her foot and palpated her ankle, as Deke remained at her side, not touching her, as she'd asked.

Morosely, she continued to massage the joint, wondering how to alleviate this tension between Deke and herself. They were both frustrated. Frustrated and angry and hurt.

"This is ridiculous," Addie mumbled, her palm braced at her side on the gazebo's smooth floor. "I've gotten into wrecks with horses and cows that knocked the wind out of me, and got up, brushed myself off and kept goin' for another six hours without doing anything more than wrapping a bandanna around whatever was throbbin' worst to keep the swelling down.''

"Well, even if it's not serious, like you said, you might want to get a cold pack on it right away, just in case,'' Deke suggested. He had settled a few feet away from her, leaning back against the other post. "And keep it elevated for a while.''

He paused. "At the risk of soundin' fresh, do you want me to carry you back to the house?''

"Thanks, really, Deke, but I can manage,'' she said hastily. Heavens, if she hadn't already been sitting down, the mere thought of being in those strong arms, her hands linked behind his neck and her face inches from his, would have made her weak at the knees.

And if she didn't have the ability to leave, she at least had to get him out of here!

But it seemed, once again, that her choices were limited, and this time she had no one to blame but herself. No one to blame for her falling in love with Deke Larrabie again, even with all the old frustration, anger and hurt still there between them.

"Honestly, Deke, you don't have to stay,'' she said. "I'm just going to sit here a minute till I quit aching so much. My ankle, I mean.''

This time, instead of hurt, the look on Deke's face was again impassive. Even in the glow of the moon, she could see that.

Still, he set one boot on the top step, his other leg bent at the knee with his wrist resting upon it. "I'll wait here with you, just to make sure.''

Addie's mouth fell open. She couldn't remain here with him. She just couldn't. The heat virtually radiated from him, with that particular scent mixing rawhide and the outdoors that she'd always identified as being uniquely Deke's.

Yet it came to her that she was helpless to leave—and not simply because of her sprain. His openness today with Connor and Jace and herself that had made him so vulnerable again was like a tonic to her. She couldn't have refused it, so much did she need that from him. She had a sudden insight that, as long as Deke—as long as she, too—didn't turn away from those emotions, as long as he continued to meet them head-on, then they *would* have a chance to resolve any issues they had with each other. And perhaps move on.

Was that what he meant about taking a risk?

Deke said nothing, but leaned his head back against the column. He lacked that ever-present Stetson of his tonight, and despite how well he wore it, she realized that the view of him without it was just as powerful, his wide forehead completing the sculpted curve of his jawline, his thick eyebrows lending a new element of expressiveness to his face.

And then there was that shock of dark hair falling over his forehead that reminded her not of her son, but of that half-boy, half-man to whom she'd given her trust, her innocence, her heart seven years ago, in an act of utter vulnerability that she'd never repeated.

Yes, she *had* risked it all—and had come out on the short end of the stick. How could she go there again?

"Honestly, Deke," Addie said softly, still studying him. "I didn't come here tonight spoiling for another fight with you." She sighed. Somehow that was how things inevitably ended up between them.

"Then, what did you come here for?" Deke asked as quietly.

"I—I told you—to thank you, for what you did for

Jace. And for me. And to apologize for putting you in that position in the first place.'' She tucked her chin. ''It made me think of the night your dad died.''

There was a long pause, and then he said stiffly, ''Yeah, I thought of that night, too. Of what happened here—and how I ran away then from facin'…oh, hell, a lot of things. About who I was and what I was.''

There was another interminable pause, and then he murmured, ''About who we both were, Addie.''

''M-meaning?'' she asked in trepidation, because all at once, she wasn't sure if she wanted to find out the workings of his mind and heart.

''My mom and dad…they loved each other to distraction, y'see,'' he said slowly. ''I remember times, like when we'd all be outside enjoyin' the cool of a summer's evening, up in Montana. Mom and Daddy would be on the porch, side by side on the swing, her with some mending in her lap and him sippin' the last of his coffee, while I messed around in the ranch yard, showin' off my roping skills or just cuttin' up like little kids do in front of their folks. And I'd turn and catch the two of 'em looking at each other, and somehow it'd give me a sense deep down of comfort and uneasiness, both at once. It was that intense. That wild and uncontrollable. Like…an addiction. So that when he lost her, it ruined his life.''

His voice fell to a whisper. ''I didn't understand how that could happen to a man, not then, not until I met you—and felt those same kind of feelings with you.''

He reached out and caught the edge of one finger under her chin, lifting it so that she could look into his eyes, look into his heart, in a moment of rare revelation.

''That's why I really left, Addie. I gotta be truthful

with you there. It was partly because *I* was scared—runnin' scared—that I'd somehow fail you by not doing what was best for you. That somehow it would be the destruction of you, as my dad's taking Mom to Montana was the death of her. But I left mostly for myself and my own concerns. I was just deathly afraid that if I ever did lose you, I wouldn't survive it, like my dad had been destroyed by Mom's death. So I left, rather than ever have to face that day. Or have you face that day.''

Almost absently, he caressed her chin with his thumb as he went on in a rough whisper. ''Because you deserve more, Addie. More than a man who doesn't trust love.''

She could only sit in stunned silence, staring at him as her body thrummed at his touch—while at the same time her spirit ached. Miraculously, he was opening up to her, as she'd so prayed he would. But oh, what it was inside him that he wanted her to know!

And oh, what she must tell him in return.

''I u-used to—'' she swallowed ''—I used to wonder where that young girl went to—the one who gave herself to you so freely. Sometimes I—I can feel her, like when I watched the twirl of your lariat a moment ago, or feel your touch branding my skin right now. But she's gone, for the most part.''

She took a deep breath. ''You see, in my own way I've been as untrusting as you, Deke—holding back from the people in my life, while I try to control my emotions and my life, to wrap them up in a nice convenient bow, just like y-you s-said....'' A sob of despair escaped her lips before she could pull away from him and cover her mouth with her hand.

''Addie, I'm so sorry,'' Deke said, his own raw aching in the roughness of his voice. "God knows I never meant to hurt you, never meant to be the cause of so much of your unhappiness...."

But you have! she wanted to tell him. *You have, and I'm so very afraid of being hurt again by you—whether you leave or stay. Whether you love me or not.*

But she simply couldn't let it happen! Not again. It had nearly killed her before.

Angrily, she swiped away a traitorous tear. "I promised myself I wouldn't do this!"

"Wouldn't do what?"

"That I wouldn't cry over you ever again!" Her head came up with fierce determination. "Because yes, I cried rivers over you, till I was ill, till I thought I'd die! Damn it, it took me two years to stop my heart from pounding out of my chest at every ring of the phone or trip to the mailbox, another two to keep myself from lookin' for you in every passing pickup truck. And I won't do it again! *You* can't do this to me again. I told you from the first, Deke, you can't come barging back into my life and m-make me—"

She broke off, robbed of her breath, her heart thundering out of control.

"Make what?" he persisted.

She scraped at her wet cheeks. "Damn it! Make me love you again!"

They stared at each other, the nearness of him making her so aware of every breath she took. Indeed, she was still very much alive, gloriously so in every inch of her skin as she yearned toward him, unable to stop herself.

Her eyes pleaded with him. For what, she couldn't have said. Perhaps that he would have the strength she herself lacked to turn away from this destructive path they were on.

But then, he'd just admitted to her that he hadn't that ability. Or was he trying to show her that he did?

Then Deke's gaze fell to her trembling lips.

"Yeah, well," he muttered, "I promised I wouldn't touch you ever again, but what the hell."

And in the next instant he pulled her close, bending his head to take her lips with his.

Chapter Eight

Oh Lord, what that wild mouth of his did to her!

Kissing Deke was like being inside a firecracker, with a million explosions of sensation going off at once, all of them sizzling and incendiary, setting off another round of explosions even more powerful.

And just as hard to douse once they'd been set off.

He was insatiable as his lips played across hers, first rough, then tender, with the nip of his teeth followed by the soothing stroke of his tongue. She clutched his shirtfront in both fists, pulling at him as he pulled her closer with his hands in her hair. The pins holding it up came loose, and it spilled onto her bare shoulders in a purely sensual sensation that elicited from both of them groans deep in their throats.

She'd have thought the feelings between them would have changed, ripened or somehow tempered themselves in the years since they'd loved each other so passionately. For both she and Deke had lost so much of their innocence since then, about so many things: life, love, happiness. But the emotions were as fresh and frantic and raw as ever.

Never breaking their kiss, one large hand splayed on her back, he laid her back against the hard, cold plank floor just as he had on that uncomfortable, narrow bunk seven years before. She didn't care, though, and found the primitive harshness fitting—like the palms of his hands, toughened by years and years of hard, honest work, which chafed the skin on her bare arms. They were rougher still as they slid up to her shoulders and across her upper back, exposed by her sundress. His mouth was hot and fierce as it kissed a path across her jawline to her earlobe and down the side of her throat in a journey that made her writhe beneath him.

But that was just the beginning. Her breath caught in her throat as he edged one finger beneath the thin strap of her dress and tugged it down over her shoulder, and she thought she'd die with the slow sensuality of it.

Then he slipped one finger inside the bodice, caressing the sensitive slope of her breast before delving deeper and bumping across its taut, aching peak.

"Oh, Deke," Addie moaned as she shamelessly tugged his head downward, where his fiery mouth branded her collarbone, the slope of her breast and lower. All the while he pulled the zipper at the back of her dress down just enough so that when his lips reached her nipple he could taste her, his tongue making a slow undulating swirl.

Desire nearly rent her in two.

Fingers buried in his thick hair, she held him against her as his lips tugged first at one breast, then the other.

The night breeze whispered over her damp, exposed flesh, making her dimly aware that she and Deke were covered only by the darkness of the night. He had always been able to do this to her, from the very first—make her abandon every caution and forget everything but the two of them and this pounding need for each other that went against logic, against judgment.

At least for her. He had been able to hold back, to try to take it slow, to cool down some, to call a stop altogether when the passion between them threatened to rage out of control.

Except for that last time, when he'd made love to her.

Wild and uncontrollable. That was how he'd said his feelings for her were. That was how she had needed him to be, though—both then and now.

Because heaven help her, Addie now surged against Deke in the same silent, aching plea of that long-ago night.

Yet her action seemed to have the opposite effect, bringing him to his senses.

"No," Deke rasped against her breast. He shook his head as if to clear it. "No—you're right. I can't do this to you again, Addie."

He lifted his head, and she'd never seen a man more torn, except on the very evening they'd been in this situation before—the evening of his father's death.

Rolling away, he sat on the edge of the step, his breathing jagged. His hand shook as he drove it back through his hair. "No, I won't do this to you. And I won't do it to myself, either."

"Do...do what?" Addie choked out, clutching at the front of her dress as she pushed herself up on one elbow.

"This!" He gestured between them. "You're promised to Connor Brody. And this feud between the Brodys and Larrabies has got to stop here and now. 'Cause as much as Mick might believe it, it's not the Larrabie way to steal another man's woman away in the middle of the night. Or...to steal away from her."

He rose and paced to the opposite side of the gazebo, and in shock she wondered if he would leave her again, without explanation. Then he whirled around, and in the illumination of the yard light, she saw just how tormented he actually was. Beads of perspiration stood out on his forehead, and those intense eyes of his were shadowed and as haggard as those of a man who grappled with the most insidious of demons: himself.

At that moment, he looked exactly like his father, D.K.

"It's gotta stop here." He pointed at the floor in front of him. It was almost as if she weren't there. "I am *not* my father, getting so caught up in a woman I can't think straight, can't do what I know to be right for...for everyone."

His voice was chilling in its desolateness, hollowing out a similar emptiness in her, especially when he whispered, "I won't do it. I couldn't face my son if I did."

Yes, Jace. In the heat of the moment, she herself had forgotten about their son, and she could tell Deke had, too. But now it was as if the boy stood between them, forever binding them—and, she realized in a flash of insight, forever keeping them apart.

"And if it weren't for Jace...what would you do, Deke?" Addie had to ask. "What would happen then—between us?"

He blinked as if coming out of a trance.

"We wouldn't be having this conversation at all," he said bleakly. "Because I'd be gone—and out of your life for good. Wasn't that what you wanted, why you stopped looking for me after only nine months? It's what we've been talking about, Addie. You *knew,* even at seventeen. I knew it, too. And it was as clear to me today at the barbecue as it was then, that no matter what I did, leave or stay, it was a no-win situation, no matter what feelings we shared. Either way, I was bound to be the destruction of you."

His gaze hit hers, and suddenly, they understood each other in a moment of perfect clarity. She could see how wrong it was for them to be here together.

They continued to stare at each other for several moments. Then he gave a nod of understanding. And he was gone.

And Addie, still clutching her dress to her breast, laid her head down on her arm to do what she had vowed she never would again. She cried her heart out over Deke Larrabie.

Addie climbed out of the Bar G pickup truck and shut the door behind her as she scanned the ranch yard at the Tanglewood for signs of life. She saw none.

Of course, she'd arrived in the morning's waning hours. Most every available man would be out with the herd working—including, she hoped, Mick Brody.

Good. When she'd chatted with Connor earlier this morning over the phone, he'd mentioned he planned to spend the day at HQ working on the ranch's books. It was the one area of ranch work, she knew, that he already felt competent at, and to which he could make a contribution as he strove to learn the rest of the skills needed to run the Tanglewood—and to help her run the Bar G.

At the thought, her chest tightened in regret. This was going to be one of the most difficult things she'd ever done.

But she had no choice—not if she wanted to be fair to everyone involved. And she did want to be fair, if nothing else.

Feeling dragged out as she had for the three days since Deke's encounter with Mick—and since her encounter with Deke—she entered the ranch office with a short knock on the door, which brought Connor's attention from the computer screen to her. Catching sight of her, he gave her a smile of pure sunshine.

Addie experienced another of those squeezes on her heart that were becoming so much more frequent these days.

"Well, this is a surprise!" he said, rising and coming around the side of the desk to give her a kiss and a hug.

She hugged him back, a catch in her throat as she said, "I'd hoped to find you here."

He pulled away to peer into her face. "Is everything all right, Addie?"

"Actually, I needed to talk to you, Connor. That's why I'm here."

His brown eyes filled with concern. "Sure. You know you can come to me any time 'bout anything, don't you?"

"Y-yes." Addie took a seat on the fancy cowhide sofa that she knew Connor disliked, as he did the rest of the office's ostentatious decorations. Showily displayed in glass-fronted solid oak cases were Mick's antique guns and knives, along with his prized Western belt buckle collection. The brass-studded leather-topped desk looked big enough to float a load of cattle down the Brazos.

But then, this was still Mick Brody's domain, and would be for several years, even though he was training Connor to take over Tanglewood.

Somehow, she couldn't imagine Mick yielding control over anything until he was laid in the ground.

Connor sat next to her and took her hand so tenderly it had her madly batting back tears.

"Lord, Addie, what's wrong?"

She drew in a deep breath, gathering her strength. Addie squeezed his fingers. "Ever since what happened at the engagement party, Connor, I've been thinking."

He made a sound with his mouth. "I know, that was pretty awful for everyone. Like I said, I am sorry as all get out for what happened with my dad. It shouldn't've happened, and I told him so. How's it been with Jace?" he asked.

The sympathy in his voice made her sniff back tears again. She'd cried more in the past few days than she had in years, she realized. And now that the faucets had been opened up, it seemed there was no shutting them off.

"Oh, difficult, as you can imagine," she answered him. "F-for Deke, more than me." She made herself look him in the eye. She owed him honesty—owed him a lot more, truth be told. "That's why I'm here. With all that's got to be resolved with Jace…and Deke…I just don't see how I can marry you, Connor."

Releasing her hand, he sat back, clearly nonplussed. Clearly hurt.

"Ever?"

"I'm so sorry, Connor." She choked.

He hunched forward, elbows upon his knees, fingers clasped so tightly that she could see the knuckles turn white, and for a moment Addie wondered exactly how Connor *would* react. She'd never known him to be anything but kind and honorable, but he *was* Mick Brody's son....

She shook her head, instantly ashamed of her thought. Connor was no more prone to Mick's vices than Deke was to D.K.'s. Or her son to his father's faults.

"I guess I just have one question," Connor finally said, turning his head to look at her. "Are you still in love with Deke Larrabie?"

She didn't immediately respond, not knowing if there was an answer to such a question. Perhaps a better one might be this: Did it matter whether she loved Deke or if he loved her, when it seemed impossible that either of them would ever be able to trust in that love?

She'd done a lot of thinking since their meeting in the gazebo. Once again, it was as if the years-old hurt she'd nursed had created a blind spot that made her ignorant of her own heart. The truth was, she had worked herself into such a huff at Deke that it had caused her to be shortsighted about her own faults and mistakes. She'd realized it with Jace, in keeping the knowledge about his father from him. And now she realized it about herself—that she actually hadn't shown Deke the faith in their love that she accused him of holding back from her.

That was why she was here: she couldn't make yet another mistake with Connor. For while they might grow together through the years, he would realize that he didn't have all of her heart, and it would hurt him deeply. She couldn't do that to him.

But neither did she know how she would deal with the echoing hollowness inside her that came from loving a man who could never give her all of *his* heart.

Addie spread her hands. "Even if I were in love with Deke, it takes a lot more than love to make anything work in this life, whether it's running a ranch, keeping a marriage going, or bringing up a child together. And with Deke and me, there's so much hurt that's gone on, so much broken trust, between so many people...."

The office was quiet but for the hum of the computer, which seemed so out of place amid the Old West decor.

Connor sighed. "Aw, Addie, I know it's been tough for you—"

He took her hand again, and she clung to his, her heart so full.

"I'd just kind of hoped that I'd be the man able to mend some of those hurt feelings."

Thoughtfully, he rubbed the band of her engagement ring with the pad of his thumb. "This doesn't come out of the blue, I guess. You've changed since Deke came back. Jace's changed. Hell, it seems like the whole damn county, includin' the livestock, has changed since he came on the scene."

"Just like a rainmaker," she murmured. But in the story about the rainmaker, the hope he'd placed in the townspeople's hearts had been based on a confidence game.

Except...in the end, hadn't it been a woman's leap of faith that had redeemed him—and brought him and her, the whole town even, the very thing they most wanted in life?

But it had taken more than faith—it had taken love, unconditional and accepting, innocent and unstinting.

And forgiveness for faults, on both sides.

Tenderly and with great care, Addie slid the ring off her finger and folded it into Connor's palm. "There'll be someone for you, Connor, I know it. And I'd be as selfish as a kid with two ice-cream cones to hold on to you and keep you from finding that woman."

He didn't say anything, his eyes downcast and his features wearing an expression of bemusement. And worry.

"This is going to send your dad over the moon, isn't it?" Addie asked abruptly.

"Oh, ya think?" he quipped with a wry smile. He shrugged unworriedly, not entirely carrying it off.

"I'm sorry, Connor—"

"Sorry for what?"

Addie jumped three inches off the sofa, for this hadn't come from Connor. She turned to see Mick Brody standing in the office doorway.

His shrewd gaze went from her to his son and back again. "Sorry for what, Addie?" he repeated in a friendly, interested voice that fooled no one.

Before she could speak, Connor drew himself to a stand.

"Sorry, like I am," he said candidly, "that things aren't going to work out." He squared his stance. "Addie and I have decided to call off the engagement."

At another time, Addie might have felt some measure of reparation at seeing the shocked dismay on Mick's face—if it hadn't been so quickly followed by a frightening anger.

"Wha— Why?" he demanded, striding into the

room. "What blamed fool notion has gotten into your head now?"

This was directed at her. She started to rise in protest, but Connor set his hand on her shoulder, staying her.

"It's my decision, too, Dad. Sure, Addie and I have come to care for each other, but after takin' another look at things, we just don't feel it's enough to marry on."

Mick scrutinized Connor like a bug under a microscope, and to his credit, Connor stood up under the examination, although his fingers had a death grip on her shoulder.

"Bullcrap," Mick finally barked. "There's no way in hell this is your idea, so don't lie to me."

He turned on Addie, pointing a finger at her. "It's because of Deke Larrabie, isn't it."

"No, it's not." She managed to answer him levelly enough, but the blush she couldn't prevent from rising to her cheeks betrayed her.

Seeing her embarrassment, Mick's mouth twisted. "He's come back sniffin' around, hasn't he," he stormed, taking such a threatening step toward her that she couldn't stop herself from recoiling. "And you haven't got the decency to do right by my boy and tell that deadbeat cowboy to hit the highway again!"

"Dad, stop," Connor said, this time moving between her and his father. "I won't let you talk to Addie that way—"

"Oh, you won't?" his father jeered, his face crimson with rage. "But you sure'll lay down like a whupped dog and let another Larrabie come along and steal a Brody woman!"

This time, Connor didn't dignify Mick's accusation

with a response. Neither, Addie could see, would he disrespect his father. Instead he just steadily faced Mick down, until it was the older man who dropped his gaze.

"Hell, I don't care what you do, just get out of my sight," he snarled, dismissing them not only from the room, but almost, it seemed to Addie, from his life, as if they no longer existed to him.

But as she allowed Connor to usher her out of Mick's office, something told her that it would be the most foolish thing she'd ever done, believing Mick Brody would forget any wrong done to him.

The time had come for this particular pilgrimage.

Deke leaned a shoulder against the massive trunk of the cottonwood, contemplating the etching on the small granite grave marker set into the ground at his feet.

In memory of David Kenneth Larrabie, cowboy, it read. Nothing more.

So that was the extent of his father's legacy, Deke thought. But then, that pretty much summed it up, didn't it?

He'd wondered at first why there wasn't more—the date of his father's death, at the very least. Then it hit him: Maybe there were others, aside from him, who'd not wanted that reminder of the real legacy D. K. Larrabie had left behind.

Suddenly, the reality of the fire struck, and Deke experienced all over again the crushing disappointment.

Drawing in a deep breath, he cast his gaze upward at the maze of branches and leaves. The tremendous cottonwood provided almost total shade from the hot late-May sun, at least on the side of the tree he stood under. Much of the other side had been burnt away in the fire, leaving the ruins of the breeding facility exposed to the heat and rain and years. Now they resembled nothing so much as the bleached and rusted remains of a Conestoga wagon on the grassy plain, with as many hopes and dreams lying in the dirt.

And in the same way, the whole scene seemed to Deke to symbolize the Bar G, and Addie and himself, even the very nature of hope. People suffered the devastating loss of hope, then bore the terrible scar of that loss. And still, somehow, they managed to lift themselves up from the ashes and go on.

Yes, he must remember that. Somehow, they would all go on, even if they might not dare to hope again.

The scuffle of falling stones on the other side of the cottonwood brought his chin up. He peered around the rough-barked trunk.

There, amid the rubble of brick and cement and sun-bleached wood was Jace, poking through the wreckage.

What was he looking for? Deke wondered, pressing himself back against the trunk and out of sight. There was little left of the building but the slab foundation, weeds and exposed rebar sticking up through the cracks like the petrified ribs of an animal carcass on the prairie.

Yet, maybe Jace's showing up here was actually a lucky happenstance that Deke could use to his advantage, especially since he hadn't had a whole lot of other opportunities lately to make the father-son connection.

His heart throbbed painfully at the thought. Immediately after the Tanglewood barbecue, it had seemed the boy was progressing, however slowly and with much strain, toward coming to terms with him. Jace's curiosity, he could see, was stronger than his hurt.

But then a few days ago, Jace had closed himself off

to Deke. Wouldn't talk to him, look at him, cut so wide a swath around him that Jace practically made a tour of the county whenever he saw Deke coming.

And Addie, when he managed to corral her for a word, would only offer the advice to give Jace time.

Time? Hadn't she told him that night, too, how time had only made things worse for them, instead of providing a healing touch?

No, time wasn't a commodity Deke felt inclined to let gather interest, not when the prospect of Addie's marriage loomed on the horizon like a debt coming due, bringing ever closer the day when his son would go to live on the Tanglewood—and be within arm's reach of Mick Brody.

That thought near to made Deke sick. Almost as much as did the thought of Addie within the arms of Connor Brody.

Deke squeezed his eyes shut, remembering how it had felt to hold her, touch her, kiss her—and to experience her undeniable response. And how it had felt as he, too, once again traversed that razor's edge, sharp and sweet, between pleasure and pain, that cut much too close to the bone, brought him much too close to giving in and losing it all.

But he hadn't. He must remember that. *He* hadn't surrendered to the inevitable. And he hadn't lost anything—or anyone. Yet.

This time, however, there was no running away from confronting his weakness. No running away from confronting himself. It was more evident to him than ever that while Addie Gentry might crave that connection with him, so sure and strong, he could not give her the one thing she needed from him that Connor Brody could: a certainty in his ability to stay, and a trust in his word that he would.

And as if the fates had heard his thoughts, just when Deke was on the verge of stepping around the tree and approaching Jace, he heard a different step, one as recognizable to him as his own. Deke hesitated, the air stopped in his chest as if bottled with a cork.

"Jace," Addie said softly. "What are you doing here, hon?"

There was a moment of more scraping and the scuff of a boot in the debris, then Jace said, "Nothin'. Just messin' around."

"Well, this isn't the best place for kids to 'mess around.' You could get hurt."

More silence, except for a faint *chink* of a thrown rock making a landing.

"This is where he died, ain't it?" Jace finally burst out. "Deke's daddy."

It was the precise topic Deke himself had hoped to discuss with his son, but obviously the boy didn't feel he could bring it up to him.

Tick-tick-tick.

He wondered briefly if he should make his presence known, except that he felt himself held captive behind the cottonwood by some force as strong as the one that had driven him away.

"You knew that, hon," Addie carefully answered the boy. "I told you the story long ago."

"Yeah," Jace reluctantly allowed. "But you din't tell me...I din't know then that he was...you know. Who he was."

Deke heard her sigh. "Come on over here and have a sit," she said.

After a moment, Deke hazarded a peek around the

tree trunk. Addie had taken a seat on one of the concrete steps that had led up to the door of the building, her long red hair pulled back into a ponytail that trailed down her back from under her straw hat. His own hat tilted back on his head, Jace slouched next to her, his profile revealing obvious reluctance as much as compelling curiosity.

"Well, let's see," she began, arms linked around her bent knees. "I guess I was about sixteen when D. K. Larrabie and his son came to the Bar G from Montana. They were such able cowboys that Daddy—Granddad, that is—hired 'em both on the spot, even though…"

"Even though what?"

She hesitated, then gave a deciding shrug. "Even though D.K. had worked here on the Bar G before, back when he was just about Deke's age—twenty-one or so. That's when he met your grandmother, Lorna Keene."

"That was her name?" Jace said. *"L-O-R-N-A?"*

Addie looked at him with the same puzzlement Deke himself felt. Why had the boy spelled the name? Unless he was trying the concept on for size.

"Yes, Lorna." Addie laid her palm on Jace's back in a gesture obviously meant to reassure him as she revealed "She was promised to be married to Mick Brody."

Still, the boy whipped his head around to look at her, so that Deke could no longer see his expression. He sure enough heard the shock in Jace's voice, though, loud and clear.

"Y'mean Deke's daddy *stole* her from Mr. Brody, like a cattle rustler?"

Addie's lips turned down at the corners in a rueful frown. "Not exactly," she said tartly. "From what I'm told, Lorna Keene definitely had a will of her own. Maybe that was why runnin' off with D. K. Larrabie made more sense to her than marrying Mick,'' she added, almost to herself.

Absently, she rubbed Jace's back, her other hand cupping her chin as her elbow rested on her knee. ''She was goin' to school north of here at College Station and met Mick when she came down to Houston to visit a mutual friend. The way the story gets told, Mick was plain bowled over by her from the first. But after D. K. Larrabie came on the scene, Lorna had eyes for no one else, even though her kin threatened to disown her if she married him.''

Deke could barely hear Jace over the rustle of cottonwood leaves. ''What's that mean—*disown?*'' he asked suspiciously.

Addie's husky tones, however, still managed to ring in his ears as she said, ''To…to say you won't claim someone as your own.''

There was a beat of silence.

''You mean like Deke did with me,'' Jace said bitterly.

''Not exactly, son.'' Her fingers collared him around the back of the neck in emphasis of her words. ''Lorna'd made her choice, y'see. She was in love with D.K. and wouldn't have a word said against him. So the two of 'em eloped, takin' off for Montana.''

Jace picked up a stone at his feet and chucked it out into the weeds. ''Is that what happened to you, Mama? Didja fall in love with Deke like that? You know, so's you wouldn't listen to nothin' said against him?''

Her voice turned musing as she slowly brushed a lock of hair off her cheek in a purely sensual gesture that made Deke swallow, hard.

"I was…awfully young. We both were."

"Is that why ya din't run off with Deke?" the boy pressed. "'Cause of bein' too young?"

Deke leaned forward, clearly in Addie's line of sight, should she glance up. But he didn't care; he couldn't miss what she said next.

"No. It was because I…because Deke had left already before I—"

She broke off as Jace shot to his feet like a bronc from a chute, and Deke drew back an inch, startled.

"Then it's true, ain't it? It's gotta be!"

"What's true?" She reached out a hand to him, but he shook it off, radiating indignation.

"Deke's nothing but a good-for-nothin' cowboy—just like his daddy!"

Deke watched Addie stiffen in shock even as his own shock blasted a hole through him.

"What?"

"I heard tell that Deke's daddy caused the fire right here!" He faced his mother angrily. "And how Deke weren't man enough to stay and take 'sponsibility for his kin bein' so careless. That's why the Bar G's got all the problems it does! And now he's back and he's gonna wreck ever'thing for us again. He's got his mind all set to steal you 'way from a Brody, just the way his daddy did, and then leave like before! He don't got it in him to stay!"

Deke wondered if it'd be too much trouble to have the world end right then and there, as his fingernails dug reflexively into the cottonwood's gnarled bark. Hearing such a condemnation from Mick Brody, seeing it in the eyes of half the county—that was one thing. He could hold their censure at bay, knowing he was doing his utmost to make up for those wrongs.

But to stand here and listen to his own son call him a good-for-nothing cowboy just like his father, when he'd spent seven long years working to disprove such a verdict, if only to himself, and trying to drive such thoughts from his head... Well, Deke had to wonder whether there was much reason for life to go on.

His gaze homed in on Addie as, on tenterhooks, he waited for her response. If she confirmed such an appraisal of him, Lord, he really didn't know what he'd do.

"Where...where did you hear such things, Jace?" Addie asked when she'd recovered herself.

The boy's chin jutted defensively. "From Mr. Brody."

"Connor?"

"No—his daddy. Tuesday, when I went to town with Opal, he came up to me while I was waitin' in the truck."

"He did?" Addie exclaimed, clearly as disturbed by this revelation as Deke was.

"I din't want to believe him!" Jace blurted out miserably. "But just now, you said it, too, Mama."

Damn Mick Brody! Deke silently cursed. He should have known! Why couldn't the man leave him alone? After all, the Brodys had won, hadn't they? D.K. had sure enough paid for his wrong against Mick, and Connor was marrying Addie. So what pound of flesh was the man still aiming to have from him?

As if on cue, the answer was revealed to Deke, as Jace chewed on his lip, his expression one of utter forsakenness that called to Deke from the very bottom of his soul.

"I don't want nobody like that—nobody like Deke Larrabie—for my daddy."

Chapter Nine

Even if he'd had a bucket of ground glass passing through his gut, Deke couldn't have experienced any more pain than he did at that moment, hearing Jace's confession.

How had it happened? How, despite all efforts of his to keep history from repeating itself, was he now standing here with a son who felt for him the same way he'd felt for his father?

Yes, he'd been ashamed of D.K., of his weakness for the wife he loved and lost that drove him to another weakness: his drinking.

Oh, he should never have come back! How could Jace's anguish at knowing for certain his father's most damning faults be better than his not knowing? The boy would have been better off believing his father was dead.

So dazed was Deke that when Addie looked up, he

hadn't the wherewithal to move out of sight, to mask his expression, and she saw him standing next to the tree. He wondered if she'd detect the turmoil roiling through him right then, or if the shade of the cotton-wood, the shadow of his hat brim, the iron mask of his expression, would obscure her view of his eyes. For they alone would tell her in no uncertain terms how badly he wanted to leave at that moment. Leave, as she'd exhorted him to, and never look back. Certainly, no other sign betrayed the death spiral of emotion tak-ing place inside him; years and years of self-imposed control over himself had assured him of that.

But would Addie know, simply because she knew him? And expect nothing different?

Without missing a beat, she shifted her gaze to Jace, whose back was now turned to Deke, tension radiating from his small body.

"Both Deke and his daddy have their faults, that's true," she said. "But like I've told you, it was a tragic accident how he perished in the fire on this very spot. How could it have been anything but?"

Her arm swept around in a semicircle, painting a mental picture. "You should've seen it, all shiny and new and pristine. Everything you'd need to get the job done and then some. It was the talk of the county. When it was finished, D.K. had almost popped his but-tons, he was so proud of it, prouder of it than even Granddad! And as for Deke—well, Deke was not just made in the image of his father, he was a better man. I'm not just talkin' about him being one of the finest, natural cowboys you could ever hope to see. Lord, when he'd take off across the range a-horseback after some cow, holdin' on by nothing but his spurs, that lariat of his swinging around his h-head—"

Her voice cracked, and she dropped her chin briefly, then lifted it and went on with a new sureness. "It was poetry in motion. Still is. But Deke also had a way of lookin' out for those who were within his care, whether it was the land or animals or p-people, and puttin' their welfare above his own…. I guess what I'm tryin' to say, hon, is that looking back, I realize that…that he and his daddy were simply…who they were, meanin' they were cowboys, in the best sense of the word."

"But D.K. burnt the building down!" the boy protested mulishly. "That wasn't the best, that was the worst."

"Not on purpose," she reminded him, placing a gentle hand on his shoulder.

"No—it happened 'cause he was a drunk! A drunk cowboy!"

"Aw, hon." She sighed. "Faults and flaws and mistakes don't make people bad. It just makes 'em…people."

Jace didn't seem to hear her, though, as he shook off her touch. "No! Deke left you on purpose, and he didn't come back."

"He *did* come back, Jace. Granted, it took him seven years, but he did come back."

"But how could he leave in the first place? How could he leave *me!*"

Deke couldn't do it. He could stand there no longer, held captive by his inaction, damned by it as much as by any deed he'd come to regret.

Because even if it damned him again, he couldn't let Addie face this moment alone, not again.

This was their son.

He stepped forward, and at the faint sound of his

boot crunching on the gritty concrete, Jace started
to turn.

But Addie caught him by his shoulders, preventing
him from seeing Deke. He understood why when she
said in a rush, as if she'd lose her nerve in the next
instant, "Deke didn't know about you, Jace! I didn't
tell him. And I asked him not to tell you that, or that
he was your father. That was the promise he
made…the one he wouldn't tell you about."

Even without seeing Jace's expression, Deke could
tell the boy was as stunned as he'd have been if she'd
told him she was once abducted by aliens and just now
recalled the episode.

Deke saw Addie swallow.

"I was hurt, Jace. Terribly hurt when he left without
an explanation, no matter why he felt he had to go.
A-and hurt, too, that when he came back…that it
wasn't for me. So I made him promise not to tell you."

Mother and son stared at each other in mute agony,
as Deke's own Adam's apple worked in his throat. No,
it wasn't worth coming back—not if it meant Addie
might lose Jace's trust in her, and Jace might lose his
trust in anyone or anything.

Staunchly, she continued with the dignity he'd always prized in her.

"It was only going to be for a while, Jace, until…oh,
I can't even remember why now. Because holding him
to such a promise…it was wrong. I can see that now.
I made a mistake—and if I want to be forgiven my
mistakes, I think I'd best be for forgiving those wrongs
against me, shouldn't I?"

She looked directly into Jace's eyes. "And
won't you?"

"I don't want to forgive nobody, Mama," Jace admitted in a shamed whisper.

"I know. Rare's the person who chooses to forgive a wrong done to them, especially when the hurt's still so raw. And merely sayin' you do doesn't make it so. But it does help to start fences bein' mended. Look—" she crossed her arms over her knees, eyes on a level with his "—you don't have to give all of your trust right away. That wouldn't be right for anybody. Small steps, though. Small steps will do the trick, eventually."

Her face was a study of compassion—for what Jace was going through, certainly. But, Deke knew, also for him and what he'd gone through. And for her own journey on the bitter road she'd traveled. For it was only in forgiving oneself that forgiveness for others could happen.

Jace didn't immediately respond, obviously still reluctant, his stance as tense as a guy wire stretched taut, too taut. And in that instant Deke felt he looked at D.K., fighting himself in a battle that couldn't be won. Because no matter what part of him triumphed, some part had to break.

It was an impossible situation, with impossible choices.

Then Addie lovingly reached out to their son and took his face between her hands. "It's okay if you can't forgive Deke or me right away, hon, really it is. Just…don't let your hurt hold you back from reachin' out in faith when the time is right, and giving everyone, includin' yourself, a chance to be happy. Will you promise me that much, son?"

"I—I guess," Jace whispered.

"All right, then." She straightened. "Now, run on

back to the house. I heard Opal say something about baking a couple of fresh blueberry pies this morning.''

''Yes, ma'am.'' Jace pushed to his feet and took a few hesitant steps, then turned and flung his arms around Addie's neck, clearly the beginning of the boy's own forgiveness of his mother.

''I love you, Mama,'' he said.

Deke felt his throat tighten as he watched her squeeze her eyes shut and hug their son.

''I love you, too, son,'' Addie whispered back. Then she released him with a fond swat on the seat of his jeans to send him off.

She gazed after him until he was out of sight, then stood and walked toward Deke with that long-legged, assured gait of hers.

Oh, he had never loved her more, this fine, strong woman! For he knew he hadn't imagined the beginning of her own forgiveness that he'd heard in her voice. And he knew then that he had never stopped loving her, would never stop loving her for as long as he lived. *That,* God help him, was why he couldn't leave again, no matter what.

It would be a living hell for the rest of Deke's life to have to see her married to another man, to see her grow closer to Connor, build a life with him, bear his children....

Oh, he didn't doubt that his soul would be improved with the effort over the years, but at the moment the mere thought drove him crazy.

She stopped in front of him, and he spoke first.

''Thank you, Addie. For tryin' to redeem me in Jace's eyes, even at your expense.''

She shrugged, but he detected the uncertainty in the

gesture that told him she knew there was still much more repairing to be done yet between her and the boy.

"Jace has never been one to hold grudges."

"And I'm here to tell you that neither am I," he said softly. "I'm not gonna try and steal you away from Connor to spite Mick *or* just because I can, like Jace said. I may be a cowboy, through and through, but I'm not that kind of man."

Even though, he thought but didn't say, it was taking everything in him at that moment not to pull her into his arms here, now, proving to them both that it *was* beyond both their wills, this connection between them.

Still, he knew that while in the short run he might find satisfaction in knowing that the passion that had always been between them was as undeniable as ever, in the long run it wouldn't be good for anyone.

He gave himself a short, reinforcing nod. "And I want to respect your wishes about how you see runnin' the Bar G. Jud kinda forced me on you, and while I still feel I've got a lot to offer the operation, I'm not the boss of this outfit. So I'll be clearin' my gear out of the bunkhouse in the next few days—"

"You're leaving?" Addie interrupted, her eyes wide.

"Just the Bar G. There're any number of outfits in the area I can probably sign on with. It probably won't be the steadiest work in the world, but at least it'd keep me close by. I may not be makin' the best job of it, Addie, but I am trying to do what's best for everyone— and tryin' to accept, too, your choice in marryin' any man, Brody or not."

"I know." She became very interested in picking at a patch of bark on the cottonwood's trunk. Then she said, "Actually, Deke, I'd like to take a look at some of your ideas for instituting an AI program here on the Bar G.''

Deke shook his head as if to clear the wax from his ears, because he honestly wasn't sure he'd heard her right. "You would?"

She seemed fixated on her idle task. "Mind, it'll have to be on a budget, which I need to have laid out in complete detail. The bank'll need it, too, if there's some financing required. And I want to see a step-up plan that implements the program in stages," she added briskly. "We're not jumping into anything headfirst again."

Even more puzzled, he frowned. "I'd be happy to get you anything you need, but what about your plan to wait till fall when there'll be plenty of money for all kinds of improvements?"

"That's not going to happen now." Finally, she turned her gaze to his. "I'm not marrying Connor."

You could have tipped him over with the flick of a finger. "But I thought…you know…that everything was set and your mind made up."

"Yes, everything seemed to be tied up didn't it?" she said ruefully. "I truly was trying to do what *I* thought was best for the Bar G and Jace when I said I'd marry Connor. Now, though…"

Her voice trailed off, and Deke, on a precipice of sheer suspense, asked, "Now…what?"

She gazed off into the distance, blue eyes shimmering under the brim of her hat. "Now, I see that I believed I didn't have much other choice. And that's not a good enough reason to do anything, e-especially marry someone."

She'd faltered on that last assertion, but then she bravely looked him in the eye. "Just as feeling I didn't have much choice left to me has never been a good enough reason to cut you out of Jace's—and my— life.''

She smiled absently, almost sadly, and Deke realized it was a different Addie standing in front of him than the one he'd encountered when he first came to the Bar G. To be sure, she was the same woman in her loss of youthful innocence and trust that he'd pinpointed as owing to him. But while that Addie had felt the loss keenly, bitterly, this new Addie seemed to bear the burden with a certain world-wise acceptance that bent without breaking.

''So when…when did this come about, the break with Connor?'' He had the nerve to persist.

''Tuesday.'' The span of time sunk in to them both at the same moment. Tuesday was when Jace had said Mick approached him in town. Deke couldn't help being glad the boy would have even less contact with Mick from now on.

''All right,'' he said with a brisk nod. ''I've already been working with Jud on the database for the AI program, so we've got a head start in that area. We'll develop a schedule for takin' checks on the reproductive condition and history of each heifer, best we can, and get the hands doing that part.''

Excitement built inside him, first rumbling and coughing like starting a long-idle motor, then evening out to a steady purr that felt good. Damn good.

''I looked at what equipment's on hand,'' he continued, ''and we've already got a squeeze chute that can be modified. I'll look into purchasing supplies of syringes and some secondhand liquid-nitrogen cylinders.''

No, this AI program wouldn't have all the expensive

bells and whistles the other one had had, but that wasn't what the Bar G needed. And an AI program wasn't the only thing the Bar G needed, either.

"That can't be our only line of defense, though, Addie." Deke went on. "You and Jud and me should sit down as soon as possible and talk about what other strategies we can use to cut costs and improve production."

In his earnestness, he took a step forward, to within a few inches of her. "I want as much as you do to see the Bar G succeed, you know. For Jace's sake."

And yours, he almost added.

While she didn't retreat at his advance, she did drop her gaze under his too-personal scrutiny.

"That, I've never doubted," Addie murmured. "And it would be pretty shortsighted of me not to take advantage of your offers of help and your expertise while I can."

He should give her more space, he knew, but he sensed he was on the cusp of another discovery here— about Addie. About how she felt about him.

"So…am I forgiven, Addie?" Deke asked, glad she wasn't looking at him, for he was afraid his whole heart showed in his eyes.

"Forgiven," she said, "as I hope I am by you."

"Don't give it another thought," he told her huskily.

He automatically extended his right arm, meaning to shake on it, but she briefly slid her left hand into his palm, partner-like, and he noticed that it lacked Connor's ring.

Before he even had a chance to get used to the warmth of her touch, she pulled away.

Still, as they walked back to headquarters side by side, despite himself and his better judgment, Deke felt the hopes and dreams he'd left in the ashes on that very spot seven years ago rise up like a phoenix.

The day was typically Texan. Not just hot and steamy, but hot and steamy in spades, with both the temperatures and humidity in the high double-digits. Deke wondered if one could literally melt with the heat, like a slab of lard on a primed and ready griddle.

He did know for sure that such weather made for some rough ranch work as the hands herded the spring calf crop into the branding corral, where, amidst the constant crescendo of bawling critters, the boys were expected to engineer the vaccinating, tagging, branding, dehorning and castrating of a few hundred cattle.

By early afternoon, however, the Bar G crew had nearly completed the job and was cleaning up, shutting down the propane-fueled branding fire and washing the blood-spattered equipment as the buzzards spiraled overhead.

Leaning an elbow on the top rail of the fence, Deke lifted his sweat-soaked straw Stetson from his head to wipe his forehead with his red bandanna. He watched Addie, her own hat rim dark with perspiration, check on one newly steered critter who'd bled out more profusely than his fellow beeves.

He had to hand it to her. She'd directed all the action today from horseback like Sam Houston leading the troops at the battle of San Jacinto.

Hell, she didn't need him to keep the Bar G going; she didn't need anyone. Under her direction, he couldn't imagine that the Bar G would ever go under, although the ranch might scrape bottom at times.

But that was the nature of ranching. The risks were always there. Addie knew that—she had simply lost her nerve for a while, on account of what had happened with D.K. and the breeding facility. On account of what had happened with him.

Obviously, though, she had come to terms with those fears, as he had so despaired her ever doing. But since she'd been able to, maybe it was time for him to move on, too, in his own heart.

Addie looked around and spied him standing outside the corral. Turning Keno, she rode over.

Deke obligingly opened the gate to let her ride through, then latched it behind her. "Looks like you've got a good crop of calves this year."

"Yup. All we can hope is that beef prices don't bottom out by fall." She nudged Keno backward as he stuck his nose through the fence rails to graze on the carpet of moldy straw the hands had scattered to absorb the blood. "I've got six heifers who came up dry for the season. I'll be sending them on down the road next week."

"Well, depending upon what we've got comin' up for first-time breeders, this fall might be a good time to check out a couple of auctions." He tipped his hat back on his brow so he could better see her. "Although we might want to wait to do any buyin' till after next spring's calf crop drops."

Addie gave a noncommittal shrug. "I'll see what makes sense once I know what the fall brings."

Deke felt his mouth thin into a stiff line. *I,* she'd said. Not *we,* as he put what he hoped to happen.

Oh, it wasn't that he expected once they'd come to terms with each other that every loose thread would tie itself up nice and neat and they'd go on as if neither of them had ever had a wrong word between them. But he could tell that some piece of business continued to worry Addie.

Was it Jace? Turning, Deke squinted against the late-afternoon sun at his son, who continued to linger in the corral. Deke was positive it was because today was the first time Jace had been allowed to fully participate in this ranch ritual. Even now, when he had to be dog-tired, the boy continued to practice his roping using a post from one of the portable chutes that had yet to be taken down.

He'd gotten pretty good at hitting his mark, Deke thought with pride. The youngster's windup was steady and sure, and his technique when he let that flat loop take off was…well, it was pure poetry, as Addie had called Deke's own skill with a rope.

"He's come a long way in just a few months," Addie observed beside him, adding gently, "in more ways than one."

"He's sure still his daddy's son, though," Deke answered without a bit of sympathy for himself. "Not much bend in the Larrabie backbone. It won't stand him in very good stead as he gets older, if he doesn't learn to give a little, without feelin' he has to give all."

"He is what he is, Deke." Her voice was soft.

"What you mean is that he's a bred-in-the-bone cowboy. And not necessarily in the best sense of the word."

She said nothing, and he peered up at her stoic profile. Stoic—and accepting of the inevitable.

That's when it hit him.

"You don't believe I'm gonna stay, do you, Addie," he asked with sudden comprehension.

She merely gave a shrug, although it was an uncomfortable one. "I don't believe it's somethin' one has any say about—even you."

"But I *do* mean to stay."

"I know you do, Deke. I'm not saying you don't believe that you will—"

"But I shouldn't make promises about it—is that what you're sayin'?"

She wouldn't look him in the eye, and on impulse he caught her ankle in his hand. Even through layers of denim and leather, he could see how his touch instantly broke through her defenses. Her blue eyes flashed at him, partly angry and partly pleading.

So what if he did break through? Would it be such a terrible thing for either of them? She'd told Jace that she had been hurt, terribly hurt, by his leaving. Deke saw now, however, that she'd been even more hurt by his return—a return that hadn't been...on account of *her.*

Or so she believed.

"Addie—" he said, his voice low, the promise on his lips.

"Bull! Look out, y'all! Bull in the pasture!"

Deke released Addie's ankle, whipping around to where the commotion was. Sure enough, a big, black Angus bull had somehow broken through the far fence.

The cowboys scattered, each heading for the fence. Yet he knew without looking that his gaze and Addie's were simultaneously seeking out Jace's small figure among the blur of legs and flying hats, wondering which of the ranch hands had scooped him up and gotten him to safety.

Deke's blood drained to his toes when he spotted the boy standing stock-still and alone in the middle of the corral—alone except for half a ton of hotheaded beef, which at that very moment focused on his target.

"Jace!" Addie screamed. "Oh my God."

Deke sized up the situation instantly. Two of the hands on the far side of the corral had heard Addie's scream and, realizing that in all the confusion they'd forgotten about the boy, started toward him at a dead run. Addie herself was hauling back on her horse's reins to turn him around even as she reached for the rope coiled around her saddle horn, and Deke realized her intent. She was going to jump the fence and head the bull.

She'd never pull it off. Even if Addie were able to get a loop over the bull, at the speed it was going there'd be no stopping its turf-tearing beeline toward Jace and the ranch hands. In fact, the momentum would likely wrest Addie from her saddle or bring Keno crashing to the ground.

Which meant any way you looked at it, someone would get hurt—and badly.

Unless the bull were distracted off his course.

On that thought, Deke bounded over the fence and took off toward the mad beast at a run, whooping and hollering and waving his hat and his own lariat for all he was worth.

The bull didn't even seem to hear him as his legs churned like well-greased pistons, eating up the ground, eating up precious seconds.

"Heeya! Heeya!" Deke yelled frantically, drawing to within twenty yards of the beast, trying to keep one eye on what was going on at the other side of the corral. At least Addie had realized his plan and gone for Jace, he could see that. But oh, was it really his lot that he should have to watch helplessly as one or both of

the people he loved most on this earth got killed right in front of his eyes?

"Heeya!"

Miraculously, the massive head turned, the hooves ground to a halt in the turf. Sides heaving, the beast narrowed one bloodshot eye at Deke, who sent a dubious prayer of thanks heavenward.

But none of them were out of the woods yet, he knew. Somehow he had to keep the bull distracted until Addie had gotten the boy and herself safely on the other side of the corral fence. Once they were, he'd have to get himself out.

One of the hands heaved Jace like a sack of potatoes onto Addie's saddle in front of her. The boy caught hold of the horn with both hands as his mother's arm clamped around his middle. They were all heading for the fence line, when Jace's high-pitched voice rang out.

"Deke! He's gonna get Deke!"

At the sound, the bull swung around, snot blowing from his nostrils as he sized up the situation on the other side of the corral. He gave a mighty bellow that sounded to Deke like frustration—and pain.

Was the animal hurt? he wondered. For that matter, how had this bull, which had to be Mick Brody's, even gotten through the fence Deke himself had checked only yesterday?

"Oh, what's it gonna do, Mama?" Jace's voice again pealed out. The hulking beast zeroed in on the sound, indecision in his stance.

Deke judged it a prime opportunity to give him a little help making up his mind. Uncoiling his rope, he gave the loop one, two twirls above his head, then let it sail. It caught the bull by the horns, and Deke gave a mighty yank, not just pulling the beast's head around but tugging him forward a couple of steps.

The effort wasn't for naught; the bull's focus shifted back to Deke, who gave another powerful jerk on the rope, just for good measure, dragging the bull's nose downward into the ground.

In fact, he got the distinct impression he'd been too successful, as, with a vicious snort and a rake of his hoof in the turf, the bull charged him.

Deke hesitated only a split second, making sure that the ornery critter was well and truly on a mission to make mincemeat out of him, then turned and headed for the fence at a sprint, legs pumping for all they were worth.

He was fast; the problem was, the bull was faster. Deke became aware of the ranch hands on either side of his mark standing on the bottom rail of the fence, waving their arms and beating their hats against their thighs. That alone would have been a sure sign he'd left himself too little wiggle room, even if he hadn't heard the thunder of hooves drawing nearer, hadn't felt the rumble of them beneath his heels with every step he took.

The fence—and safety—were still yards away.

So—was *this* how it was going to end? he thought wildly. Not with himself seeing his loved ones die, but with Jace watching in horror as the father with whom he'd so many scores yet to settle was run through by a bull in another fatal miscalculation?

Was this how it would end, too, for Addie, with her having no other choice but to pick up the pieces again, being left alone by him to raise their child?

He'd only been trying to do what he believed was

best for them, both then and now! It wasn't a mistake, distracting the bull, even if it did mean losing his life.

Even if it meant he'd be leaving without either of them knowing how much they meant to him.

Sucking air into his burning lungs, Deke kept his eye on the top rail of the fence, every muscle in him straining toward it. He didn't need a rearview mirror to know that the bull was practically in his back pocket, that one false step, one wrong move, one hesitation, no matter how slight, would mean certain death.

With a fierce lunge, he grasped the pipe railing with both hands, vaulting over the fence just as the bull crashed into it. The force of the impact shook the railing so hard Deke lost his handhold and went flying. An instant later he made contact with the ground in a jarring landing, flat on his back, that drove the wind out of his lungs and made him black out for a second.

When he came to, however, he couldn't care less that pain shot through every bone in his body. He'd landed on the outside of the pasture, safe and alive.

And where a mere second ago he'd have forsaken that life, now Deke wouldn't give it up for anything. Because that's when he heard something he thought he'd go to his grave without ever knowing the sweet joy of.

"Dad!" Jace cried, flinging himself on top of him, driving the rest of his breath clean out of him, hugging with all his might. "Dad, are you okay? Are ya?"

Amazingly, there must have been some air left in his lungs, for laughter bubbled up from their recesses. Deke lifted his arms to enfold his son in as fierce a hug.

"Yes, Slick, I'm fine," he said. "Just fine."

Chapter Ten

It took another hour for the hands to subdue the bull and run it into a smaller enclosure where it wouldn't be able to hurt anyone.

By that time Addie's nerves were stretched as tight as a banjo string. It was all she could do to keep the ranch hands on task to finish up in the branding corral. With the morbid fascination that human nature has for such things, everyone wanted to cuss and discuss Deke's near miss at getting made into shish kebab.

Everyone except Addie. Standing at the edge of the corral, arms crossed, she called out to her top hand. "I swear, Harley, if I find even one piece of equipment that hasn't been thoroughly disinfected and put back in its place, I'll have the cowboy who's responsible busting sod way out in the farthest corner of the Bar G for the next three weeks."

"Yes, boss," Harley called back, hustling the hands

along. It wasn't often she got into a mood like this, but when she did, look out.

All Addie knew was that if she let down her guard, if she showed any concern or was shown any, she'd burst into a storm of sobbing that would *really* scare the hell out of the boys.

She herself wanted nothing more than to forget that horrifying, frightening moment when it seemed Deke was not going to escape the bull's deadly wrath. In fact, for an endless few seconds she thought the beast's horns *had* struck Deke, throwing him over the fence. With Jace tight against her in the saddle in front of her, she'd cut a mad path through the hands gathered at the fence as she tore around the outside of the corral to where Deke lay deathly still in the grass.

Once there, however, she couldn't bring herself to go to his side, to do anything but slide from the saddle and watch Jace do what she'd have given her right arm to do.

She managed to hold up fine through the rest of the afternoon's cleanup, through a supper that she barely tasted with Jace and her father. Yet even a long, hot shower didn't dispel the twanginess of her nerves.

So she went looking for Deke.

Addie found him in the tack room off the stable, hunched over something resting on one thigh, and for an instant she wondered if he had gotten injured after all.

"Deke?"

He turned, and she saw that he held his lariat.

He noted the direction of her gaze. "It got pretty beat up during all the commotion today. What with getting stomped on by one churned-up bull, drug through the dirt, and wrapped around just about every fence post on the place, I'm thinkin' it's not gonna be fit for active duty again.''

"Really?'' Addie walked forward, and he handed the rope to her for her inspection. She ran its length across her palm and could see what he meant. There were at least half a dozen spots where the nylon filaments were frayed if not split. Even one such weakness in the fibers was reason to think twice about retiring even your best catch rope.

She glanced down at him. ''I'm sorry, Deke. You've had this rope for years.''

"Since before my dad died,'' he confirmed tonelessly, as she handed the coil back to him. ''Well, I was surprised to find it had any kind of life left in it when I came back to the Bar G, so I guess it's no great loss.''

His eyes were downcast as he stroked the tips of his fingers over one loop in a way that brought a dangerous sting to the back of Addie's eyes.

"You could still use it for show,'' she suggested hoarsely. ''Couldn't you?''

"I suppose.'' He looked as if he'd just come from a shower. His dark hair glistened in the light like a horse's chestnut coat. ''But if a piece of equipment's not up to snuff, I'm not one for keepin' it around for sentimental reasons. It's too risky. You saw it today— you can't have any weak links in this business...and that goes for people, too.''

He tossed the rope onto the nearby worktable with much more vehemence than his tone had indicated. Then he rose, his back to her, hands set on his hips, looking clearly disturbed. Clearly on the brink of... of what?

Apprehension sprang up in her all over again. "Deke, what's going on? What is it? Tell me!"

He said nothing for a few moments. Then he burst out, "Damn it, Addie, I checked that section of fence myself a few days ago, in anticipation of just such an accident happening!" He whipped around, one finger pointing emphatically at the floor. "I *knew* we shared the fence with the Tanglewood, and I wanted to make sure none of our cows got a wild hair, broke through to Mick's pasture and gave him reason to get even more het up at us and the Bar G."

"Well, I called over there a little bit ago." Addie made herself speak reasonably. "Mick wasn't there, but I spoke to Connor. If it helps, he said he was pretty sure his dad had taken a ride out to that section of fence the other day, too. So who knows how Mick's bull got through it. Things like this happen in ranching."

Remarkably, she almost believed herself.

At least Deke seemed to.

He sighed gustily. "I guess so. He was sure riled enough to bust through a wall at Fort Knox, wasn't he." His hand drove through his hair, making the cowlick in front more prominent. "I wonder what got into him. I thought there'd be no turnin' him off his heading once he got Jace in his sights. Hell, once he got *me* in his sights—"

"Could we not talk about it anymore?" Addie broke in. She shoved each of her fists under the opposite arm, trying to still the sudden tremors in her hands. "I've had it up to here with all the hashing and rehashing of the 'Wreck that Almost Happened.' Heavens, you'd think people almost wish you *had* taken a body blow from that bull!"

He gave her a hard look. "Well, at least I'd've gone out a hero in front of my son instead of a failure."

So. Once again, Addie realized, this was about that damn cowboy pride of his! Well, it was high time he got over it!

She strode straight up to Deke so she was nearly riding his boot tips. "Is that what you wanted today, Deke Larrabie? To *die?* And wouldn't that have made a nice, handy exit, right when your son's obviously accepted you as his daddy! Oh, I've heard of cowboys who'd take off without their last paycheck and leave their best cowpony behind to avoid havin' to deal with some sticky situation they got themselves into, but this takes the prize!"

His head jerked back as if he'd been slapped. "What in hell are you talkin' about?"

"You! You and your infernal cowboy-ness, your damn Larrabie Way!"

"You think I *wanted* to check out today, like my daddy did?" he demanded, lightning forming in his eyes. "Good God, Addie, I know you've got your doubts about me, but that's not fair!"

"Isn't it?" she challenged recklessly. She knew she was being irrational, but she couldn't stop now. Unable to prevent herself, she grabbed his shirtfront in both hands, yanking him off balance, so that he had to grasp her upper arms. "Don't you dare do it, Deke! I won't let you do this to Jace! I won't, do you hear me?"

"Do what?" he asked in complete bafflement.

"You almost got *killed* out there today!"

His eyes narrowed dangerously. "Are you sayin' I shouldn't've done everything I could to save you and our son? I had to do what I did, Addie. And I'd do it again!" His fingers tightened on her arms. "What, would you've had me not do everything in my power, beat a path to hell and back, to protect Jace, to protect you? Is that what you're saying?''

''No!'' She realized tears were pouring down her cheeks, and she let go of him to bury her face in her hands, shocked to her core at how she was behaving. She literally couldn't stop herself. And that was what scared her most.

Oh, how had she managed to return to this place in her heart again, when all she had ever wanted was to move on?

''I don't know what I mean,'' she mumbled into her fingers.

''What?'' Deke took her wrists, tugging her hands away from her face.

''I don't know what I mean!'' she cried, eyes squeezed shut and head turned against her shoulder, almost in shame. But what did she have to be ashamed of? ''Just that…I finally know how awful it must have been for you, that night your father died. I mean, really know. It was fairly radiating from Jace. When I saw him realize that he might lose you…it was like when I saw you realize that your own daddy was gone, after h-how you'd both hoped for so much more…and with so much to be settled between you yet. The look on your face, in your eyes, was pure horror at what'd just happened.''

''What…what *had* just happened?'' Deke repeated, his voice barely a whisper—and filled with dread.

''You lost him, Deke, that's what. It was there in your face how alone you were—'' A sniff camouflaged a sob. ''And I wanted to c-comfort you, tell you that you weren't, you weren't alone.'' The sob burst from her, anyway. ''You h-had m-me-ee…but that wasn't enough. My love wasn't enough to heal the pain and keep you from leaving—''

With a gentle grasp of her chin, he turned her head, and through her tears she found not the forbidding Deke of late, but the boy she'd fallen in love with—vulnerable and strong, tough and tender at once.

''Addie, I didn't leave because you didn't love me enough. Believe me.''

''Are you sure, Deke?'' Her own heart lay as exposed. ''Because that's all I've got to give you now, to get you to stay. And all I know is that I almost lost you again today, Deke, and I can't lose you, not again.''

His eyes flared for a moment, and then he pulled her into his arms. She clung to him as she'd wanted to for the past four hours. For the past seven years—which only made her cry harder, for she cried for him, the boy he'd been, the man he'd had to become on that smoke-filled night. And she cried for herself, too. For the woman she'd had to become. That was what he'd been trying to tell her for weeks, what he'd been trying to tell her in his leaving years ago. For what had divided them wasn't the trials they'd had to deal with that came to everyone; it was the true loss of innocence: finding out that even if they'd seen those trials through together, their love for each other still might not have been enough for them to make it.

''Hush, now,'' he murmured into her hair. ''I'm not goin' anywhere.''

She lifted her head, could barely see his face through her tears. ''That's just it, Deke! You promised me you'd stay before, and then you broke your promise.''

With the edge of his thumb, he brushed a tear from her cheek. ''Actually, I only broke half of my promise—and even then, I've tried to make good by coming back.''

Blinking furiously, Addie struggled to pull away from him, but Deke was having none of it. "Don't play technicalities with me, not now."

"How'm I doing that?" he asked, with what she thought was maddening obtuseness.

She managed to poke a finger at his chest. "Don't think I don't remember every word you said, how you promised you'd never leave me—"

"Yeah. That's the half I'm sayin' I broke—"

"And that you'd always love me…"

Her voice trailed off, and Addie stared at Deke, stared deep into those amber-green eyes of his, searching for the truth as moments before he'd searched hers. Because she had to have it! She had to have it, would settle for nothing less.

"W-what are you saying, Deke?" she asked.

He took her face between his hands. "I'm sayin' that I love you, Addie Gentry. I never stopped—and believe me, I tried. Tried to forget you with every bit of strength I had. But I couldn't. I didn't have a choice in the matter."

Addie blinked. "You didn't?"

"That's right." Leaning his forehead against hers, he murmured, "And if that damns me—damns us both—back into a living hell, so be it."

Then he was kissing her. Not just kissing her, but taking prisoner her lips with swift and utter command, as if he knew every vulnerable spot in her heart. Which he did. He had always known….

She'd changed into a cotton dress after her shower, and now was glad she'd done so, as every hard angle of him imprinted itself on her tender flesh through the thin material. Her nails dug into his shoulders as he found the sensitive spot behind her ear that she herself had forgotten existed. Warmth poured through her abdomen like honey, then quickened, just like that, to licks of fire as his hands splayed on her bottom. And she thought she'd die as she tilted her pelvis against him and felt the solid length of him.

"Oh, Deke, please," she whispered. "Please…"

It almost brought her to tears again when he pulled back, although he still held her in that push-pull of emotions that she understood so well.

"I can't…we can't…" he rasped, his arms trembling with the effort. "I won't do it to you again, Addie. Much as I want you, I won't make love to you—"

Her heart stopped still, until he went on raggedly, "—I won't make love to you, not without protection."

"But it's all right, really. I-I'm on the pill."

He went still.

"I only went on it after Connor and I became engaged," Addie hastened to explain, "thinking that, after all, this was the man I was going to marry, and it might be possible that we'd, you know—"

"You don't need to explain, Addie. Honest," he said. His nostrils flared with the extent of his struggle to control himself. Then he sighed. "Damn it, I know I've got no call to be jealous. But I am, jealous as hell."

"Good," Addie said, surprising both of them. She snaked her arms around his neck again. "I daresay your soul could do with the improving of a good struggle with such a sin…but that can wait until after you make love to me, cowboy."

With a low growl he lifted her into his arms and

strode into the small bunkroom. Next to the narrow cot, he slowly set her on her feet, easing her down against him, inch by glorious inch.

Unable to wait any longer, she unbuttoned his shirt, slipped her hands beneath its edges to ease it over his broad shoulders. His body was different, while still being entirely the same. He'd filled out in the shoulders and chest; the hair there had grown thick as it arrowed down to his navel—and beyond.

Overcome by a shyness she didn't entirely understand, Addie stopped.

"What? What is it?" Deke asked.

"I...I don't know," she confessed. "I guess for a long time I lived on memories of that night we made love. Sometimes I'd want to wipe it from my mind so badly I cried. Sometimes, though, I went over each and every detail, over and over again, not caring that it drove me crazy. But then, I've never had any other experience to take its place. And now...now I'm afraid. Afraid there's been too much that's happened to me, to both of us...."

"But we don't have a choice, do we?" he said.

"No. We've got no choice, no matter what happened, but to go forward. And it scares me, Deke. That's all I'm sayin'. It scares me to death."

His tongue stroked the inside of her bottom lip, the suction of his mouth tugging at hers, tugging at her core.

"I know, I know. If only we knew whether what's to come will be for the better..."

Inevitably, though, she was pulled along, as his palm slid the length of her thigh, rucking up the hem of her thin dress, in a slow, hot caress. Edging his hand under the elastic edge of her panties, he cupped her bottom, his fingertips stroking her intimately.

Addie thought she'd come undone with the intensity of it, and knew she was lost.

Her hands shaking but purposeful, she slid his belt from its buckle, undid the button on his jeans and slid the zipper down. She slipped her hand inside, pressing her palm against the shaft of him.

Deke groaned, and she knew it then: he was lost, too. For better or worse.

In one motion, he gathered her dress and tugged it up over her breasts, then shoulders and arms, and completely off, taking her bra with it. Quickly he shed his clothes, and laid them both down upon that familiar—and narrow—bed.

He frowned ruefully. "This cot is damn confining, isn't it? Kinda cramps my style."

"Do you have a style?" Addie asked, eyes downcast.

He nudged her chin up with the edge of his index finger. "I won't say I've been a monk, but no, I'm not a love-'em-and-leave-'em cowboy. I never was."

Then he lowered his head to flick his tongue across the taut peak of her breast, creating a slow, sweet ache low in her abdomen, as he tantalizingly caressed her rib cage, then her abdomen and beyond with the nudge of his hand on her inner thigh. Again his fingers found her with a sureness that made her writhe as he wielded that sure hand that was pure poetry.

No, he was no longer the uncertain young man who had little experience touching a woman's body, and strangely, she yearned to have that boy back, just for an instant, and nearly cried with the want of him.

"Sweet," he murmured against her neck. "Ah, sweet Adeline, what you do to me."

Tears started in her eyes again. It was his old nickname for her—the one shared only between the two of them in moments of intimacy.

"I wondered if you'd remember," she choked, cradling the back of his head, relishing how good it felt to have his long, lean body against her again.

He lifted his head, his eyes dark with passion. "And just how under God's heaven was I supposed to forget?"

Yet when he slid inside her, she got the strangest sensation, as if it weren't him but she who'd been away a long, long time, and was at last coming home.

With that thought, her own uncertainty and awkward movements became as sure as his. With fevered purpose, she clasped his shoulders, urging him on desperately, and Deke wouldn't see her denied as with a powerful stroke they both reached the peak, the highest of mountaintops where the air was so rare, the rush so great that it took them even higher.

And just as before, the connection brought her a measure of peace, impossible as it seemed. How or why that could be, after all the disappointments and disillusionment they'd both endured, she didn't know. It simply was.

Deke lifted his head for a moment, the blacks of his eyes huge and hazy with the strength of emotion, and Addie knew he was experiencing the same thoughts that she was.

Tenderly, she brushed back that cockscomb of dark hair, realizing only then the reason she'd come to cherish it in her son.

It was because she had first come to cherish it, and always would, in his father.

Deke lay very, very still, simply absorbing the sound of Addie's soft breathing as he held her in his arms on the narrow bunk.

His calf was very close to getting a cramp in it, his arm had fallen completely asleep, and there was something hard and pointy in the old mattress that poked him in the ass. But he wasn't moving.

No, he wasn't going anywhere at all, not if he could help it.

How in heaven's name had he been able to live for seven years not knowing the sweetness of her body next to his, the sound of her soft breathing against his neck? How had he walked a step, thought a thought, accomplished a single deed without her at his side?

It was simply beyond him to comprehend it. Beyond him to believe he had ever chosen to leave her, for whatever reason.

Deke tugged Addie closer, as if that were possible, stifling a wince at the twinge of a sore muscle in his back. It seemed like a decade ago that he'd been in that tussle with Mick's bull. Damn, but the critter sure took after its owner. Deke had rarely seen a more ornery, ranker beast. Of course, after he'd gotten it contained this afternoon, he'd been able to get a good look at the bull's underbelly, where he'd noticed it bleeding from a wound on the inside of its right flank. That was likely what got it riled in the first place—the animal had somehow managed to get in a scrape with the barbwire, and it had sent him into a frenzy.

Except, it occurred to Deke now, from what he'd been able to tell from a safe distance, the bull's wound didn't look like the other scrapes and scratches on its hide from barbwire. This cut had been long and deep and clean.

And about the fence. He'd lay his reputation on the fact that it had been stretched as tightly and securely as any ever strung on the Bar G or Tanglewood. If it hadn't been, Mick would have hunted him down like a bounty hunter after checking the fence himself.

Unless Mick hadn't been there, as Addie mentioned Connor had said, to spot weaknesses in the fence—but to make them.

In a flash of insight, Deke knew the bull's wound wasn't caused by barbwire. And that being so, there could only be one explanation. Someone at the Tanglewood had deliberately injured the animal, inducing it to go on a tear across the pasture—right through the hole in the fence and into the Bar G's branding corral.

Funny, but Deke didn't need to be a mind reader to know who that person was or why: Mick Brody was out to get Deke—because of Addie.

Deke tensed, causing Addie to stir against him. "Deke?"

"Yes, darlin', I'm right here," he soothed, rubbing her back as he would that of a fractious child. She sighed and settled back to sleep.

How could he not have seen this coming? Of course Mick would jump to the conclusion that he'd stolen Addie away from Connor, just as D.K. had stolen Lorna from him. Hadn't Mick already tried to poison Jace against him, accosting the boy when he was in town?

That was about as low as you could go, working on a little kid when there were no adults around!

Or was it? Because if Mick would do that, to what

further depths would he sink to take his revenge out on a Larrabie?

Horror crept through him like a deadly scourge, for that's when Deke knew the worst. That bull hadn't been meant for him, not entirely. Such a tactic was too easy, trying to pick him off. No, Mick had meant for Deke to suffer more than that.

The bull had been meant for Addie or Jace.

Deke stared out the small, high window at nothing, Addie cradled in his arms, his thoughts churning on top of each other, as he tried to find—prayed he'd find—some hole in the fabric of his suspicions that would make them disappear. But there was none to be found. None at all.

He turned toward her with a heart full of fear, and Deke felt his hand almost involuntarily go to Addie's breast in a featherlight touch that caused her nipple to peak reflexively. His mouth, also as if it had a will of its own, kissed its way down her temple, over her silken-soft cheek to find her lips, unconsciously pouting in her sleep. He traced them with his tongue, first delicately, then with more and more urgency, while his fingers tugged gently on her pebbled nipple.

"Deke?" a drowsy Addie whispered again, and this time he didn't soothe her back to sleep.

He wanted her awake and knowing when he took her again.

"Wake up, Adeline," he said against her mouth.

"What is it?" she asked.

"It's what it's always been," he told her, pressing the length of himself against her, which sure enough got her eyes to open wide. "What it'll always be," he whispered, reaching down to stroke her intimately.

"Oh…yes." She sighed and opened up to him.

And so he made love to her with all the passion and feeling he had in him, powerless to keep from doing so, to keep from loving her in every way possible—even while he knew in the deepest, darkest recesses of his soul that he would have to be very, very careful if he did not want to end up like his father.

"Pancakes *and* gravy *and* biscuits this mornin', Addie?" Jud asked, eyeing the mountain of food on his daughter's plate.

She hid her blush under the bustle of fetching the pitcher of orange juice from the fridge, sidestepping out of Opal's way as the silver-haired housekeeper set a platter of sausages on the table.

"Well, you got to admit I didn't eat much at supper last night after that near miss in the branding corral," she defended herself.

Even now, the thought made her stomach curdle.

It settled down nicely, though, at the memory of what had come after.

Deke had roused her shortly before dawn so the two of them could dress, and had seen her to the back door. He'd been quiet, almost preoccupied, but the parting kiss he'd given her had been as intensely Deke as ever, his hug goodbye as fierce as if he expected never to see her again.

"From what I heard, that were some kind of scare," her father admitted, lifting his coffee mug for another dose of caffeine from the pot Opal offered. "Good thing Deke was there."

Yes, Addie thought, taking her place at the table and tucking in to her breakfast. It had seemed almost prophetic that in such a dire circumstance the quick thinking and agile cowboy work that was signature Deke

Larrabie had been there to save the day. Few cowboys could have done what he did, for few would have known what she would do without asking. They'd worked as a seamless team to save Jace's life, as perhaps only those who were his parents could have, so strong was the tie between them.

The realization brought her up short, a forkful of hash browns halfway to her mouth.

As if on cue, there came a knock at the screen door, and in walked Deke. He doffed his hat with a nod toward Opal and Jud before his gaze found her as inexorably as hers sought his.

Addie blushed again, this time in an all-over tingle of sensation at the memory of his hands and mouth and body on her skin.

Heavens, would it always be this way with him, that with one look he could make her weak with want, pounding with emotion?

Oh, she hoped so! Hoped against hope he would always be here to do so.

"'Mornin'," he said.

"'Mornin', Deke," she returned with an almost girlish bob of her head.

"Cup of coffee?" Jud offered, thankfully oblivious to the byplay going on between the two of them.

"Don't mind if I do."

He took a seat opposite her as if it were the most natural thing in the world for him to be there. Opal even set a plate before him without asking.

"How's that bull this mornin'?" Jud asked, after Deke had helped himself to the fixings. "Calmed down some, I hope, otherwise there's no way Mick'll get him trailered."

Deke tucked his chin for a swallow of coffee from

his full mug, and it was only then that Addie detected something different in him this morning, beyond the intimacy they'd shared that seemed to have changed her.

It was a drawing back, ever so slight, as he distanced himself—again.

"I just checked on him a minute ago," he said easily enough, though. "Poor critter seems to be in some pain."

"What, from a few bob-wire scrapes?" her father persisted. "Most bulls got hides tough enough to take those kinds of nicks and scratches. Unless there's a worse problem you noticed."

"Where's Jace this mornin'?" Deke asked abruptly.

"Still sleeping," Addie answered, trying to draw Deke's attention to her so she could get some indication of what was going on. "He had quite a bit of excitement yesterday."

Deke only nodded, seeming more preoccupied than ever.

The sound of a car door slamming sent Opal to the window to investigate. "Here's Mr. Brody now."

For some reason, Deke was instantly out of his chair and out the door, as if he expected a confrontation. More puzzled than ever, Addie followed him, with Jud behind.

Once outside, she didn't know what Deke had been so edgy about. Mick Brody stood in the middle of the ranch yard, an expansive smile on his florid face. Connor was just climbing out of the driver's side of the Tanglewood dually, and Addie recognized Doc Johnson, the local veterinarian. Mick had probably brought him along to sedate the bull if it was needed.

"Damn, Jud, what a scare y'all must've had yesterday!'' Mick said, coming forward to shake her father's hand. ''No one got hurt, you said?''

Her father gave a jog of his head toward Deke. ''Well, Deke here's movin' kinda slow after nearly gettin' tossed over the fence by that critter of yours.''

Strangely, Mick didn't respond with any kind of comment to Deke. Instead, he barely gave Deke a glance as he remarked, ''I suppose we better get the devil loaded up and out of your hair 'fore he causes any more trouble.''

But as he turned to call Doc Johnson over, Addie got a look at the rancher's face. There was something about his bland expression that set her on her guard, too.

The group walked in silence to the pen where the bull was being held, the early-morning sun in their faces. The temperature really hadn't risen much yet. Still, Addie felt a trickle of perspiration slither between her breasts. She tried to hang back to have a word with Connor, but Deke for some reason seemed intent on placing himself firmly if surreptitiously between her and both of the Brody men. Neither would he look her in the eye, his face that familiar impassive mask.

She was trying not to worry about what it might mean, but it was pretty evident to her that she was worrying as the perspiration continued to warm her and chill her at once.

Once at the pen, they all watched Doc climb warily over the fence to administer a shot of sedative, while from the outside a couple of the hands did their best to keep the bull in check.

The poor animal seemed to have lost most of the frightening fury he'd displayed the previous afternoon. His eyes were glassy and bloodshot, and his broad sides heaved with his ponderous breaths. Addie couldn't help wondering if perhaps there was something wrong with the bull that had made him so loco.

It was apparent Doc spotted something not quite right, as well.

"This animal's wounded," he said, bending down to inspect the bull's underside.

"Wounded?" Mick exclaimed, almost a little too quickly. "What do you mean, Doc?"

"It looks like a pretty deep one, too. Almost like the belly's been impaled with a sharp object."

The vet moved to one side, trying to get out of Mick's light so he could see better. Stepping up to the fence, Addie caught a glimpse of the glistening cut on the animal's belly near his right hind leg, still oozing blood. Looking closer, she could see the dried blood on his flank, nearly invisible against his black hide.

Apparently, everyone else could see the blood, too—including Mick.

"How could this've happened?" he demanded.

The vet straightened. "I'm sure I don't have a clue, Mick. I'd have to clean the wound and take a closer look at it—"

"Damn it!" Mick interrupted explosively as his fist came crashing down on the pipe railing, making it vibrate under Addie's palms. "This animal's worth a good ten grand. An injury like this could keep him from ever bein' used for breeding again! Could he have done it when he came through the fence?"

Doc readjusted the set of his Stetson, apparently thinking. "Maybe—if one of the posts split."

"But anyone checkin' that fence would've seen whether a post was pulling apart like that." He turned to Jud. "I'll admit, none of my boys have been out to inspect that section in a while. I probably should've had them on it.''

Addie's gaze shot to Connor, who, she only now noticed, had been curiously silent, standing in the background as if he didn't want to be seen there. Hadn't he told her last night that he was almost certain his father had been out along that fence line only a day or so ago?

And Deke had definitely been out there. He'd been ready to blame himself last night for nearly getting someone killed, but even with only one of two such practiced eyes as his and Mick's looking the fence over, surely any possible problem would have been spotted.

It was just as she'd said last night, though. These things happened sometimes. Like when Deke's father had accidentally set off that fire. It was tragic, it was regrettable, but a person could make herself crazy believing that she could control every bit of her life.

She tried again to catch Deke's gaze and failed, as Mick went on, glancing around at the ranch hands who'd been drawn over to the pen by curiosity. ''Come to think of it, though, ain't that line of fence up to the Bar G to keep up?''

''It is.'' Deke stepped forward, and despite herself Addie got a very definite sense of foreboding. ''I checked that fence not two days ago, since I knew we'd be using that corral for branding.''

''Really?'' Where a moment before he'd acted as if the younger man hadn't existed, now Mick zeroed in on Deke like a cat watching a mouse hole. ''How'd it look then?''

''I sank a new post and stretched the wire myself.

That's why I went out earlier this mornin' to look at the break—''

He paused, although it wasn't for effect, she knew.

''The post is splintered clean down the middle,'' he admitted flatly.

The ranch yard went so quiet you could have heard a flea sneeze.

''So,'' Mick said in a low, deadly voice. ''Why didn't I already know it had to be a Larrabie's sloppy, slipshod work and inattention to business that's again responsible for nearly bringin' about a world-class disaster?''

Around her, the low buzz of cowboy murmurings— ''Well, it don't seem right, but what else could've happened?'' ''How's a post that's just sank get split like that?''—spread the first seeds of doubt against Deke that she wanted more than anything to nip in the bud. What she desperately needed Deke to do at the moment, however, was look at her!

What in heaven's name was going on here? Sure, Deke had been ready to blame himself last night for not spotting a potential weakness in the fence, had even talked about how, if he hadn't gotten away from the bull, he'd at least have gone out a hero instead of a failure in front of his son. But missing something so obvious as a post beginning to split—a new post he'd have inspected thoroughly—*was* next door to negligence.

The situation was almost an eerie repeat of the night D.K. had died in a fire of his own making—right down to Mick Brody's cruel damning of the Larrabie name.

For that was when the big man lifted one arm and, pointing his finger at Deke as a revival preacher would have at the most vile of sinners, let go with a string of abuse. "You may not be a drunk like your daddy, but you're cut from the same cheap cloth, no doubt about it. Just another reckless, incompetent cowboy steppin' above his rank. It's obvious you don't got it in you any more than D.K. did to be a real rancher—and much less a real family man to this gal here and the boy you left her with to raise on her own. Of course, leavin' her was a mite better than what your daddy done."

Mick stopped for breath, but before anyone could jump in to stop him—as if everyone wasn't too stunned to do so—he charged on. "I mean, correct me if I'm wrong, but wasn't it D.K.'s spiritin' Lorna Keene off to some godforsaken two-horse farm in the wilds of Montana that caused your mama's death?"

Chapter Eleven

Around him, Deke was aware of a collective gasp of shock from the gathered assemblage. As for himself, he felt no emotion, nothing. He'd detached himself so completely, it was as if he hovered above the scene, and he saw himself standing in front of Mick and saying not a word in his defense to contradict the slurs against him.

Because Deke saw himself, too, standing alone, as he had that evening seven years ago. He was aware of the looks from the hands, good men who'd become his friends over the past several weeks, who'd accepted him on his own merits and hadn't held any lacking in his father against him.

But he knew they knew the story of what had occurred between Mick and D.K., and between Mick and himself, and the ill will it had fanned to flames on two different occasions. And while he wasn't under the slightest delusion that the hands believed Mick Brody's accusations, still Deke had heard the shadow of a doubt about him in their voices.

That wasn't the killer, though. Not by a long shot. No, it was when, from the corner of his eye, he caught sight of Addie's slow, stunned lift of her hand to her mouth, a gesture that fairly shouted at him her own doubt. That's when he knew he hadn't any control at all, not really. No, he was within a hairbreadth of all hell breaking loose inside him in that tick-tick-tick, tick-tick-tick of the second hand, inching ever closer to its moment of truth.

Desperately, he fought that inching movement— fought himself, for himself, tried to find the precious distance that would keep him from completely forsaking what little control he did have.

"No," he said with a shake of his head, not so much in denial as to clear it. "The feud's got to end *now*."

He raised a hand, palm out, as if actually calling a halt. "I'm sorry, Mick. I can't change the fact that my dad took the woman you loved from you years ago. And I can't change any of the mistakes D.K. made, for which I am heartily sorry. Can't change the mistakes I've made—just like you can't change the mistakes you own."

He bit down on the inside of his mouth, hoping the pain would keep things real for him, for once again he needed to walk that fine line of keeping enough distance but not too much. "You'd like to think you could, though—oh, not so much change what's already done, but…somehow make up for the damage done— to your loved ones. To yourself."

He paused, while the two sides of his nature crashed

up against each other in his chest. He couldn't stop now, though. He had to press on.

"But you can't make up for such mistakes. I can't. I can only do my best from here on out. So that's why the blaming's got to stop. It's time, Mick."

And with that, feeling as if the actor were an entirely different man from himself, he held out his hand to shake on a truce.

Mick only stared at him as if he, too, saw not Deke Larrabie but a stranger straight out of another world. Then he flushed even redder, if possible.

He exploded. "He knew it himself, didn't he. That's what you're talkin' about. D.K. knew he had no one to blame but himself for Lorna's death. Just like you've got no one to blame but yourself for the damage you've done here."

Spit flew from his mouth as he shouted triumphantly, "Well, he's by God payin' for his sins now, ain't he? *Ain't he?*"

Just as suddenly as he'd removed himself, Deke experienced a coming back into himself. He realized then, in a flash of stark insight, just how deep Mick's bitterness and hatred for the Larrabies actually went.

Mick Brody had killed his father.

The fact was there, in the older man's face, flushed a vivid, violent blood-red. In his eyes, black with malice. Deke didn't know how it had happened, had no clue if it could ever be proven for sure, but Mick was somehow responsible for D. K. Larrabie's death.

Which would mean, then, that his father *had* overcome his alcoholism...that he had been able to triumph over his inclinations—to reconcile himself to a love lost—and go on with his life.

Or am I simply fooling myself? Deke wondered. Was

he grasping at straws, at any handhold or toehold he could fasten onto, rather than face up, fully, to the truth, not about his father's nature but about his own?

For on the heels of his shock came fear in a roaring stampede not unlike that bull yesterday. He knew it, too, without a doubt:

There was no way now that he could stay.

Addie felt as if a giant fist had crushed her heart within its grip. And if she were experiencing this kind of pain, she could only imagine what Deke must be going through.

Palm pressed to her mouth, she watched him stand with ominous stillness, hand still mechanically extended, so that the older man's rage seemed more apoplectic than dangerous.

But she knew what it was costing Deke to remain calm—and to keep from retaliating in kind, even now. He hadn't, though, not even to show Mick up with his righteous anger as he had before. And he hadn't walked away, either.

Oh, her proud, honorable cowboy! Impossibly, she knew she had never loved Deke Larrabie more than at that moment.

She was aware of her father's own shock as he stood beside her. Even Connor, standing behind Mick, seemed so thoroughly disbelieving of his father's behavior that his face had gone completely slack. He stared at Mick as if he'd never seen him before in his life.

And it was, really, like looking at a stranger. For all of Mick's overbearing, arrogant ways, this display was way over the top even for him. Her respect for Deke had shot mile high with his appeal to Mick's better nature in that offer of peace. It had been a futile effort, though, for it was obvious that Deke's implying Mick might have some hatchet-burying of his own to do clearly made the older man more furious.

"You want the blame to stop, Larrabie?" he sputtered in his rage. "And so it will. Well, Jud—" he turned to his lifelong neighbor "—I'd say you're damn lucky your daughter and grandson are alive this morning, no thanks to Deke Larrabie. It's up to you, but if you choose again not to take any action against him for the grief he's caused, that's your business. As for me, even if the damage done to my prize bull can be fixed, I'm not gonna stand by and let this cowboy get the chance to cause any more trouble for people. Soon's I can, I'm puttin' in a call to Sheriff Davies, asking him to bring Deke Larrabie up on criminal charges for reckless destruction of property—*and* child endangerment!"

He whipped back around to Deke. "'Cause you know it, too, Larrabie. What with how you put Jace smack in the middle of danger through your own carelessness? Well, you've only proved yourself your father's son, once and for all."

"And what if he has!"

Addie was as surprised as anyone to realize the question had come from her. But now that she'd spoken, she wasn't going to let the opportunity to support Deke pass her by again.

She strode to his side. "What if Deke's shown himself to be D.K.'s son? No, I don't mean by being careless, because I've never known a cowboy to be more conscientious than Deke Larrabie. He didn't have to come back here, after all those years. But he did. And he's stayed even when every odd has been stacked against him.''

She turned in a circle, making each and every hand look her in the eye. ''As for how that bull got through a fence Deke had just mended, well, all of you know how risky this business is, how things like that can happen to the best cowboy or rancher, even after taking every caution and precaution! I can't begin to count the number of times I could've taken any one of you to task for some slip, and you know it!''

To her satisfaction, she'd elicited some embarrassed ducking of chins and shuffling of boots in the dirt. *Good.* Oh, she was glad to have this opportunity to stick up for Deke, as she hadn't had the wherewithal to do at the barbecue, or seven years ago. Glad to give him all her support, loyalty—and love.

Not that he evinced any reaction. His eyes remained on Mick, as if he expected from the rancher some twitch of his hand that signaled the lightning-quick drawing of a six-shooter.

But this wasn't some Old West showdown, where disputes and disagreements and yes, even feuds, could be solved with a shootout that didn't end with the best man winning, but the one with the quickest reflexes, nerves of steel and sheer luck.

She hurried on. ''What I'm saying is that anyone can make a mistake. That doesn't brand them a failure forever, does it? The provin' is in how people come back from their failures and go on. And if anyone's done that, it's Deke Larrabie.''

As she had seven years ago, she laid her hand on Deke's arm, in a show of support and sympathy. At the contact, she felt his muscles tense under her palm. This time, though, she wouldn't be put off by his drawing away from her. She wouldn't allow him to, no matter what.

But then, instead of bending upon her that look of impassiveness that told her he was anything but, Deke turned to Addie with the leisurely pace that suggested complete control over himself. His gaze met hers, and what she saw in those amber-green cat-eyes chilled her.

It was cold, clear, implacable calculation.

Addie gasped, snatching her hand away as if she'd been burned.

"You might as well save your convincin' for a cause that you can win, Addie," he drawled. "I sure enough've got the message that that's what I need to do."

"What…what do you mean?" she asked, stricken.

"I mean, Mick's right. *You're* right. The Larrabie name is mud in these parts, and there's nothin' I can do to change the fact. I can see that now. But what has changed is me. I know now when to cut my losses, pack up my gear and head for home."

Deke shrugged philosophically. "It was worth a try, I guess. Now that I know I've given it my best shot, though, I can move on."

"You mean…you mean you're leaving?" she asked point-blank, not even caring that practically the whole ranch was privy to their intensely private conversation. "You'd leave me again, after what you said last night? After you promised me you wouldn't?"

"Yeah, well, if it helps, I thoroughly meant it at the time—"

He gave her a half smile that was pure wayward cowboy and that made her stomach drop two stories.

"But you and me, darlin', as a permanent thing? I think we both know it wasn't meant to be."

He actually reached up and trailed a finger down her cheek in a gesture so calculated to charm that she was repulsed by it.

"Try not to take it too hard," he said. "It wasn't the end of the world before, and it won't be this time, either."

Addie could only stare at him, her whole body slowly turning numb, as if death crept over her. *But it was almost the end of the world!* she wanted to scream at him. And he'd made her a promise!

What kind of bizarre nightmare was this? Oh, had she really misjudged him so drastically that she'd made the most fatal of mistakes herself, trusting him again, believing in his rainmaker promises, letting him not only back into her heart, but into the heart of her son— *Jace.*

With a cry, Addie spun on her heel, ready to run for the house. There, however, on the other side of the corral stood Jace, his shirt half buttoned and hanging out of his jeans, the legs of which were shotgunned in his boots, as if he'd jerked them on in a hurry. And on his face the look of a lost soul.

There was no doubt: the boy had seen and heard everything.

If ever there was a picture of shattered trust, Jace was it.

Anger, pure and sharp, rose up in Addie like a crimson tide. Yes, she would survive, as Deke had said. What was the saying? *What didn't kill you only made you stronger.*

But Jace—oh, her little boy! She feared it would kill him, would sever in him any hopefulness and trust…like the shearing off of a vital limb.

Next to her, Deke made a sound. Addie turned, her

words of anger dying on her lips as she saw something nearly as heartrending as Jace's expression.

And that was Deke's. He stared at Jace, naked despair ravaging his face, before it turned to stone again so swiftly that Addie wondered if she'd actually seen it.

Jace pivoted and ran back toward the house. Even from a distance, they could hear the screen door slam in his wake.

"Deke—" she began in confused anger, but he cut her off.

"If I do aim to move on down the road," he said curtly, turning to go, "I better start wrappin' things up around here."

"Oh, yeah," Mick agreed. "Just like a Larrabie to clear out before the law shows up. I bet you don't have the guts to stay long enough to face the music. In fact, I've got a hundred dollar bill here says you'll clear out before the end of the day, just like you did before."

His back to Mick, Deke lifted one shoulder ever so slightly, as if to dislodge the demon sitting there and whispering in his ear. Then, sparing her not another glance, he headed for the ranch office.

Mick was willing to share a smug grin with any takers.

There were none, thank goodness. Even if no one would stand up in Deke's defense because the consequence might be earning Mick Brody's undying wrath, neither would anyone ally themselves with him. And he knew it.

"Fine," he snarled. "You're all a bunch of losers, anyway."

"That's it. Git your bull loaded, Mick," Jud said, standing more erect than Addie had seen him in years, his shoulders straight instead of rounded and his head held high without a bit of trembling.

It was like looking at the Jud Gentry of old.

"Then git yourself off my land."

With a scowl, Mick obliged, and within minutes the sedated animal had been trailered. Yet when Mick yanked open the dually's door with a barked "You comin', Connor?" everyone was surprised when the younger Brody actually hesitated.

"Mr. Gentry," he said, holding out a hand to Jud. "Addie. Please accept my sincerest apologies—"

"What the hell are you apologizing for now?" Mick interrupted.

Connor didn't even glance at his father as he went on. "—for the damage our bull caused to your fence and property...and for nearly killing Deke. It should never have happened. The Tanglewood is as responsible as the Bar G for checkin' that fence, especially one that important—"

"That's enough, Connor!" his father blasted him. Mick bent the full brunt of his malignant gaze upon Connor, who, to his credit, didn't flinch. "I swear I've had it up to my eyeballs with your apologizing! You didn't do nothin'—but then, that's pretty much the way it's always been, ain't it? You doin' *nothing*. I don't know why I've even bothered tryin' to make a man out of you."

Connor blanched. Then, setting his mouth, he walked around the front of the truck and climbed inside.

"So, Adeline, what do you intend to do?"

She whirled to find her father standing behind her. "Do?" she echoed. "About what?"

"About Deke's leavin' again."

Addie bit her lip, her thoughts in a jumble. Yes, that was the $64,000 question, wasn't it. What could she do if Deke really was willing to give up again and walk away—even after he'd seen how it would crush Jace?

Oh, she didn't know if she could ever, ever forgive him for that.

The thought renewed her fury and pushed the pain back. "You heard Deke, Daddy," she said, standing straighter. "He's giving up without a fight. I—I might have expected more from him, but what can I do if he has?"

Yes, what could she do but pick up the pieces of both her heart and Jace's, and go on?

"I survived Deke Larrabie leaving before, I'll survive it again," she vowed around a throat so dry she could hardly swallow.

But oh, how lonesome and barren her future appeared without him in it!

"Or you can take the other choice you've always had at your disposal," Jud said reasonably. "Fight for him."

She stared at her father in disbelief, wondering if he'd fallen under the rainmaker's spell completely. "How? It's pretty clear the love Jace and I have to offer him isn't enough!"

"Sure, it is, darlin'," Jud contradicted calmly.

"But he doesn't believe it is." She gave a huff of pure frustration that ended on a dry sob, and pressed the back of her fingers to her lips, afraid she'd break down in the middle of the ranch yard. "Oh, Daddy, I don't know how to make him believe!"

"So you're just gonna let him walk away from you again, and take your happiness and your son's happiness with him?" Her father pointed his cane toward the ranch office where Deke had headed. "Damn, daughter, have you learned nothing in the past few months?"

"Daddy!"

"You wanna be happy in this life, you gotta take some risks, reach out for it with both hands. Don't you know Deke Larrabie by now?" he demanded. "You know it's always when he's tryin' to do right by the people he loves most that he's left everything he holds dear in this life?"

Addie turned her head in the direction he pointed. Could her father be right? It made a convoluted kind of sense, didn't it? And she hadn't mistaken the look of pure pain on Deke's face at Jace's anguish.

But that had been for Jace. She'd always known Deke's son held a special place in his heart. So did she, though; she *hadn't* mistaken Deke's meaning last night. He had come back for her, he told her.

What if she was wrong? Even if Deke loved her, was it enough to make him stay?

Wasn't it worth the risk of laying everything on the line to find out?

"So what're you gonna do, Adeline?" Jud asked again, breaking through her thoughts.

Eyes still glued to the doorway Deke had disappeared into, Addie set her mouth with the kind of grit and determination that would have done her pioneer ancestors proud.

"I'm goin' after Deke Larrabie," she said. "And this time, even if he does leave the Bar G, he's gonna know up front I'll spend the rest of my natural days hunting him down."

The bang of the office door jolted Deke from his contemplation. He'd been gazing out the window, where on the distant rise stood the cottonwood, half living and half dead.

He'd expected to have another go-round with someone on the Bar G before all was said and done, although he'd counted on it being Jud.

He was surprised—and dismayed—to turn and find Addie standing across from him, her color high and her blue eyes blazing. The flamed tongue of fear licked at him again.

"Well," he said unconcernedly, "I suppose you've come to give me my marchin' orders right now, instead of leaving it to me after I've tied up the loose ends." He shrugged. "No matter. You'll be able to figure out without much trouble what needs to be done on the AI program and go to it. You've always been sharp that way...knowin' how to move on without much trouble. This temporary roadblock I caused should barely break your stride."

He spoke with deliberate insolence, hoping to put her off her intent, the nature of which he could guess. He couldn't let her take one step in that direction, so tenuous was his hold on himself.

"You're not leaving, Deke," Addie said without flinching under his words.

"Yes, Addie," he said with perfect calm, "I am."

"No." She strode forward and slapped her palms on the desk that separated them. "You're not."

The movement made her work shirt gap at the neckline, revealing just a tantalizing sliver of cleavage. At the sight, Deke felt his body surge in remembrance of how only hours before he'd drawn his tongue down that cleft of flesh and beyond....

He jerked his gaze away, in a panic that she might

have noticed its direction. "Yes, I am," he answered her, but even he detected the drop in conviction in his voice.

Addie must have heard it, too, for she came around the side of the desk. Despite himself, Deke took a step backward at her approach, damning himself even as he did so.

"So you'd leave again?" she asked measuringly. "Leave Jace right when you've gotten his trust back?"

Oh, but that was a knife to his vitals, hollowing him out in one clean sweep.

"Not after today, obviously," he said hoarsely, holding not a bit of sympathy for himself. He realized he had a death grip on the back of Jud's office chair. "I believe I've pretty much had my last chance at winnin' his regard."

"He's your son, Deke. You'll never run out of chances to redeem yourself in his eyes, just like your father never ran out of them with you."

He squeezed his eyes shut, trying to close out the pain her words evoked in him. Trying to close out her nearness, which made him as weak as a newborn calf.

But it wasn't to be, for she went on. "You've only got to give him a reason to believe. Just one reason. And you can do that by staying." She laid her hand on his arm. "For both of us."

As always, her touch sundered his resolve.

"Damn it!" Deke opened his eyes and glared at her. "Don't you see, Addie? I've got no choice!"

"You've always got a choice," she said gently.

"Not this time! It's pretty damn clear Mick's not gonna even begin to let this matter go. And it's too dangerous to stay—Mick's already shown he'll stop at nothing to bring me down."

"What do you mean?" She dropped her hand.

He pointed out the window. "That fence post was *solid,* the wire stretched on it tight as a drum. I know it was. There's no way Mick's bull could've broke through it. And the bull's wound—I didn't get a good look at it, but it wasn't accidental. I'd stake my reputation on it. The animal was in unholy pain, I'm sure, but he didn't get that way from chargin' through a fence."

"You think that someone on the Tanglewood had a hand in causing that near tragedy yesterday?" Addie's mouth turned down in contemplation, then went rigid as his implication hit home. "Mick *did* go out to check the line of fence, just like Connor thought. And Connor knows it, too. After you left the ranch yard, he apologized to Daddy and me about the break, and Mick went ballistic on him almost as bad as he did on you. It was frightening. I mean, the Larrabies may be his sworn enemies, but Connor is Mick's kin."

Her words had him gritting his teeth to bite back his fear, but he made himself go on before he lost his nerve. "That's just it, Addie. I...I've got a gut feeling that somehow, Mick caused my dad's death seven years ago."

Once expressed out loud, though, the notion sounded far-fetched even to his own ears, and Deke wondered for a moment if she would upbraid him again for letting his own dislike of the Brodys cloud his judgment. Then he saw how she stared at him in such shock it was as if she'd had a bucket of ice water thrown in her face.

"I just remembered something," she whispered, stricken. "You said at the barbecue that your dad always drank Jack Daniel's. Deke, I could swear the labels on the bottles Mick said he found in your dad's pickup were Jim Beam. I could swear it.''

Now Deke drew back in shock. ''And at the barbecue...''

She swallowed. ''Mick had been drinking Jim Beam.''

Abruptly, he pivoted away from her. He had to, in order to hide his thoughts from her—or was it to avoid facing some realization that he dare not consider too closely, lest it truly sway him from the course he knew he had to take?

And that was to walk away!

But Addie had already put two and two together, even if she still lacked the whole equation. ''You think Mick was trying to kill *you* yesterday, and that's why you'd leave the Bar G?''

His hand was unsteady as Deke drove it through his hair, for he had decided to lie to Addie. ''For lack of a way to prove it or what happened with that fire seven years ago...yes.''

''But there's got to be a way!''

''Yeah, and what would you suggest?'' he demanded, swinging back around. ''Walk into Sheriff Davies's office with only the evidence of my claimin' that the section of fence I fixed had been tampered with, or your remembering after a half-dozen years that there'd been two different kinds of whiskey labels? It'd be our word against Mick Brody's. And me against him, in a game I can't win.''

Her blue eyes were desperate—desperate to believe in him. ''We can at least try to prove he was behind that near accident yesterday.''

''And if we prove Mick did it?'' he asked harshly. ''He'll get a slap on the wrist that'll make him so mad at me it'll only be a matter of time before he tries somethin' else. No, it's not worth the risk, Addie.''

"But it *is* worth the risk, Deke!" She took a fearless step toward him. "It is. Won't you even try? Can't we try—together?"

He held his ground this time. "No. If I go, he'll believe he's won the feud and it'll be over."

"But leaving's not the answer!"

"Isn't it?" The words burst out of him of their own volition, opening the way for the next rush. "'Cause believe me, if it *were* just a threat to me, I'd stay and give Mick Brody as good as he gave, and damn the consequence." He took her by her arms. "But it's not just me, Addie. Mick was trying to hurt you or Jace yesterday. I know it in my gut. And you want to talk about something that'd drive me out of my everlovin' mind? If something happened to either of you because of me, I wouldn't be able to live with myself. So yes, by God, I'm leaving again!"

"I don't care!" She shook her head fiercely. "You can't do this to me again, you can't do this to Jace! I won't let you! We'll come after you...come with you."

"Leave the Bar G and Jud and everything you love? Damn it, Addie, it's no better solution than it was seven years ago—no better than it was when my father took my mother away."

Her eyes were huge and questioning, and he would have given anything to have the answer to her questions at his fingertips. But there was no answer.

"Addie," he said raggedly, "maybe...maybe you and me, it was never meant to be—you know?" He fell back on the line he'd used on her in the ranch yard, but this time, when it was only the two of them, he couldn't quite carry it off with the same flourish. Instead he sounded just plain desperate. "I mean, I don't regret Jace, and I could never regret loving you. But so far as us trying to make a go of it, being happy together…it doesn't seem to be the Larrabie way. It's not about needing to move on. It's about it never being the best thing for me to stay."

Her mouth worked with the strength of her emotion; her blue eyes were even brighter with pain. Damn, but this was some kind of hell on earth! How was it that he was continually faced with hurting those he loved most?

Then Addie asked, "Not even…not even for this?"

And without warning she reached between them, grabbing the front of his shirt and jerking it open with a string of pops as the snap-buttons came undone.

Hesitating not another half-second, Addie plunged her fingers into the hair on Deke's chest, raked her nails down his pectoral muscles to his flat, washboard stomach to grasp his belt with both hands and yank him flush against her abdomen.

Deke stiffened but didn't pull away, as with a slow undulation of her hips, she rubbed against his fly, not caring how wanton she must seem.

"Addie, please." He grated out the words, his hands clenched on her waist, not pulling her closer, but not pushing her away, either. "Don't…do this."

"Do what? Hmm? This?" she whispered, sliding her palm down the length of his thigh, then upward along the inside of it to cup him familiarly, wresting a groan from him. "Or maybe this." She closed her fingers around one of his wrists and drew it up to press his hand over her breast, his thumb going unerringly to her nipple, producing her gasp of resistance and surrender.

At the sound, Deke cursed, softly and with vivid explicitness. "This isn't fair, Addie! Not to me—" The hand on her waist drove downward, grasping her bottom, fingers curling to caress her as familiarly as she did him. "But not to you, most of all. You deserve better."

"The thing is, Deke," she said with her last bit of sanity, "it's not about fairness." She stroked the edge of her own thumb the length of him. "It's never been about fairness."

Bless him, he still tried to resist—for one bare instant. Then he gave an explosive groan that fleetingly put in her mind of a bomb bursting, a depth charge of such violent emotion. For some reason, it frightened her so much she drew back, suddenly unsure of anything that she'd have staked her life on a split second before.

Then he was covering her mouth with his, and the fury of desire within his kiss wiped away all fear as she wrapped her arms around his neck and answered him with every fiber of her being.

His hand fumbled between them as he struggled to undo the buttons of her shirt while still kissing her. His fingers were sure and swift, however, as he found the front clasp of her bra and opened it to splay his hand over her naked breast.

"Yes." He groaned as her hand covered his. "God, yes."

She was unafraid, unashamed and unrepentant. If she had to use his weakness for her to get him to stay, she would, without a shred of regret.

He bent and swept her into his arms. In half a dozen strides he was through the doorway of the tiny bunkroom, kicking the door closed behind him and setting her down on the thin, narrow mattress. Swiftly, he latched the door, then returned to the side of the bunk.

But he didn't lay down with her, only stood over her, hands fisted at his sides, eyes dark and troubled, his chest rising and falling with the strength of the war that still raged within him—and perhaps, it struck her, always would. For the way he looked right now was the way he'd looked that long-ago tragic night when she'd put her hand on his arm in silent empathy: as if he'd been betrayed by his own nature.

"I can't promise you anything," he said, sounding as if he were forcing the words out through a throat welded shut. "Even if we make love, I still can't promise you anything. So it's got to be your choice if we do."

She stared up at him. It was the opposite of what had happened before, when he had made her a promise that she'd taken on faith.

Unhesitatingly, Addie pushed herself to her knees on the mattress and flung her arms around his waist, pressing her cheek to his chest.

"Make love to me, Deke," she said from the bottom of her heart. "Make love to me, or I'll surely die."

He stiffened, then wrapped her in his embrace. "Addie," he said raggedly, "do you have any idea, any idea at all, how much I love you?"

"Yes," she said, her voice muffled against him. His belt buckle cut into tender flesh, but she couldn't have cared less. "Yes, I think I finally do."

She turned her head, kissing his flat stomach, etching a path to his navel. His belt was promptly disposed of, yet when she reached for the zipper tab on the fly of his jeans, Deke stayed her, gripping her wrists.

"No," he said firmly.

Addie froze.

"No—if this is going to be what it's meant to be, for both of us, we've got to go together."

With that, he stepped back, and of a silent accord they undressed, their gazes locked, their movements almost a mirror of each other.

Then he was laying down next to her, both of them on their sides and faces an inch apart. Again their movements were in tandem as they caressed each other with the leisurely stroke of a thumb along a jawline, the tickling trail of a finger down the side of a neck and across a collarbone.

Without speaking, they told each other where they wanted to be touched—Addie with subtle circling of Deke's flat nipple with her fingertip; Deke with his slow, gentle rubbing of tender, sensitive flesh between her legs—until they were both writhing mindlessly, completely at each other's mercy.

Yes, she was as lost in him as he in her. It wasn't about weakness, she knew that now. It was, for what it was worth, simply the way it was.

"Please, Deke," she begged him. "Please."

Then he was on top of her, inside her in that most perfect of complements, filling her with his strength of passion and love that had drawn her to him from the first, that half-boy, half-man who could not hold back, never hold back....

Some instinct told her to open her eyes, and when she did she found Deke staring back at her, those jungle cat-eyes ravaged with savage desire, to be sure, but ultimately, absolutely sane and whole.

With a cry, she exploded, felt him surge within her, too.

Afterward, he lifted his head, their eyes meeting in understanding.

"You're leaving again," she said without inflection.

"Only if I have to, Addie," he whispered jaggedly. "Mick said he'd be contacting the sheriff today to bring charges against me. That means I don't have much time if I'm gonna figure out how to prove he cut the fence and deliberately wounded his own bull so it'd charge through the Bar G's branding corral on the exact day we were usin' it."

He shifted to his side and into a sitting position, giving her a hand to help her up, too. Gathering up her clothes from the wood floor, he passed them on to her.

"I'll head out to take another look at that fence and see if I can tell how it was tampered with," he said as they dressed.

"And I'll see if I can find out how that bull got wounded," she volunteered, pulling on her jeans.

Deke's grip on her shoulder brought her head up. "You're not to do anything of the sort, Addie. Mick can't get wind of our suspicions."

"But—"

"No buts. It's too dangerous. If it looks like the situation's gonna turn even uglier with Mick, I'll back off and back down. And leave. Whatever I need to do to convince him he's won."

She stared up at him. "Deke, he may have killed your dad! You could go without trying to bring the man who did that to justice?"

"If I have to, Addie, I will. I'm not gonna take any chances, not with your welfare and Jace's to think about."

She had never seen him look more coldly implacable. Then he surprised her yet again by pulling her to her feet and into his warm, strong embrace.

"You're just gonna have to trust me," he whispered into her hair.

She hugged him back with all her might. "I do, Deke," she murmured against his shoulder. "I just can't help feeling that if I do let you go, somehow I'll lose you forever."

He said nothing; he just held her so tightly it hurt. But the last thing she wanted was for him to let go of her.

She knew it was the last thing he wanted, too.

So. Once again she was going to have to give this man her trust. And this time it would be with no promises.

Chapter Twelve

The sun was a red-hot ball on the horizon when Deke finally made his way back to ranch HQ. After leaving Addie, he'd returned to the break in the branding corral fence for another look. He'd even taken a chance of word getting back to Mick by asking a county deputy to come out and look at the split post. But the deputy had taken the information, and the Polaroids Deke had made him take, with a stoic business air that bordered on indifference.

Or so it struck Deke. He should have known better than to think he'd get any kind of help from lawmen in the county where Mick Brody had lived all of his fifty-five years.

So he had spent the rest of the day trying to come up with some other way to make a definite case against Mick. Now, eight hours later, he was worn-out and worn down. It didn't look good for him.

And he had to assume things were about to get worse as he spied Addie walking toward him across the ranch yard. Trailing in her wake was Jace.

Jace. Lord, in all the excitement he'd clean forgotten about his son. Or, more accurately, he'd deliberately shoved into the farthest corner of his mind the mental picture of that moment when Jace had had his world come crashing down around his ears with the total destruction of his faith in his father.

But how could Deke have prevented that from happening? He'd had to make it seem he wasn't staying, to protect both Jace and Addie. He wondered now, though, how much better it was for the boy to go on living with that spirit-breaking experience dogging him the rest of his natural-born days. For even though it appeared now that his own father might be innocent, in Deke's mind, he didn't see how he could ever make any kind of comeback with Jace, despite Addie's assurance to the contrary.

It seemed, however, that some kind of reckoning was to take place, for Deke froze when Jace, with a nod from his mother, trudged up to him, the heels of his boots scuffing in the gravel and kicking up dust.

Oh, he could see the boy's doubt and naked hurt in those eyes that were mirror images of his own, and it nearly tore Deke to shreds. As ever, though, he couldn't walk away from whatever confrontation was to come, no matter what.

Jace said nothing, just stood before him, that hat of his sitting like a stovepipe on his head, its brim wide enough to shade his small shoulders. Deke noticed he had something wrapped in a blue polishing cloth in his hands.

"What've you got there, Slick?" he asked, for lack of a better opening.

"It's...it's a belt buckle," Jace divulged readily enough.

"A belt buckle?" Deke echoed, puzzled.

"Yeah. I found it up under that cottonwood where the fire was." He squinted up at Deke. "And where your daddy's buried. Y'know?"

"I know the place," Deke admitted, his gaze glued to the cloth in Jace's hands, his heart suddenly pounding, although he couldn't have said why.

"At first, I din't think it was nothin'," the boy said. "It was so black and dirty. But then I got a rag and started rubbin' on it, and I could see the letters on it."

He dug a boot toe in the dirt. "I found it a long time ago and din't tell no one about it. Then...then when I found out about your daddy...and mama...I got it out. I showed it to Mama this morning, and she helped me shine it up."

He thrust the cloth-covered buckle out to Deke, avoiding his gaze, his mouth tight with emotion. "I thought you might want it, if it was your daddy's. Y'ought to have it, to remember him by...wherever you go. Y'know?"

"I—I know," Deke whispered, overwhelmed by his son's gesture of unselfish love, even in light of what the boy understood him to be—a cowboy leaver.

He wanted badly to take his son in his arms, but didn't trust that he'd be able to let Jace go again. And he might have to, as much as he could barely stand the idea. Might have to let both his son and Addie go.

His hands shaking, he opened the cloth to find a brass belt buckle bearing five letters: *L-O-R-N-A*.

More puzzled than ever, Deke ran the pad of one

thumb along the scrolled engraving surrounding the name, carved in a script as delicate as he remembered his mother being.

"Jace, I appreciate your findin' this, and taking such care with it, but—" He broke off, sudden caution bidding him to bite back his next words.

For the buckle hadn't belonged to his father. Deke had never seen it before in his life.

Curious, he turned it over. On the back, down along the lower curve, he could just make out two letters—initials, he realized.

M.B.

Like an electric charge, shock fired from the tips of his fingers, through his hands, up his arms and all the way to Deke's heart, which gave a stutter step. Could it really be…?

Glancing down, he found his son gazing up at him with those gold-and-green eyes that were so much like his own. Except now, Deke saw not himself in Jace's eyes, but Addie. It was in their expression, in how—despite the heartrending disappointment and disillusionment—they continued to convey support and hope. But most of all love.

And if Jace was still able to feel such love, Deke knew it was because of Addie. Addie and her love.

It was humbling. It was uplifting. It was everything to him.

The crunch of gravel under tires brought his head up in enquiry, even though there could be only one person who'd be pulling into the ranch yard right now. Turning, Deke moved protectively in front of Jace, although never more than right then did he fear he hadn't the ability to protect any of his loved ones.

The door of the red dually opened, and first one large

black boot, then the other, planted itself on the ground next to the truck.

Across the ranch yard, Mick Brody's eyes met his.

"So," the older man said. "Still here, are you, Larrabie?"

"That would be correct." A strange calm settled over Deke. He noticed the crowd that was congregating, as ranch hands, having heard Mick's truck pull up, moseyed closer, their curiosity getting the better of them. He caught sight of Jud hobbling over to stand next to his daughter.

"I suppose you've contacted the sheriff and filled him in on all the pertinent details," he said simply, as Mick sauntered closer.

"Actually, I had Connor take care of that," Mick said.

Deke's gaze turned to the younger man who had followed his father like a reluctant shadow. Disturbingly, he refused to look at Deke.

"I sure did," Connor said in even tones. "Told him everything I knew." He hesitated briefly, then gave a firm nod, almost to himself. "Now let the chips fall where they may."

"That's right," Mick agreed heartily, hitching his jeans up by the belt loops, obviously pleased by the audience that had shown up for his grand performance. " 'Let justice be served' is what I always say. And it's about damn time it was. Finally, the Larrabies'll get what's comin' to them."

Deke frowned. Somehow, he'd gotten the whiff of an impression that Connor had meant something quite different. He noticed Connor stood a good six feet from his father, almost as if he were subconsciously distancing himself from Mick.

"Just to make sure, though," Mick went on, "I called the sheriff myself not a half-hour ago. He said he'd be here any minute." He cast a self-righteous glance around. "Yup, the sort of reckless ruin of property and lives the Larrabies have wreaked on the county for years is gonna end right now."

He snickered, low and nastily. "That is, if you don't tuck tail and run like y'all always do when it's time to reckon up."

Beside him, Deke felt Jace bristle in indignation. Lord, he'd warned Addie not to defend him, but he hadn't even thought about Jace wanting to. The boy was set to go off like a top any second, too.

Keeping his face as blank as a slate of stone, Deke clamped his fingers on the boy's shoulder in warning, praying he'd heed the silent message. Jace's body grew even more tense, but Deke could tell the boy had understood and would obey him—for now.

"I guess I didn't think you'd be back so soon to make good on your threat," he stalled, playing for more time in which to assess Mick's mood, to figure out exactly what Mick had planned for him. If it was simply a trip to the county jail, well, it wouldn't be the greatest to have his son see him hauled away by the law. But Mick would feel he had Deke under his thumb and under his control. And at least his son—and Addie—wouldn't have to see him walk away from them, yet again.

Except, it became clear by his next words that that was exactly what Mick wanted him to do.

"Yeah, well, call me a dumb s.o.b. for not knowin' better after all these years," he said, "but you could say I'm kinda doin' you a favor, givin' you warning. You've still got time to hit the highway, if you got a mind to. You might as well leave, 'cause you've sure enough proved yourself no better than your cowboy daddy.''

The taunt hung in the muggy, heated afternoon air, just as it had on that long-ago night, so thick and hot. Then, however, the atmosphere had been thick with smoke, the heat emanating from the scorching remains of a dream, of a last shot at redemption.

And Deke knew suddenly that he could not go down in the same kind of flames. He couldn't lose all he held dear, all that he'd fought for and given up so much for.

But as before, he had to ask himself, one more time: What would be best for those he loved—for him to stay, or to leave?

In the distance, the sheriff's car turned in to the Bar G drive and started up the long lane. Deke stood stock-still, Jace at his side, but Addie knew the war still raged in him.

Certainly, she'd hoped Jace's gesture would show Deke that he didn't have to go, what he would leave behind if he did, and she wasn't sorry for prompting their son. All she and Jace had to offer Deke was their love. But would it be enough to keep him here?

For if Deke stayed and lost to Mick Brody yet again, something would die in him, as surely as something had died in his father at losing Lorna.

Over Jace's head, his gaze collided with hers, and she knew he knew what she was thinking, and that her heart was breaking for him.

Go, she tried to convey to him. *You were right— there's not enough evidence to prove Mick's the one responsible for both yesterday's accident and your daddy's death. I understand now. I understand why*

*you've got to go, because I love you too much to watch
you go through this. Even if it means losing you.*

He merely blinked and turned away.

As if awaiting the hangman, they all watched in silence as Sheriff Davies pulled up. It helped when her
father slid his hand into hers and gripped it with all his
might.

With a heaviness of movement that was strange for
such an athletic man, Sheriff Davies got out of his car.
Stranger still, his gaze took a reckoning turn around
the assembled group. Finally, it rested on Connor, and
Addie's stomach vaulted to her throat. What had Connor to do with this business?

The sheriff gave him a nod.

The younger man cleared his throat once, twice before he began to speak.

"There's sure enough some unfinished business
here," Connor said. "And I'm hoping we can settle a
few scores today—settle 'em in the right way."

His handsome features drawn but calm, he turned to
his father. "We've got some evidence here, Dad, that's
makin' it pretty clear that the accident yesterday wasn't
an accident."

Mick shifted uneasily under his son's steady gaze.
"'Course it wasn't an accident. It was clear negligence
on Deke's part, doin' such a sloppy job mending the
fence."

"It wasn't Deke Larrabie's fault, either," Connor
said with what struck Addie as incredible gentleness.
"Sheriff Davies here told me this afternoon that Deke
asked one of his deputies out to take a look at the break
and judge for himself."

The sheriff nodded. "That's right, Mick. And from
what Tom could tell, and what I could see in the Po-

laroids, that post had been tampered with. Split with an ax, not 'cause it wasn't good wood.''

More than a few of the hands could be heard to condemn outright the person responsible for such deceit, almost taking it as a personal betrayal. It was one thing to cause a ranching accident through carelessness, but quite another to be purposefully destructive in a business that was already dangerous enough.

The sheriff reset the angle of his dark brown hat, obviously uncomfortable but bound to do his job. ''Not only that, Mick, but once Doc Johnson had a chance to get a clean look at your bull's belly, he told your boy here that there's no way the wound was caused by goin' through the fence.''

''And what Doc thinks is that the bull must have been wounded,'' Connor added quickly, as if wanting to break this news himself, for his tone was still gentle, incredibly so. ''Wounded on purpose, and let loose to charge onto Bar G land.''

''Just what're you gettin' at, Whit?'' Mick asked the sheriff in a flat tone of voice, completely ignoring his son.

''Somebody stabbed that animal,'' Sheriff Davies answered. ''That's what I'm saying. Somebody on the Tanglewood.''

''*Somebody.*'' Mick spat the word out. ''Well, 'fore you jumped to conclusions, did it strike you that Larrabie here could've done it? He's wily enough to've found a way to sneak onto the Tanglewood without anyone noticin'. Most of the county knows that bull's one of my best breeders. Deke could've thought to put it out of commission, but the whole plan backfired on him when the bull crashed through his shaky fence.''

''Dad, please.'' Slowly, Connor approached his father, pure misery in every step. "It didn't happen that way."

"Well, it could have!" Mick shouted. Perspiration had broken out along his brow line, and it ran down the sides of his face in rivulets. "Who's to say it didn't?"

Stopping before his father, Connor pulled a folded piece of paper from his back pocket and held it out to him. "I've got Doc Johnson's report right here."

He cleared his throat yet again. "He says the angle of the cut…it could only have been done by someone who was right-handed. So it couldn't have been Deke. Just admit it, Dad," he finished raggedly. "Won't you just admit you did it?"

Mick's face was a study in reckoning, although what tally he could have been taking and upon whom, Addie couldn't have said.

"What if I did gouge my own bull in the belly?" he asked derisively. "Tell me where's the law that says that's a crime. And if it is, hell, I'll pay a fine if I'm liable for it. But you can't prove I did anything to warrant much else."

The angle of the sun, right in her eyes, was giving her a headache of mountainous proportions, Addie noticed. Clearly, the situation was just as Deke had predicted it would be, for only then did she realize the way they all stood in a circle around the main players in this little scene of prairie justice. Mick squared off in front of his son and the sheriff. And Deke, Jace glued to his leg, set apart as if he were the accused still on the gallows stand, noose around his neck, while before him his fate was argued without him being given a chance to defend himself.

And he had little means of protecting himself or his

loved ones against Mick Brody's even more vengeful wrath, should Mick come after any of them again. And he would—of that there was no doubt.

Well, she wouldn't give up without a fight!

"It's not just about the bull, though," she heard herself say. "There's more…more than enough reason to charge you with a real crime, Mick!"

"Addie, no," Deke said, his voice vibrating with warning.

She ignored him as she marched up to the sheriff. "I'm talkin' about D. K. Larrabie's death. I'm betting there's enough evidence to prove that D.K. wasn't drinking at all that night…and that someone may have wanted him dead."

She turned on Mick with such vehemence that he started. "Admit it, Mick. You planted those empty bottles in D.K.'s truck. The problem is, he didn't drink that brand of whiskey. He drank Jack Daniel's, just like Deke said. *You* drink Jim Beam."

Mick merely looked her up and down, a scornful smile touching his lips. "You can't be serious, girl."

"As a stroke. I'll testify in a court of law that the bottles you had that night were Jim Beam label."

She whirled on the sheriff. "Well? You already know he tried to frame Deke yesterday and almost got someone killed in the process. What'll it take to convince you he could've succeeded seven years ago with Deke's dad?"

Sheriff Davies shifted uncomfortably. "That's a pretty serious accusation you're makin', Addie."

"But it's the truth!" she said desperately.

"The truth according to the Larrabies, sounds like," Mick sneered at her. "'Cause you can't prove anything."

Addie very much feared he was right—until she heard the words ring out. "Oh, yes, we can."

It was Deke. He stooped to extract himself from Jace's grip. "Go on over to your mama and granddad," he told the boy gently.

Jace was clearly reluctant, but then Deke bent to whisper something in the youngster's ear. Jace nodded and walked quickly back to Addie, who gathered him against her, her mind overrun with questions. What was he doing? What sort of proof could he possibly have that would lock Mick away once and for all? For that was what it would take to stop his madness.

To her amazement, Deke held out the belt buckle she'd helped Jace polish.

"See this buckle?" Deke asked Mick. "It's inscribed with my mother's name. *L-O-R-N-A.*"

"Yeah? And what's that got to do with anything?" the older man asked suspiciously.

"You tell me, Mick," Deke said as he leisurely flipped the buckle into the air. It spun like a gold coin, catching the sunlight and bouncing it back over and over again, like a beacon sending a message. "Was the belt attached to this buckle the one you used to tie up my father and leave him to burn to death? Or was it used to kill him? 'Cause it was found over there—" Deke gave a nod in the direction of the cottonwood "—in the ruins of the breeding building, all covered with soot and tarnish from layin' there for seven years. Seven...long...years."

In a move so fast it made Addie gasp and Jace jump beside her, Deke hurled the buckle at Mick with perfect accuracy. It knocked the rancher's Stetson off his head and flying a dozen feet before it tumbled to a stop in the dirt. The brass buckle landed a yard or so from the sheriff's feet, and he bent slowly to pick it up.

"Take a close look at the inscription on the back, Sheriff," Deke said, his stance as relaxed as Addie had ever seen it, making her wonder what in heaven's name was going on.

She wasn't to remain in suspense long, for that's when Deke pointed out, "It's got two initials on the back—*M.B.* Couldn't be yours, could it, Mick?"

The older man said nothing—just stared at Deke as if to bore a hole in him from sheer will. Deke stared back calmly.

"*Is* it yours, Mick?" Sheriff Davies asked.

The stare-down continued for several moments before Mick shrugged. "What if it is? You're gonna believe the accusations of a fly-by-night ranch hand over the word of someone who's lived in these parts all his life, whose family settled the Brazos Valley over a hundred years ago?"

The sheriff gave Deke a long, measuring look. From atop the ridgepole of the barn, a crow cawed, the sound echoing in the still air and making Addie shiver, despite the heat, for it reminded her of a death knell.

Then Sheriff Davies spoke. "Maybe you'd better come with me on down to the county jail, Mick, so's we can ask you a few questions."

It was as if the older man had been slapped. "Come along with you," Mick repeated ominously. "Whit, you aren't arrestin' me, are you?"

"No. You got to admit, though, that what with this turn of events yesterday, how it could look like you've got the means and the motive. Everyone knows it's never set well with you, D.K.'s taking away Lorna."

Mick stared at him so hard that Addie thought his eyeballs would dry out.

"You don't know what you're doin', Whit. Haul me down to the courthouse for any reason, and you'll sure enough get an appreciation for what don't set well with me."

"No, he won't."

Heads turned in unison as Connor took a step toward his father. "There's not going to be any more retaliation. It's got to stop now, Dad—this hate that's destroying everything and everyone—"

"Shut up!" Mick snapped. "Don't you know by now when to shut up?"

"I guess not, Dad, if keeping quiet means seeing innocent people get hurt."

"You're no son of mine!" Mick shouted, slashing his arm through the air between him and Connor as if forever severing the tie that binds. "Everything you do, you make a hash of. Can't ranch worth a lick, can't keep your woman."

Clearly shaken by his father's condemnation of him, still Connor stood tall and resolute. "Maybe I can't. But that doesn't change that what you're doin' is wrong—as wrong as anything can be in this life."

Mick turned in a slow circle, eyes narrowed like those of a caged wolf searching for the weakest link in the group surrounding him.

"What the hell do any of you know," Mick finally said, his florid face for once pale, ominously so. "None of you can begin to know what it was like to watch the only woman you ever loved get charmed by a two-bit cowboy who didn't deserve to shine her boots. And then, when it came back to Texas how she'd died— out on some two-horse *farm* that she'd worked like a dog to help keep from failin'? Well, tell me, *tell me* that wouldn't make the best of men turn loco.''

"It did," Deke said. "It drove my father to drink. But it didn't drive him to take his misery out on another."

"That's 'cause he knew!" Mick shouted at Deke. "He knew she should've married me. You should've been *my* son!"

As pale as he'd been before, his face drained completely of color now at his obviously inadvertent admission. Then blood flooded his features as he lunged at Deke, who didn't lift a finger to protect himself.

The blow caused by Mick's fist rocked Deke's head back and set him off balance—but only for a second. Calmly, he righted himself, wiping away the blood at the corner of his mouth with the edge of his thumb.

"I won't say there was never a Larrabie who didn't have that comin' to him," Deke said quietly. "But that's it, Mick. The feud's over and done with. It's time to move on."

Amazingly, Mick came at him again, but this time the sheriff had the wherewithal to catch Mick from behind, pinning his arms to his sides.

"Don't make me put 'cuffs on you, Mick," he said.

The older man struggled briefly in a last act of resistance. Then, with a muttered "To hell with you all," he allowed himself to be escorted to the sheriff's car, looking neither left nor right.

Addie looked around to find Connor standing only a few feet away, his expression uncertain—and torn.

"Thank you, for what you did today."

This, to Addie's amazement, had come from Deke, who gazed at Connor with new respect.

Connor merely waved him off. "No thanks needed. There never is when there's wrongs to be righted."

"It couldn't have been easy, though, by any stretch of the imagination. I know."

They shared a look of complete understanding. "No-oo." Connor drew the word out on a sigh. "And it's not going to be easy for a long time, if ever."

"Well, I hope you know you've got my lifelong gratitude and support, wherever I am—"

Addie wondered if she were the only one to detect the tremor in Deke's voice, although it was sure and true as he went on.

"It's a blessing to me to know that my father wasn't a victim of his lesser inclinations, that he could redeem himself, no matter the crimes of love he'd committed. That we all have that ability in us, given the chance, to change."

The last was said with an emphasis that Connor couldn't have missed.

"I'll remember that," he said to Deke.

There was an awkward pause during which both men's right arms stiffened at their sides before all hesitation disappeared and they grasped hands for a long, heartfelt shake.

Yes, the feud was over at last, Addie thought, the tears again welling up in her eyes. Now, perhaps, the healing could begin in earnest.

Deke watched Connor go. Then he turned toward her, and something in his gaze struck a whole new definition of fear into her heart as she wondered whether such healing would come with a price. After all, Deke had made no promises this time—oh, not about staying, but about being able to trust that love would be enough. Enough to find hope among the ashes and build a future upon it.

Bless his heart, Jace must have picked up some of the same vibrations, for he cut loose from her and ran to his father, though he stopped short of throwing himself at Deke.

"So are ya…are ya leavin' still?" Jace asked.

Addie swallowed painfully, even took a half-dozen protective steps toward her son as she heard hope, as ever, warring with doubt in his voice.

Deke dropped his chin, and her breath stopped in her lungs, until he answered.

"No, Slick. I know that's what I said I was going to do—even had an ironclad reason for believin' it would have been the right thing for you and your mom."

She watched his profile as he gazed solemnly down at Jace, and saw every bit of the tough and tender cowboy she loved.

"But when it came down to it…I simply couldn't. Not for anything in the world."

Then he raised his head and looked at her over their son's head, with those golden-green eyes she loved so well. "I can only ask that you—and your mom—forgive me for the hurt I've caused you. I can't promise that I won't disappoint you again sometime."

"But you won't never leave again?" the boy asked.

"Never, Jace."

Yet Jace seemed to be waiting for something further, and Addie realized what it was.

"I believe that's one promise you can take to the

bank, hon—'' she said, her own voice cracking. ''Deke Larrabie wouldn't lie to you.''

Jace smiled then, a smile of such untouched innocence and trust that Addie knew a small miracle had just occurred—knew she was not the only one with tears in her eyes at that moment. Dropping to his knees in the dirt, Deke enfolded his son in his arms, as without reserve Jace gave as good as he got.

And then suddenly Deke wasn't hugging Jace but had caught Addie to him in a fierce embrace.

''Addie. Oh, Addie,'' Deke muttered into her hair, his voice husky with a relief that told her how harrowing was the emotional gauntlet he'd run today.

''Deke'' was all she could manage to say, hugging him back. ''I was so scared—''

''It's over now,'' he murmured. ''It's over. I'm home.''

And when she looked up into Deke's amber-green eyes Addie saw everything she'd ever wanted or dreamed of. He was at peace.

''I believe I need to thank someone else for doing some pretty fervent convincin' to the sheriff,'' he said in a low, sexy drawl just for her, ''even after that someone had promised me she'd sit tight.''

''You're not the only one, Deke, who did what he had to do,'' she defended herself staunchly, linking her arms behind his neck. ''And I'd do it again—*all* of it—in a heartbeat.''

He laughed, the sound like the bells of freedom ringing. She knew she'd never again hear a sound so joyous, so wonderful.

''Lord, Addie. If you *are* my biggest weakness, then

I'll gladly take the consequences for losing myself in you. Because,'' Deke whispered against her lips, ''heaven knows, you're my greatest strength, too.''

And when he kissed her, they both knew that this was one cowboy who'd come home to stay, once and for all.

* * * * *

Connor Brody finally finds a love
of his own and gives Lara Dearborn

THE RANCHER'S PROMISE (RS #1619)

next month in Silhouette Romance!

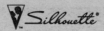

SPECIAL EDITION™

**Was it something in the water...
or something in the air?**

**Because bachelors in Bridgewater, Texas,
are becoming a vanishing breed—fast!**

**Don't miss these three exciting stories of Texas
cowboys by favorite author Jodi O'Donnell:**

Deke Larrabie returns to discover
someone *else* he left behind....

THE COME-BACK COWBOY
(Special Edition #1494)
September 2002

Connor Brody meets his match and gives her

THE RANCHER'S PROMISE
(Silhouette Romance #1619)
October 2002

Griff Corbin learns about true
friendship and love when he falls for

HIS BEST FRIEND'S BRIDE
(Silhouette Romance #1625)
November 2002

Available at your favorite retail outlet.

Where love comes alive™

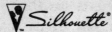

Available in November!

So This Is Christmas

Celebrate the season with three brand-new stories by three bestselling authors!

"The Perfect Holiday"
by

Sherryl Woods

A matchmaking aunt sends a perfectly handsome—and perfectly grumpy—man to her single niece. But will the wealthy bachelor become a groom by Christmastime?

"Faith, Hope and Love"
by

Beverly Barton

After one passionate night, a love-struck beauty finds herself pregnant with her sexy bodyguard's child—and hopes this secret gift will be the beginning of a lifetime of love.

"A Rancher in Her Stocking"
by

Leanne Banks

A spirited schoolteacher opens her home to a ruggedly handsome rancher for the holidays and discovers the tight-lipped cowboy is all she needs to live merrily ever after!

Silhouette®
Where love comes alive™

If you enjoyed what you just read,
then we've got an offer you can't resist!

Take 2 bestselling love stories FREE!

Plus get a FREE surprise gift!

Clip this page and mail it to Silhouette Reader Service™

IN U.S.A.	IN CANADA
3010 Walden Ave.	P.O. Box 609
P.O. Box 1867	Fort Erie, Ontario
Buffalo, N.Y. 14240-1867	L2A 5X3

YES! Please send me 2 free Silhouette Special Edition® novels and my free surprise gift. After receiving them, if I don't wish to receive anymore, I can return the shipping statement marked cancel. If I don't cancel, I will receive 6 brand-new novels every month, before they're available in stores! In the U.S.A., bill me at the bargain price of $3.99 plus 25¢ shipping and handling per book and applicable sales tax, if any*. In Canada, bill me at the bargain price of $4.74 plus 25¢ shipping and handling per book and applicable taxes**. That's the complete price and a savings of at least 10% off the cover prices—what a great deal! I understand that accepting the 2 free books and gift places me under no obligation ever to buy any books. I can always return a shipment and cancel at any time. Even if I never buy another book from Silhouette, the 2 free books and gift are mine to keep forever.

235 SDN DNUR
335 SDN DNUS

Name	(PLEASE PRINT)	
Address		Apt.#
City	State/Prov.	Zip/Postal Code

* Terms and prices subject to change without notice. Sales tax applicable in N.Y.
** Canadian residents will be charged applicable provincial taxes and GST.
  All orders subject to approval. Offer limited to one per household and not valid to
  current Silhouette Special Edition® subscribers.
  ® are registered trademarks of Harlequin Books S.A., used under license.

SPED02   ©1998 Harlequin Enterprises Limited

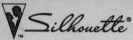

COMING NEXT MONTH

#1495 SEAN'S RECKONING—Sherryl Woods
The Devaneys
While fighting a deadly blaze, Sean Devaney rescued a precious
five-year-old boy—and was hell-bent on blaming the tot's mother
afterward. But hardworking single mom Deanna Blakewell was
nothing like Sean expected—and *everything* he'd been looking for
in a woman. If only he could convince proud Deanna to accept his
help…and his heart!

#1496 MERCURY RISING—Christine Rimmer
The Sons of Caitlin Bravo
Falling for a bad boy? Bookstore owner Jane Elliott had been there,
done that—and then some! Jane swore she'd never again try to tame
the untamable, but she didn't reckon on meeting gamblin' ladies' man
Cade Bravo, her new next-door neighbor. Could Jane possibly say no
to this baddest of bad boys when her heart kept screaming *yes*?

#1497 MONTANA LAWMAN—Allison Leigh
Montana Mavericks
Deputy Sheriff Holt Tanner had a murder to solve, and painfully shy
Molly Brewster seemed to hold the key. But before a suspicious Holt
could unlock Molly's mysteries, he had to face his growing attraction
to the secretive librarian. When Holt finally learned the truth about
Molly's past, would he be able to solve the crime and help Molly heal
old wounds?

#1498 THE STRANGER SHE MARRIED—Crystal Green
Kane's Crossing
Two years ago, rancher Matthew Shane disappeared, leaving his
wounded but tough-as-nails wife, Rachel, to fend for herself. Then
Matthew returned…with amnesia! Would coming to terms with their
rocky history lead Matthew and Rachel to another painful
estrangement…or a bright new future?

#1499 AN AMERICAN PRINCESS—Tracy Sinclair
Shannon Blanchard had just won on a game show—and her grand
prize was two weeks in the kingdom of Bonaventure hosted by Crown
Prince Michael de Mornay. Sparks soon flew between the suave royal
and the pretty virgin. But Michael assumed he could never provide
family-loving Shannon with the one thing she wanted. Until she got
pregnant with his baby!

#1500 THE AMBASSADOR'S VOW—Barbara Gale
Dutiful Daniel Boylan was the very successful American ambassador
to France, but he'd never forgotten the true love he'd lost: pianist
Katherine Harriman. Ten years after their controversial romance, the
handsome diplomat and the elegant single mom reunited at a concert.
With passions rekindled, what would Daniel do when he learned that
Katherine's son was *his*?